HIGHER EDUCATION

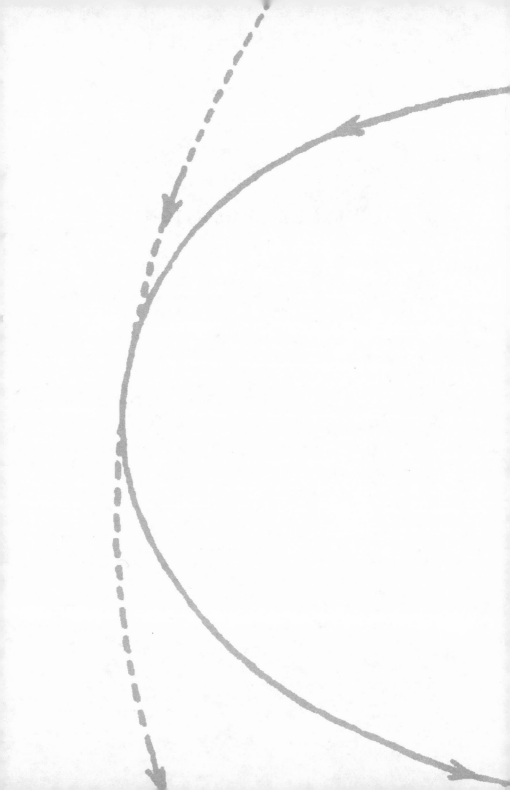

HIGHER EDUCATION

A *JUPITER*™ NOVEL

CHARLES SHEFFIELD

AND

JERRY POURNELLE

A TOM DOHERTY ASSOCIATES BOOK · NEW YORK

This is a work of fiction. All the characters and events
portrayed in this novel are either fictitious or are
used fictitiously.

HIGHER EDUCATION

This book is printed on acid-free paper.

A Tor Book
Published by Tom Doherty Associates, Inc.
175 Fifth Avenue
New York, NY 10010

Tor Books on the World Wide Web:
http://www.tor.com

Tor® is a registered trademark of Tom Doherty
Associates, Inc.

Design by Sara Stemen

Library of Congress Cataloging-in-Publication Data

Sheffield, Charles.
    Higher education / Charles Sheffield & Jerry Pournelle.
        p.   c.m.
    "A Tom Doherty Associates book."
    ISBN 0-312-86174-5
    I. Pournelle, Jerry. II. Title.
PS3569.H39253H54   1996
813'54—dc20   95-52875
                                                         CIP
First Edition: June 1996

Printed in the United States of America

0 9 8 7 6 5 4 3 2 1

To the long-suffering schoolteachers of America

A modified version of this novel was
serialized in *Analog* magazine.

HIGHER EDUCATION

CHAPTER ONE

AT SIXTEEN, Rick Luban's life was about to end. He didn't know it yet. He thought he was all set for a good time.

The first period had gone no differently from usual. Mr. Hamel had been teaching high school for thirty years—forever, in Rick's eyes. Hamel looked like an old turtle, and like a turtle he had developed his own survival techniques. Nothing got to him; not talking in class, or eating, or farting or sleeping. Gross and direct rudeness or violence, too much even for him to ignore, he passed up the line at once to the principal's office.

Hamel's rule: No fuss, no muss. And if that meant no work and no learning, too, he would settle for it. He usually reached that understanding with a class before the end of its first week.

"Test today." Hamel took no notice of the half-hearted groans. Failing an Act of God, biology tests in his class came every Tuesday and everyone knew it. "Read the questions, mark the answers. You have forty minutes."

More out of boredom than anything else, Rick put on the earphones attached to the desk and slipped the written sheet of questions into the reader.

"Question one," said the voice in his ear. "Five point credit. One of the animals on your screen belongs to a different class from the others. Indicate which one. For assistance on the biological definition of *class*, or for name identification of any of the animals shown, touch the empty box."

The TV screen in front of Rick was divided into six rectangles. The first was empty. The second through sixth showed an ant, a butterfly, a mosquito, a spider, and a caterpillar. They were all in color, and all moved in natural settings.

Rick saw Dim Willy Puntin, Puntin the Pumpkin, reaching out to poke the icon of the caterpillar. It certainly looked grossly different from the other four. Rick snorted to himself. That was just like Hamel, trying a trick question. Rick had hardly been listening to the lesson about larval insect forms, but even a five-year-old knew that caterpillars turned into butterflies; and insects all had six legs.

Rick reached forward to touch the icon of the spider, at the same moment as Juanita Cesaro, two seats in front of him, removed her headset. She raised her hand and then stood up. Hamel left the raised podium and moved over to her at once. Rick eased the earphones away from his head. Juanita was dim, but she was hot stuff. Half the boys in her year—including Rick—had been through Juanita; but you'd never know it from seeing her in class. She always sat demure and quiet, doing so poorly in every subject that her teachers all had trouble passing her. She *never* caused trouble.

"These." Juanita waved her hand vaguely at the headset, television, and reader. "Not working."

Hamel came around the desk and leaned over to examine the television picture. He was very careful not to touch Juanita, and careful to stand so that this fact would be apparent on the classroom videocamera recording.

Wily old turtle. No sexual harassment charges for you. Rick could see the empty box and the five icons on Juanita's screen, just like on his own. Another clapped-out reader, it had to be. The readers were junk, breaking down all the time. Even when they worked they would only handle one size of page. School was too cheap to buy decent stuff. Not like the school the phone company ran. That place had great equipment, but it was just for kids whose mothers or fathers worked there. His mother had got herself fired for drugs six weeks after she started with them, so Rick had only been to company school for a little while. That was back in first grade, but he still remembered it well.

Hamel had apparently made up his mind about the reader. He was glancing thoughtfully around the class, finally gesturing to a girl at the back. "Belinda. For this period I want you to change seats with Juanita."

Rick had expected that action, well ahead of the teacher's taking it. Belinda Jacob was one of three people in the class who could read well enough to handle the test from the printed sheet, without using a reader at all. *So see what reading does for you,* Rick thought, as the two girls changed places. *Not a damn thing.* Belinda was Hamel's star student. She had probably been halfway through her own test before she had to move—and now she was forced to start over, while Juanita would get the benefit of her right answers.

Rick grinned to himself as he settled back to listen to the rest of the questions. Unless Hamel went to the trouble of noting the point where the two had changed over, which wasn't at all likely, Juanita for the first time in her life was going to score—on a *test.*

The broken reader was all that the first period could offer to relieve the boredom. That was predictable with Mr. Hamel. Dullness was the rule. What Rick and his friends had been looking forward to for a week was second period. They were supposed to get a new civics teacher then, right out of training.

"Willis Preebane, his name is. An' if I can't have some fun with him, I'm losing my touch."

Screw Savage was speaking. Any one of the three might have offered the same statement, but Screw had special credibility. He was a school legend. Two years before, by a mixture of near-inaudible insult and off-videocamera dumb insolence, he had made a new teacher take a swing at him on her very first day. She had been fired on the spot. Screw was provided with a groveling apology from Principal Rigden. His parents had sued school and county anyway, and been paid a hefty out-of-court settlement. Now Screw tended to get high grades without ever doing homework or handing in tests.

"But we'd all like to have first go at him," Screw went on, "so we do it fair, an' draw lots."

Rick and the other two were walking between classes, heading for Room 33 with Screw Savage leading the way. The corridors were their usual confusion with backed-up lines in front of the metal and plastique detectors. Hoss Carlin, walking next to Rick, took a step to his left and reached out to brush his fingers over the breasts of a girl walking the other way. She slapped his hand away, but she turned to give him a big smile and said, "See you tonight."

"Watch it, Hoss," Rick warned. "You're in deep shit if they have that on camera."

"Nah." Hoss jerked his head upward. "Checked already."

The ceiling videocamera for the corridor was ruined, lens broken and body a shattered hulk. It was like this all over the school. Every time a corridor camera was repaired, within a day or two it would be smashed.

"Anyway," Hoss went on. "Jackie'd be on my side if they did see me. She'd tell 'em I was swattin' a wasp off her tit or somethin'."

The three youths were almost at Room 33. Most of the class was already there, standing waiting outside the locked door.

"Mebbe Preebane's not as dumb as you think, Screw,"

Hoss said. "He knows at least that much. Lockin' the door stops us givin' him a welcome."

"So one of us has to get real inventive once we're inside." Savage turned around, three toothpicks sticking up from between the knuckles of his closed right fist. "Short one has first go at Papa Willis. Who wants first pick?"

"Me," Hoss said, and grimaced with annoyance when the toothpick he pulled was full length. "Lucky with women, unlucky in the draw. Go on, Rick. You got one out of two chance now."

Rick plucked the toothpick from between Savage's first and second finger, and grinned when he saw it was a fragment only an inch and a half long.

"Lucky bastard." Screw opened his hand to reveal a third, full-length toothpick. "You get Preebane all to yourself."

"Aha!" The voice, thin and with a definite lisp, came from behind Rick. "And do I hear thomeone taking my name in vain?"

Rick turned and stared. The man waddling along the corridor was too good to be true. He was pale, short, and grossly overweight. He had watery blue eyes in a pudgy face, and he sported a flat, gingery-brown moustache that looked as though it had been poorly dyed and pasted above his full upper lip.

Preebane's very appearance was an opportunity to have fun. If Rick didn't get in quickly, some other class joker certainly would.

In fact, it was already happening. Rick heard a whisper, deliberately loud, from among the group of waiting students: "Quiet now. Here comes our new PE teacher."

Preebane, heading for the classroom door, paused uncertainly. After a moment he decided to pretend he had not heard the comment. He unlocked the door and waved the students inside. Rick, contrary to his natural instincts and usual practice, went to sit in the middle of the first row. Preebane, belly wobbling, moved to stand beneath the video-camera right in front of Rick. He beamed directly at him.

Rick gazed back and waited for inspiration. He, who usually had a thousand ideas for baiting teachers, suddenly found his mind a blank. Goaded to physical violence, Willis Preebane looked like a man who would drop dead from the exertion before he could land the first blow.

And that voice. "Good morning. I am Mr. Preebane, and I want to welcome you to my class on introductory civics." Or rather, it was "Mr. Pweebane," and "my clath on intwoductory thivicth."

"I told Pwinthipal Wigden of my appwoach, and she agweed with it completely. Begin by forgetting evewything that you have ever been told about the Conthtituthion."

"Done," said a girl's voice from the back of the room, followed by a loud male whisper, "Hire the handicapped."

The others were starting without Rick. He could feel Screw and Hoss glaring accusingly at his back. And still his brain was empty. It was an enormous relief to hear the click of the PA system, right above his head, and a voice saying, "I am delighted to announce that we have been paid an unexpected visit by Congresswoman Pearl, who as I am sure you know serves on our Board of Education. All students and teachers will please assemble at once in the main hall."

Principal Rigden didn't sound delighted to Rick. She sounded ready to shit bricks. But the interruption would give him time to think. He stayed in his seat until everyone except Mr. Preebane had left the room, then he moved out and held the door for the teacher.

Preebane nodded his thanks. Rick closed the door; was careful not to lock it; and hurried after the rest of the class ahead of Preebane. He caught up with them as they were filing into the hall.

"What about some action, dipshit?" Screw Savage didn't wait until they were seated. "If I'd known you was goin' to just sit there like a dried-out dog turd, I'd never have held any draw. You can't hang old Willis out to dry, what the hell can you handle?"

"His dick." Hoss stood on the other side of Screw. "He's done it too much and softened his brain."

"Don't you believe it. I know what I'm doing. And it's something special." Rick glared at both of them. "But I need a little bit of help from you. You have to go sit down near the front."

"And where will you be?" Screw sounded suspicious.

"Right at the back. Near the door. The classroom's not locked, Screw. I was last out, I made sure it was that way."

"Ah!" The other two understood at once.

"What do you want us to do?" Hoss asked.

"Wait 'til the principal is ready to introduce Congresswoman Whats-it. It should get real quiet. Then you drop something."

"What?"

"Hell, I dunno. Anything. Anything that makes a decent noise."

Hoss dived into his pocket and came up with a handful of change. "This? People will scrabble around after 'em, too."

"Perfect."

"But the Rigger will have my ass in a sling for interrupting her."

"For dropping money and losing some? Don't think so. Anyway, if you're going to help, get going. I can't wait much longer. Have to find a seat near the side door."

Hoss and Screw nodded. Rick turned at once and started easing his way against the main flow of students. The seats at the back, usually filled first, were today half empty. Everybody wanted to see Principal Rigden wriggle and grovel, the way she always did with Board of Education visitors. Rick sat at the end of a row he had almost to himself, close enough to the open door for a quiet getaway.

He waited impatiently while the stage filled with the senior teachers. Willis Preebane was up there with them—that was surprising for a new and junior staff member. The honor didn't seem to make him comfortable; maybe because his ass would hardly squeeze in between the arms of his chair.

There was one student on the stage, too. Daniel Rackett. As valedictorian (vale-*dickhead*-torian, as Hoss usually put it) Danny would be called upon to say something to welcome their guest. He didn't look comfortable, either. He was peering at the headset that was supposed to read his speech into his ear. From the expression on his face it wasn't working right. Even from the back of the hall Rick could see his Adam's apple bobbing up and down.

Finally Principal Rigden appeared, smiling broadly and leading a large, red-haired woman in a green pantsuit. They moved to two empty chairs at the front of the stage, Congresswoman Pearl sat down, and the principal turned to face the students. "I would like—"

There was the clatter of two dozen small coins falling onto the wooden floor. Some of them were still rolling when Rick quietly rose and slipped out of the side door.

The principal would speak, then Danny Rackett, then the visitor. Rick probably had at least half an hour. But that wasn't long for what he had in mind.

First he headed away from Room 33, keeping his eyes open for working videocameras. The contraceptive dispensers were down by the cafeteria entrance. They needed a student name and ID code before they would operate, but Rick was prepared for that. He entered "Daniel J. Rackett" and "XKY-586", waited as the valedictorian's ID was confirmed, and took the packet of three condoms. He did it twice more. Nine should be enough. If anyone checked today's records, Danny would get quite a reputation.

The corridors were deserted as he hurried back toward Room 33, opened the door, and slipped through. The trick now was to disable the classroom videocamera without being seen by it. The cable ran along the ceiling, well out of reach. Rick scaled the open door and balanced precariously on top of it. He had no knife on him—anything that might form a weapon would never get past the school entrance—but his nail clippers were enough for this job. He crouched on top of the door, reached up, and delicately snipped the thin grey cable.

He lost his balance as he did so and had to jump, but he landed easily. And finally he could close the classroom door. There was no way of locking it from the inside, but he felt a lot safer once it was shut.

He blew up eight of the condoms and tied their ends. They formed great balloons, a couple of feet long and nine or ten inches wide. He taped them all around Preebane's desk, stepped back, and surveyed his work.

It was a start, but it was not enough. He could imagine Screw Savage's sniff and critical comment: "Kindergarten stuff." He had to try for the rest.

Rick went to the door, opened it, and looked along the corridor. He had no idea how much time had passed, but everywhere was still silent and deserted. He left the door unlocked and hurried along to the washroom at the end of the corridor. He placed the end of the remaining condom over a faucet, held it in position, and turned on the water.

It took forever to fill. Rick put in as much water as he dared, until he was sure that the thin skin would burst under the weight. At last he tied off the end. The bloated condom had become amazingly heavy. He cradled it in his arms and headed back to the classroom.

The most difficult part still remained. Somehow he had to balance the monstrous condom right above the door, so that it would burst as the door swung open. And he had to get out, himself, after the trap was set.

It sounded impossible. Rick puzzled over it, increasingly sure that he was running out of time, until at last he realized that he was trying to solve the wrong problem. He didn't have to leave the room at all. There was going to be total confusion after the door was opened. He could hide behind the desks at the back of the room, and leave when the excitement was over.

He spent ten nervous minutes arranging a harness of tape around the condom, then placed thumb tacks through the ends of the tape. Finally he dragged a chair over to the door and lifted the condom into position. He pushed the pins into the wall and made delicate adjustments. When the door was opened, its rough top had to just scrape the bottom of the condom enough to break it. But the condom felt so distended and tight, he was almost afraid to move it now.

At last he realized that he was doing more harm than good. The changes he was making were loosening both the pins and the tape. He returned the chair to its original position and forced himself to retreat to the back of the room. He found a place which allowed him a narrow view of the door, with a very small chance of his being seen.

And then he waited. And waited.

What could be going on in the hall? There was no way to know how long Congresswoman Pearl would decide to speak. Certainly, Principal Rigden would not dare to interrupt a visitor who was a member of the Board of Education. Suppose that she went on right until lunch time, and the class did not return to this room?

Rick's legs were stiff and his knees sore from crouching on the hard floor when at last he heard the sound of footsteps clattering along the corridor. He tensed. He had not been able to lock the door, as he had originally intended. Maybe Preebane would notice that.

Apparently not. The metal handle on the inside was turning. The door opened its first inch and Rick heard Preebane's voice saying, "After you, Aunt Delia. I am weally glad that my clath will have you—"

The door swung open. Rick had one glimpse of Willis Preebane, ushering a large, green-clad figure ahead of him into the room. Then the giant condom, scraped by the top of the door, burst with a soft, subdued plop. Water deluged down.

Rick, peering through the narrow slit, had the sudden feeling that the flood had decapitated Congresswoman Pearl. He could see her red hair, sodden with water, lying on the floor.

Then he heard her scream. She clutched at her head. The hair beneath the wig was revealed as short-cropped and grey.

Behind the congresswoman and Preebane, crowding now into the doorway, came Rick's whole class. They were buzzing with excitement and delight. Delia Pearl's secret would be all over the school by lunch-time. Rick saw Screw near the front, standing open-mouthed with astonished glee.

He felt a huge satisfaction. He had promised; and he had certainly delivered.

CHAPTER TWO

RICK also believed that he was safe from discovery. In the melee that followed, the classroom had been total confusion. No one noticed when he joined the rest—even Hoss and Screw didn't realize that he had been in the room, and they had no idea how he had managed the trick until he explained.

It was a total shock to Rick when he was called out of class right after lunch and taken to Principal Rigden's office.

The principal was there. So was Congresswoman Pearl, the three assistant principals, Willis Preebane, and two other people whom Rick did not recognize.

The congresswoman had managed to dry her wig, and she was wearing it. That was a mistake. After its soaking it looked like a strip of cheap coconut matting wedged down onto her head. Beneath it, her blue eyes glared at Rick with undisguised hatred.

"This is the one?"

"We believe so." Principal Rigden wasted no time on formalities. She turned to Rick. "Ricardo Luban, do you know of the outrage that was perpetrated on Congresswoman Pearl this morning?"

"Yes." Rick felt uneasy, but he could not see how anything could be pinned on him.

"Will you admit that you were responsible for it?"

"I didn't do it."

"Were you in Mr. Preebane's class, before the assembly to greet the congresswoman?"

"Yes."

"And you were the last to leave that class?"

"Yes. I think so."

"Mr. Preebane?" The principal turned her head.

"He was the last. Definitely. He held the door for me."

"Did you?"

"Yes."

"And you locked the door after you, as you were supposed to?"

"Sure."

Rick felt easier in his mind. They were going to try to prove that he hadn't locked the door. He didn't think they could. And even if they did, that was a long way from proving that he had set the booby trap. But the principal didn't pursue that line. She merely nodded, and asked, "Mr. Preebane tells us that you then went on ahead of him, toward the hall. Is that right?"

"Yes." Rick was uneasy again.

"And you attended the general assembly?"

"Yes."

"And remained there throughout?"

"Yes." If they were going to ask him what happened in the hall, he was on solid ground. Hoss and Screw Savage had briefed him pretty thoroughly over lunch. Danny Rackett's headset hadn't worked right. He had tried to read his speech of welcome from printed sheets, stumbled over every word longer than one syllable, and made an ass of himself until Principal Rigden finally cut him off. She had then made a short speech herself, explaining what a wonderful person the visiting congresswoman was. And finally Congresswoman Pearl had offered her own contribution, telling the audience how pleased she was that her own nephew, Willis Preebane, had decided to teach here, how talented he was, and how lucky the school was to have him. She hoped he would be really happy with his choice.

She had said it all twice, to make sure that the principal and the other teachers got the message, added that she was looking forward to seeing an actual class being taught, and at last sat down.

If Principal Rigden wanted anything more detailed than that, Rick would plead ignorance—and be sure that half the school remembered no more than he had been told.

"So where did you sit during the assembly?"

The question was totally unexpected. It left Rick floundering.

"I dunno."

"That's silly, of course you remember. Now, where?"

"I guess maybe I was near the back. Near the side door."

"Very good." The principal turned to the screen that covered one wall of her office. "Right here, in fact." She touched the wall. "This is you, is it not?"

The screen showed a videocamera still. The resolution was not good. Rick sitting way at the back of the hall was barely recognizable.

"Yes, that's me."

Mistake. Should have said maybe, not sure. He thought of changing his story, but it was too late. The picture had flashed off, to be replaced by another, and Principal Rigden was saying, "The first image I showed was taken at the beginning of the assembly. This one was taken close to the end of it. The seat where you were sitting originally is now empty. Where are you sitting now, Ricardo Luban?"

"I moved." Rick spoke automatically, but he knew he was doomed. If they had been able to locate him on the video image . . .

"We are quite sure that you moved." The principal stepped away from the wall screen. "But where did you move to? During the lunch period we managed to identify every student in school today, in both the first and the second picture. I should say, every student except one. You are present in the first image, and absent in the second. Now would you like to confess?"

Rick shook his head. They had him on ice, but he wasn't going to admit it. He would plead innocent today, and tomorrow, and if necessary for the whole of the next two years, until the end of his time in school.

It was with disbelief that he heard Principal Rigden saying, "I quite agree with you, Congresswoman Pearl, and with the other Board Members. Guilt is established beyond reasonable doubt. Such people have absolutely no place in this school or in our school system. We will take action for expulsion as soon as the necessary signatures can be obtained and the paperwork completed."

"For the final, official decision." Delia Pearl stared stonily at Rick. "But unofficially, pending that decision, expulsion will happen today."

"Today?" Principal Rigden hesitated. "Very well. Of course." She turned to Rick. "You are expelled from this school, effective immediately. The final notification will follow in a day or two. Please collect your possessions and leave the premises as soon as possible."

"You can't do that!" Expulsion, for a simple practical joke that had really hurt no one? Rick knew a student who had broken his language teacher's arm, and another who had deliberately run over a science teacher in his car. Explosive booby traps for other teachers had been set, filled with shit or warm tar. But those people had received only trifling punishments.

"I think you must let us decide what we can and cannot do."

"I'll sue. I will."

For a second everyone stared at him. Then they all smiled.

"Sue a congresswoman?" The principal laughed aloud. "And what lawyer do you suppose will take your case? Get out, Luban. You are as ignorant as you are stupid. Go."

Delia Pearl's mouth twisted with satisfaction, and she turned to Preebane. "Willis, I do not feel that we can trust this young man one little bit. Would you please accompany him when he collects his possessions, and then escort him off the premises."

"Of course." Preebane did not even look to the principal for confirmation.

Rick was led away. He was too dazed to resist. He hardly saw Hoss or Screw or the other members of his class as he picked up his school bag, and he did not say a word when he was escorted to the front door and his ID was cancelled from the entry system. He walked out into the afternoon sunlight and stared around him as though he was on an alien planet.

He went to the side of the school, walked out beyond the sports field, and sat on the grass. He was still sitting there when school was released for the day. Occasional students passed by. No one spoke to him. He did not stir or speak to them. Only when a long afternoon shadow fell across him, and silently remained there, did he look up.

It was Mr. Hamel, more like a turtle than ever as he stood motionless with his head pushed slightly forward. He nodded at Rick.

"Caught at last, Luban. And not before time."

"You heard what happened?"

"The whole school heard. Would you like to talk to me about it?" And, when Rick shook his head, "Very well. That is your option." He began to walk away across the grass.

"Wait!" Rick struggled to his feet and hurried after him. "I don't want to talk, but I want to *ask*."

"Better yet. We learn by asking, not by talking." Hamel

continued on his way, slowly pacing out of the school grounds and into the street. "So ask."

"Why *me?* I mean, why did the motherfuckers dump on me like that? What I did wasn't any big deal compared to some of the shit that goes down all the time in school."

They had come to a bench. Hamel sat down on it and gestured to Rick to join him.

"Must you employ such language? Is your vocabulary so meager that you are incapable of other forms of expression?"

"What'll you do, expel me? You never hear people talk like that?"

"I hear people talk like that every day." Hamel sighed. "It never ceases to grate. Do you want people to wish that you were not around them? It's easy enough to do. Or do you want answers?"

"Answers. Why did they dump on me?"

"Very well. Answers you shall have." Hamel paused, studying Rick from battered sneakers to razor-cut hair. "You are not stupid, Luban. But you are a fool. For one thing, you consort with people like Savage and Carlin, who really are stupid. You are also ignorant, cynical, amoral, and unthinking. Wait a moment." He held up his hand. Rick was starting to stand up. "I am going to answer your question—or rather, I am going to let you answer it. You are—how old? Sixteen? So you have been in the education system for eleven years. And what have you learned?"

"My grades are all right."

"Certainly. Because nothing is required of you. It is easy to hit a target pasted to the end of the rifle. We are also required to make you feel good about yourself. The technical term is to 'raise your self esteem.' While you were in school

I could not have spoken to you this way, because you had to be protected from the truth. Now I can. Despite all the work that we have done to raise your self esteem, surely you must know that you've learned very little."

"I do all right," Rick protested again—half-heartedly.

"You 'do all right.' Indeed. What does that mean? Let us examine what you know.

"You can read short, simple words, but only those you have seen before. You have a reasonable speaking vocabulary—when you choose to exercise it—but you are unable to read more than half of the words that you know. You have a rudimentary knowledge of simple science, and you can do simple arithmetic. I've hammered some biology into your skull, but you know little mathematics, and no economics, geography, history, arts, or languages. You can recite all manner of juvenile song lyrics, but you are ignorant of real poetry and literature. And you would be little better if you stayed here another two years and graduated."

"Reading from books is a waste of time. Like adding up numbers. I got a calculator to do that. Reading's ancient history. The readers do it for us fine."

"They do—when they work, and when you have one available. But you miss a point. A person who cannot *read* can also not *write*. Writing—and revision—is essential for completeness and clarity of expression. But I do not want to digress. You have been in the education system for eleven years. How much, in that time, have you learned about the system itself, and how it works?"

Rick considered the question. He had never had the slightest interest in the education system. Nor did anyone else in his right mind.

"Not much."

"But you have enough information to work things out for yourself. For instance, whom do I work for—to whom do I report?"

"Principal Rigden."

"And to whom does *she* report?"

"I dunno. I guess, the Board of Education."

"Good enough. There are a couple more layers in there, but that will do. Now here's another question. How much of the county and state's total budget goes on education? I don't expect you to know the answer to that, so I will tell you. It is about four tenths. That's an awful lot of money, a huge vested interest at work. Now, who decides what that amount will be and how it should be allocated?"

"Congress?"

"For all practical purposes. Very good. So let us climb the ladder of status in society. If you play one of your unfunny 'jokes' on a teacher, and are caught, you pay a small price. But a teacher, most students are amazed to learn, is the *lowest* form of life in the school system. Do something to the principal, that's worse, and the punishment is more severe. To a Board of Education member, worse yet. And to a *congresswoman*, who is also a member of the Board of Education—"

"I didn't know I was doing nothing to a congresswoman."

"That is the plea of the foolish through all of history: *I didn't know what I was doing.* But I, speaking as a teacher, tell you that I have no sympathy for you. Is it better to insult and offend and diminish me or Willis Preebane, rather than Congresswoman Pearl, simply because the punishment is less? That is the logic of a coward."

"I ain't no coward!"

The sun was setting in their faces, and Hamel shielded his eyes with his hand. Rick could see the deep lines on his cheeks and around his mouth. Hamel seemed ancient, far older than when he was teaching his class, until suddenly he lowered his hand and turned to face Rick. His eyes were alert and astute, changing his whole face.

"I believe that you are not guilty of *conscious* cowardice. So now for some good news. Until today you were destined for two more years of schooling here. Did you have any thought of continuing beyond that?"

Rick shook his head. For the past three years he had wanted to finish school and get out of it more than anything. "Mick makes me stay in school because Mom gets the education incentive bonus in the welfare. I'd be long gone if I could."

"So now what happens to you?"

"I don't know. Sit around and watch the tube, I guess, until they throw me out. Mick's goin' to kill me. The education incentive was nine-forty a month and we only get sixty-two hundred altogether."

"So your education is a good part of the money. Of course you don't get it yourself."

"Naw. Mick takes it. He's gonna hate losing that nine-forty. Fifteen percent—"

"It is that. You do percentages in your head?"

"Sure. That's useful, you need it to play the numbers."

"An undoubtedly valuable skill. Now that you are out you will have more chance to exercise it. But suppose that you had stayed in school. At eighteen, you would graduate. Even with your minimal skills, you would receive your diploma.

Then you emerge and offer your talents to a waiting world. Did you have any plans as to what you would do?"

"Find a job, I guess. There's supposed to be plenty of jobs around."

"In laundries, or fast food places. Or running a scanner, there are usually jobs in data entry. There's also the Job Corps, makework jobs cleaning litter from parks. Plenty of those. That sound good?"

"Naw, but there's other stuff."

"Not for you. The fact is that perhaps two dozen of your two hundred classmates—twelve percent, as you will readily confirm—have skills that anyone wishes to pay for. Of course, nearly everyone has the grades to go to junior college."

Rick shuddered.

"You wouldn't learn any more there than you have in school," Hamel continued. "But it would keep you off the streets, and separate you from the genuinely stupid. Better than nothing, but still leading to a dead end."

"Bigger education incentive, too—it goes up to a thousand a month."

"A thousand a month, to stay in junior college for two years. At the end of that time would you possess any saleable skills?"

"I don't know," Rick protested. He shook his head. "The way you talk, I guess not. So who gets the real jobs?"

"Who do you think? Those who have the real skills. A few of your classmates, perhaps, but mostly students from company schools. People who know something, people who have learned how to work hard." Hamel shook his head sadly.

"It pains me that I have lived to see the transformation of the United States from a republic to a feudal aristocracy. Not pretty."

"I don't know what you're talking about."

"No, I don't suppose you do. That's part of the problem. You ask who gets the jobs. The answer is, people with knowledge and drive. There are jobs for them. Not for an arrogant, semiliterate, unfocused, troublemaking know-nothing. Not for an amoral, idle, cynical waster, which is what you'd be if you stayed here. I told you I had good news. Here it is: you are *fortunate* to be expelled from this school. Had you remained you would have wasted another two years, and at the end of it you'd have no more knowledge or capability than you have today."

Rick stood up. "I don't need to take this crap from anybody. I'm going."

"Very well. Going where?"

Rick shook his head. "I dunno. Mick's going to kill me." He knew how it would happen. When they found out that the education incentive would stop, his mother would scream and her boyfriend—Rick's "stepfather," though he certainly wasn't—would tell her to shut her yap. Then they would start in on each other. Finally when the fight between them cooled off they would gang up and turn it all on him.

"Going home, I guess. I got a truce with the gangs but I can't be out after dark unless I pay, and I don't have money."

"And tomorrow morning, when you get up and school is closed to you?"

"I don't know. Look for a street job."

"Selling dope?"

"I don't know, what else is there?"

"Theft. Shoplifting. Working as a pimp. Admittedly those don't pay as well as being a pusher, but they stay out of jail somewhat longer. Live longer, too."

Rick knew what that meant. Most rackets were controlled by gangs, or even by adult mobsters. Mick, his current stepfather, claimed to have good connections, but nobody believed him. Especially not Rick, because he had asked about getting set up in a good racket, and Mick kept stalling him. Rick was sure that Mick didn't know shit about real rackets. And if you didn't have connections you wouldn't last long. You'd get busted or shot, maybe both.

Rick shook his head. "I guess I don't know what I'll do."

"I assumed as much. However, I have a suggestion." Mr. Hamel handed Rick a small yellow card. "Can you read what is written there?"

Rick stared at the card in the fading light. "Eight-one-five-two." He paused. The numbers were easy but the words were long and unfamiliar. At last he shook his head. "Not without a reader."

"Then I will tell you. It says, 8152 Chatterjee Boulevard, Suite 500. Can you remember that, and find the place?"

"Sure." Rick stared at the card. "Say it again."

"Very well. 8152 Chatterjee Boulevard, Suite 500."

"Got it." Now that he'd heard the words he could sort of read the card, at least enough to remind him.

"If you go there tomorrow there is a possibility of useful employment."

"A job?"

"Exactly. Not an easy job, but a worthwhile one. The most rewarding jobs are always the most difficult ones. You may keep the card."

Rick studied the words, silently mouthing them to himself. "I know how to get to Chatterjee Boulevard. If I went there tonight, would someone be in Suite 500?"

"I cannot say." Hamel stood up. "I must go now. But you have the right idea. Action is usually preferable to inaction."

Rick stood up too. He wanted somehow to thank Mr. Hamel, but he did not know how. "Why are you doing this for me?"

Hamel paused. "Certainly it is not because I like you, Luban. I do not. As I said, you are a fool. And you are—"

"Ignorant, cynical, amoral, and unthinking. I heard you."

"Correct. Did I omit to say *lazy?* But you are not stupid. You are, I think, basically very intelligent. However, all forms of test that might suggest one student is more able or talented than another were long since judged discriminatory, and banished from our school system. Therefore, I have no objective basis for my conjecture. But I do hate waste. You and your friends have been wasting your lives."

"I still don't understand. You just told me I'm good for nothing."

"You are—today. I did not tell you that you lack potential. It is all relative, Luban. You believe that the antics of your friends are daring and wicked. You will be amazed to learn that this school, despite its many failings, does not come close to the bottom of the heap. Go south with me ten miles, and I will show you schools like armed camps, schools where student and staff murders and rape are a daily event. For you, with all your flaws, there may still be hope. I would like to think so."

Hamel nodded and started to walk away, a small, stooped figure in the twilight. "Do you think I'll get a job?" Rick called after him.

"I cannot say." Hamel did not pause or turn around. "But if you do, wait a while before you thank me for it."

CHAPTER THREE

MR. HAMEL had sensed the truth: Rick could not face going home. The school might not have called his mother, but somebody would have contacted her to make sure she knew there wouldn't be any more education incentive money coming in. Nine hundred and forty a month. It would stop today. He never saw one cent of it, but they would make him pay. Mick would wait up for him, drunk or drugged but anyway in a foul temper.

If only, when Rick finally had to go to the apartment, he could tell them that he already had some sort of job, some way to bring home some money. . . .

It seemed like the thinnest of straws to grasp at as he descended from the overhead Public Vehicle at the corner of Chatterjee Boulevard and began to walk along toward Number 8152. He had to push his way through crowds of young men and women, standing or wandering aimlessly along the littered street. They were part of the Pool. Not more than one in ten of the Pool would have a job of any kind—ever. Yet many of them had graduated high school and junior college, and some of them from a real college. Rick had already known most of the things that Mr. Hamel had told him. He had just never thought about them.

They didn't want us to think about them. Rick remembered what Mr. Hamel had said about self esteem. He'd heard some of that before, too, but it hadn't seemed worth bothering with. *They want us to feel good and not think about the future. And it works, too. Why should we?*

Number 8152 was a ten-story windowless building, its featureless walls made of grey lightweight carbon composite. Rick waited stoically as his ID was verified by the automatic guard and the card given to him by Mr. Hamel was read. It was close to eight o'clock at night. On the way here he had convinced himself that Suite 500 would be empty.

That conviction grew when he at last stood outside the entrance of the suite. He could see through the shatterproof glass door that it was just one room. It had plenty of computers and displays and printers inside, but no people.

He touched the attention panel anyway, and was astonished when after about ten seconds a woman's voice responded, "You are at an office of Vanguard Mining and Refining. Please identify yourself."

Rick went through the ID process all over again. He showed the little card and stumbled through the explanation that it had been given to him by Mr. Hamel, and why. The woman did not say another word, but at last the door swung open. Rick went in. The door closed behind him and one of the television monitors came alive.

"Sit down right here."

Rick took the only seat near the monitor. Now he could see the woman on the screen. She was small, thin, and sharp-featured, and somehow reminded him of an animal. A rat? No. Not quite.

She was examining something in front of her, not visible to Rick. "You are sixteen years old. You have been expelled from school. And it is eight o'clock, your time. Right?"

Each of the statements was true enough, but taken together they made little sense.

"That's right."

"I want you to tell me exactly why you were expelled from school. Take your time and give as much detail as you can. I'll try not to interrupt. If I do there will be a delay of about five seconds between what you say, and my comment or question. So you may have to back up occasionally and say things over. Go ahead."

There was a temptation to lie, or put things in a way more favorable to Rick. Some instinct warned him that would be a mistake. He recounted the whole episode, from the arrival of Willis Preebane to Rick's interrogation and expulsion by Principal Rigden. It was difficult to talk about the condoms and the booby trap. After the fact it sounded so stupid and pointless and unfunny. Rick was sure that any hope of employment with Vanguard Mining was evaporating with every word he said. He plowed on, ending with his decision to come to this office tonight even though it was so late.

"Not late where I am," the woman replied. "I got up just two hours ago. But are you tired?"

Just got up. She had to be somewhere on the other side of the Earth! The speech delay must be caused by the satellite link. "I'm not tired."

"Good. Can you read?"

"A little bit." But five seconds was far too long for a satellite link delay. Rick struggled to remember things that had never before been of the slightest interest to him. Radio signals traveled at the speed of light. But how fast did light travel?

"Can you write?"

"Just a few things."

"Hell." The woman's opinion of his reply showed more in her tone of voice than in her comment. "Well, no matter. We'll manage. I want to give you a whole set of things called *aptitude tests*. First, though, we have to deal with a few formalities. You never had tests like this in school, because they're forbidden in public programs. We're a private company but still the tests can't be given to you without suitable consent. In the case of someone like you, less than eighteen years old, that consent has to come from a parent or guardian."

Rick felt an awful sinking feeling. He was going to be sent home after all with nothing to tell except his expulsion from school.

"Problem with that?" The woman must have been

studying his face. "Tell you what. Suppose that we give you the tests anyway, see how you do. If the results are good you can get consent later and we'll postdate the tests. If they're not good, we purge the test results from our files and you're no worse off."

What she was suggesting sounded illegal—but if that didn't worry Vanguard Mining, it sure didn't worry Rick. He took a deep breath.

"I'm ready."

"Any last question before we begin?"

Rick shook his head, then changed his mind. "You said you just got up. Is it morning where you are?"

"Morning, afternoon, evening, anything you choose to call it." The woman smiled, to show small, sharp teeth. Rick suddenly caught the right animal resemblance. Not a rat, but a weasel—though he had never actually *seen* a live weasel. Mr. Hamel had somehow taught Rick more biology than either of them realized.

"I'm on CM-2, one of Vanguard Mining's translunar training stations," the woman went on, "about seven hundred thousand kilometers away from Earth. But the tests will be delivered where you are by a local program. I'll still be here if you get stuck. Don't call me unless you absolutely have to, though—the tests are timed. Ready to go?"

Rick nodded. His heart was racing and his mouth felt too dry to speak.

The woman's picture vanished from the screen and was replaced by a sequence of numbers.

"Good luck," said her disembodied voice. "Do well on your tests—and one day maybe you'll come out here and see this place for yourself."

* * *

Rick had painted a mental picture too good to be true: he would pass the tests, Vanguard Mining would offer him a job, and he would be whisked away at once to space and his new employment.

It was a dreadful shock to learn that the first set of aptitude tests was no more than a beginning.

"Not bad," said the weasely woman, whose name was Coral Wogan. She was studying a copy of Rick's efforts, and he was terribly aware that he had not managed to complete even one of the tests. "Not bad at all," she went on. "You did well enough that we'll put you on the company payroll while you take the next set."

"Next set?" It was after midnight and his brain felt like mush.

"More extensive tests. Mostly physical this time. They last about two weeks. Now, take these"—a linked batch of forms came stuttering out of a printer close to Rick—"and fill them out. All right?"

Rick took the forms and glanced at the first one. He could see at once that it was full of words too hard for him to read, but he was not going to admit that to Coral Wogan. He'd get the help he needed, if he had to go back to school and beg for it. He nodded.

"Three of them call for parental signature," Coral Wogan went on. "What's your father's name?"

"My real father? Milo Luban. But he hasn't been around since I was three years old."

"Your mother, then."

"Dora Luban."

"Right. Give her this, and tell her that there will be more coming when we receive the signed parental permissions. I rely on you to persuade your mother to sign."

Another narrow form rolled out of the printer. This one Rick could read. It was a check, made out to his mother from Vanguard Mining. For two thousand! More than double the monthly nine-forty of the education incentive.

"She'll sign."

"Good. One thing more, then you can go home and get some sleep. How soon will you be ready to start?"

Now—then I don't have to go home at all. But that would not work. He needed to fill out the stack of forms, and he needed his mother to sign.

"Will tomorrow evening be all right?" He knew what would happen if Mick saw that check. One of two things. Either there would be a tremendous fight, or Dora Luban would agree to cash it and the pair would go off on a prolonged roller-coaster ride of drink and drugs. Either way, Rick didn't want to be home for the nighttime brawl.

"Tomorrow evening should be fine," Coral Wogan said. "Here's the only other thing you'll need."

One more piece of stiff paper scrolled from the printer. Rick grabbed it and studied it. This one looked like a ticket—an *air* ticket, to somewhere with a long name. He tried to spell the word out—A-L-B-U-Q—but it was too hard.

"Albuquerque." Coral Wogan showed her first sign of impatience. "You fly there, then by shuttle bus to our facility at Tularema. You are allowed to bring up to twenty kilos of personal possessions. Don't bother with additional clothes, they'll be provided. Have you ever been to New Mexico?"

"Never."

"You'll like it. Some of the tests, though, you won't like them. I guarantee that."

She grinned—small mouth, sharp little teeth. "Any more questions?"

Rick was tempted to ask what she meant about the tests, then decided not to. "No."

"That's it then. Again, good luck."

The screen darkened, leaving Rick clutching forms, check, and ticket. He wondered how he was going to find his way home safely in the dangerous early hours of the morning.

Rick had never flown before, and he was not sure that he liked it—a bad sign for someone hoping to go out to space. Every other passenger seemed totally relaxed, while he in his window seat noticed each vibration and every whir and thump and whistle of mechanical equipment.

As the plane climbed at a steep angle and pressed him back in his seat, he stared outside at the dwarfed buildings and roads and tried to move his mind to other things. All he could think of was the bitter memory of his last hours at home.

Mick, thank heaven, had been out when Rick first got there. His mother had signed instantly, hid the check in her purse, and told him to get on with filling out the rest of the material. He had walked over to sit outside the school, struggled through the forms unaided, and delivered everything by mid-afternoon to the Vanguard Mining office.

He saw no one and spoke only with what seemed to be a computer. But everything must have been in order, because after five minutes another check came spitting out of the printer.

Rick received travel instructions and returned home to pack. Twenty kilos was more than enough—five would have done him. While he stuffed the few things he valued into a couple of plastic bags, his mother hovered over him. After signing the permission forms without hesitation she was now moaning and weeping and pretending to be heartbroken. But she could not keep her eyes off the second check that Rick had brought from Vanguard Mining. Mick had grabbed this one, the three thousand dollar "sweetener" that expressed the company's financial appreciation of Dora Luban's willingness to sign over complete parental control of her child. As for the first check, if his mother did not mention that to Mick, Rick was not about to do so.

His stepfather had been even worse than his mother. Mick hadn't pretended. He didn't try to hide his relief at getting rid of Rick, the "troublemaker" too bad even for the school system. When Rick came home and told them about the Vanguard Mining tests and the job prospect mining the Belt, Mick had asked only one question: "When do you go?"

No congratulations; no discussion of the job; no worry about possible hazards of an off-Earth assignment. No query as to how long it would be before Rick returned. Just, "When do you go?"

When do you go. Rick stared out of the plane window. Think of it this way: it sure made leaving home pretty easy.

They had reached cruising altitude and were in level flight. Rick was gazing down on stark, snow-capped mountains, their valleys already in shadow as night approached. There was no sign of buildings or roads, no evidence from up here that humans even existed. If anything went wrong with the plane, there was no place to land down there among those dark rocks.

Rick looked at the other passengers. Some were his age or younger, but they were all dressed in a very different style. It was clear that not one of them shared his worried thoughts. They were chatting, reading, playing, working, or sleeping, without a trace of interest in what lay outside the aircraft windows.

It was time to accept that life was different now. He was entering a whole new world. The old world had been washed away in the flood of water that poured down on Delia Pearl's head and took off her red wig. Rick in this new world had to learn to think differently.

He closed his eyes. He had not slept for more than a short nap in the late afternoon, and he was dreadfully tired. He smiled to himself. Say what you like, the school had a new legend now. Whenever anyone tried a trick on students or teachers, somebody would say, "Ah, but that's nothing. You should have seen the stunt Rick Luban pulled. Old Rick was the absolute wild end."

What would it take to become a legend in the world that he was entering now? . . .

The landing at Albuquerque brought Rick out of a deep and uneasy sleep. When they touched down he at first had no idea where he was. Most of the other passengers were already on their feet while he was still struggling with his seat belt. He stared out of the window at a runway dusted with white, rubbed his eyes, and groped around under the seat for his two plastic bags. One of the last people off the plane, he followed his directions through a near-deserted airport, and then outside again to look for the minibus that was supposed to be waiting for him.

Heavier snow was starting to fall. The air felt thin and cold. He understood now why Coral Wogan had told him not to bother with his own clothes—he didn't have any warm enough. But what was he supposed to do until he arrived at Tularema? Freeze to death?

The bus was one of the new autopilot runabouts, still illegal for city use. Rick had seen them on the tube, but he had no idea how they worked. Some sort of overall navigation gadget, he guessed, taking its position from a satellite receiver in the bus's roof. A radar told the onboard computer where other cars and trucks were, and how fast they were going.

Rick approached the bus and hesitated. He had seen a dozen accident videos in the past year, people killed in autopilot buses and cars that ran off the road into rivers or smashed into bridge supports and other cars. An autopilot bus was not his choice for a middle-of-the-night ride with snow and slippery roads.

While he stood there, the bus's rear door opened and a gruff voice came from the dark interior.

"You gonna stand all night playing statues? We been waiting two hours. Get inside and let's hustle outa here."

Rick swallowed his surprise—he had expected to be the only passenger. He bent his head and climbed into the bus. It was hardly warmer inside than out. Two other people were sitting on the broad seat, so muffled up in dark blankets that at first glance he could make out little more than their heads.

"Tularema?" asked the same voice. As Rick's eyes began to adjust he saw next to him a big, broad-shouldered youth, not much older than him.

"Yes."

"Vanguard Mining?"

"Yes."

"Then why don't this dumb bus get out of here?"

"Because the door is still open," the other passenger said calmly. It was a girl, sitting on the far left. She touched something on the panel in front of them. The rear door clunked shut, and at the same moment a blue interior light came on and the bus began to move smoothly forward.

Rick studied the other two, aware that they were staring at him with equal curiosity. The male was easy. He could have fitted right in at Rick's school. He was big—even bigger than he seemed at first glance, because it turned out that most of that bulk was muscle and not clothing. He had long, swept-back frizzy hair, a broad, very black face, and dark, close-set eyes. The left one was bloodshot, and he kept rubbing it. He had the same cocky, look-at-me expression as Hoss Carlin.

"I'm Vido Valdez," he said. He did not offer to shake hands.

"Rick Luban."

"You're gonna freeze your ass off in that outfit." Valdez did not offer to share the blanket sitting on his lap.

"Let's hope it's going to be a short ride," Rick said, and reached out to pull part of the blanket across his chilled legs and feet. He ignored Valdez's scowl—he could see trouble ahead there—and turned his attention to the girl who was smiling at him in a superior sort of way.

"It won't be," she said.

She was something else. For a start, she was tall and thin and pale and weak-looking, like a plant left too long in the dark. Mr. Hamel had taught the class a special word for that—eeti-o-something. Even her hair, pulled back from her narrow face, seemed weak and thin. If she was heading for the physical tests that Coral Wogan had promised Rick at Tularema, it was hard to believe she would pass any one of them.

The real shock, though, was those eyes. Rick stared at them, and had the feeling that there was nothing behind them. They were grey and wide and utterly without expression. The smile that she offered Rick somehow did not extend from her mouth to the rest of her face.

"If you're hoping for a short ride, forget it," she went on. Her voice was small and precise, a little girl's voice. Rick had the strange feeling that despite her size she hadn't matured sexually. "Albuquerque to Tularema," she continued, "is nearly three hundred kilometers. Even without stops, and I don't know if the bus has any scheduled, we won't get to Tularema until the middle of the night. It shouldn't be too bad, though. The heat comes on a lot better when we're moving." Almost as an afterthought, she added, "And I'm Alice Klein. From the Black Hills—western South Dakota."

Rick decided that, physical weakling or not, in her own way Alice Klein was as self-confident as Vido Valdez.

"I'm from Anchorage," Valdez said. "If you think this is cold . . ." He stared at Rick, and he was grinning. "I think she's right, though. This shouldn't be too bad—once we get to Tularema."

He looked with satisfaction at Rick's puzzled expression. "Didn't they tell you? Or didn't you sign up with Vanguard Mining?"

"I did sign up. Tell me what?"

"That you're out here for physical tests."

"They told me that."

"Ah, but did they tell you the rest of it?" Valdez turned, so that his smirk could take in both Rick and Alice Klein. "I guess they didn't. Don't you realize that these will be *competitive* tests? Not everyone who signs up gets a job and goes to space. We're going to be fighting against each other. And I'll tell you now: I intend to win."

Tests. Rick had been taking them in school for as long as he could remember. There was a definite technique to them.

Rule number one: find out if it mattered. Some teachers gave you tests, but there was no penalty if you scored zero or filled the screen with doodles. Then you and your buddies horsed around through the whole thing or cut it completely.

If the teacher played tough like old Hamel, you changed tactics to rule number two: sit near one of the goody-goodies like Belinda Jacob, someone who was likely to know the answers. Watch what she did, copy all you could, and deny to the death that you had cheated.

He knew within minutes of arriving at Tularema that this was going to be different. For starters, they arrived tired out and chilled in a bleak February overcast. Rick expected food and rest. Instead they were ushered at once into a grim medical facility. A man in a grey suit greeted them. Doctor Alonzo Bretherton, read his ID card, but he didn't look like any doctor Rick had ever seen—he was more like a bar-room bruiser, all muscles, jug ears, flattened nose and broken veins. He took one look at them and said, "Klein, Luban and

Valdez. Right. A quick physical, then it's track suits and a treadmill."

"We're frozen," protested Valdez.

"And starving," Rick added.

It was no lie. Even with the blankets, the night journey at two thousand meters above sea level (Alice Klein seemed to know everything) had numbed them. There had been no stops, for food or anything else.

"Exactly as you should be," Bretherton said cheerfully. "I need to catch you at a physical low point, and it's easier to do it now than starve you or keep you up all night later. Let's go. Those three cubicles."

Rick was ready to say it—*Screw you, Doc, I'm not doing no stupid treadmill*—when he saw Vido Valdez's mouth opening. They stared at each other. Finally Vido scowled and walked forward toward one of the three rooms that Bretherton had pointed out. Alice Klein had already vanished into the left-hand one.

Find someone who was likely to know the answers. That was a laugh. Rick changed into the skimpy grey gown that he found in the cubicle and stared at himself in the mirror. Wonderful. Enough to cover him to the thighs, but no matter how he adjusted it part of his ass was showing. Alice Klein was due for a treat.

Except that there was no sign of her when he emerged. Rick was shuttled along to another room, where a man and woman he had never seen before performed an hour-long physical on him. It was more unpleasant and painful than one of Mick's grade-A beatings.

"Which would you rather," the woman said when he complained. According to her badge she was a company paramedic, Tess Shawm. She was young and very attractive, but it was obvious that so far as she was concerned Rick was nothing more than a piece of meat. "Would you prefer to find out you have a problem now," she went on, "with full medical facilities on site—or find out when you're halfway to the Belt and it's fifty million kilometers to the nearest doctor?"

It was no consolation, when Rick was at last released, to see Vido Valdez and hear him grumble, "The hell with this. They were pokin' into holes I never knew I had."

Vido stared at Rick's gown and then at the close razor haircut that Rick had been so proud of two days ago, and added, "I knew you were weird, Luban, the second I saw you. You got more hair on your ass than you have on your head."

Fighting words. But before Rick could do more than raise a fist Bretherton was standing between them.

"Fun and games later, you two. Go in there and get track suits on. Time for the treadmill and the EKG."

Rick would like to have used that raised fist on Bretherton, but the doctor's bare arms were as hairy and muscular as a gorilla's. Vido Valdez was already moving away. After a moment Rick followed.

The treadmill was nothing but a sort of walking machine with an angle that could be adjusted to make you think you were going uphill. Rick waited while a bunch of electrodes were attached all over him, then the belt he was standing on began to move. He started walking. It was dead easy. He was no jock, but running the streets kept you in fair shape. He began to feel warm for the first time since he left the plane. Vido Valdez was two machines over, grunting and puffing but striding out steadily. Rick knew this test couldn't be a big deal, because beyond Valdez he could see Alice Klein, strolling easily along on her long, skinny legs.

Then he started to feel something else. It was becoming hard to breathe, and his heart was pounding away in his chest faster than he ever remembered. He put his hand to his throat.

"What's wrong?" The same man and woman attendants were with them, watching the walkers and the monitors. Tess Shawm came to stand by Rick's side.

"Can't breathe." Rick hardly had wind to speak. "And I hurt—here."

She nodded. "Where you from?"

"Simi Valley—California."

"Near sea level, right."

"Uh. Uh."

"And now you are more than a mile high. Thinner air. What do you expect?" Shawm checked the monitors. "You're all right. Heart's fine. Just keep walking."

Rick walked. The pain in his chest grew, and soon it was matched by an awful tired ache in his legs. Instead of slowing the treadmill, Tess Shawm was speeding it up and increasing the slope. Finally, when Rick knew he could not go for one more second, the machine slowed and stopped. He stood still, his hands gripping the metal bars on either side of him and his head down to his chest.

"You need to take regular exercise," Shawm said. "I'm going to make a note of that. But you'll do. You can get down now."

Rick stumbled off the treadmill. He saw Valdez next to his machine, doubled over, hands to his right side. Unbelievably, Alice Klein was still on her treadmill and still striding along easily.

"Don't get all shook up." Tess Shawm saw Rick's startled expression. "She has an advantage over you two. She went to school in the high part of the Black Hills. For the past two years she's been living up near two thousand meters. Like prolonged altitude training. She can walk both of you into the ground."

She already had. Vido Valdez and Rick went side by side to the showers in grim silence. Valdez didn't tell Rick this time that he intended to win.

CHAPTER FOUR

THERE was a temptation to say, *I've had it. You can take the tests and stuff 'em. I quit.*

But if you did that, what came next? Rick, puzzling over the words on his air ticket, saw that it had a return half. He could use it to fly back home any time.

And face his mother, and Mick, and admit failure yet again. And after that?

Things didn't seem so bad after Rick had eaten a huge

meal, slept around the clock, and woke to eat again. His legs still ached and more tests lay ahead, but he decided that, like Vido, he intended to win.

His decision was made easier when he realized what he should have known all along: he and Vido Valdez and Alice Klein were not the only three being tested. They were merely the most recent arrivals. There were fifty-two other recruits at the facility, all between the ages of fifteen and eighteen. All of them were present in the dining room when Rick appeared for his second meal, and they stared at him and at the other two new arrivals in an unfriendly way.

He found out why later that day, talking to Alice Klein who still apparently knew everything. A maximum of twenty recruits would go on to the next stage of off-Earth training. Every new arrival decreased the chances of the people already there. Vido Valdez had been quite right, the situation was competitive. Less than forty percent of the applicants would be winners.

The quality of the competition became apparent as the tests continued: manual dexterity, physical strength, speed of reflexes, hand-eye coordination, color and stereoscopic vision, ability to perform several activities in parallel. In each category there seemed to be an outstanding performer, someone who was rumored to score far ahead of everyone else. Rick was discouraged to find that he was best in nothing.

And something else became obvious. Rick and Vido Valdez might be in competition with all the other trainees, but Valdez saw the contest in more personal terms. To him, Rick was the enemy.

"I'm gonna beat you, Luban." They were eating, and Valdez was sitting opposite Rick at one of the plastic-topped tables. He was still rubbing his left eye now and again. Rick suspected that it was a nervous habit, the eye red only because of constant irritation. If it was anything real, the Vanguard Mining doctors would have done something about it. They might be ruthless and heartless, but they were certainly competent.

"I'm gonna whip your skinny ass," Valdez went on. "Remember this: anything you can do, I can do better."

"Sure. Like you beat me real good on the balance bar." Rick hadn't been present when Valdez took that test, but he had heard about it from another trainee, a loudmouth boy named Chick Teazle. According to Teazle, Vido had fallen off once, lost his confidence, and fallen off four more times before he walked it successfully. Rick had aced it on the first run.

Valdez turned red and picked up his plate of food. He was raising it high, ready to throw it at Rick, when he realized that the room had gone quiet. People all around were watching and waiting. The rule had been made clear on first arrival: say what you like to each other while the tests were going on, but start a brawl and you were out. You'd be heading back where you came from on the next autobus.

Valdez sat down with a bump and glared both ways along the table. "Don't get your hopes up, all you weenies. I'm stayin', and I'm winning." He stared at Rick. "I'll get even with you, Luban, soon as I have a chance. That's a promise. I'll beat the shit out of you. And I got a long memory."

"Your arms will have to be even longer—with you down on Earth and me up in space."

But Vido would not be drawn again. He picked up his half-filled plate, but only to stand up and carry it across to the disposal area. "Have some more food, numb nuts," he said to Rick as he left the table. "You want to be real well-fed for today's test."

That got a laugh, but Rick did not know why. He glanced down to his own empty plate. It was a favorite of his, spaghetti and meatballs, and he had eaten two big helpings. The tests of the day were not announced in advance, but did the others know something that Rick didn't? Vido was a real pig, he went for multiple helpings and he *never* left anything uneaten on his plate. Except today.

Rick puzzled over that for the next couple of hours, while he struggled to assemble sets of blocks that had been cut into peculiar shapes. It looked easy, but it was curiously difficult. It didn't help when Chick Teazle stood up after less than an hour, the assignment all done. Vido Valdez followed twenty minutes later, giving Rick a smug look as he left. Rick managed to finish, just seconds before the deadline, but then he had to hurry at once to his next assigned location: Room B-2F.

Fortunately, he knew exactly where that was. He ran down two flights of stairs, along the corridor, and entered the room exactly on time. He had half expected to find Vido already there, but the room was empty. Rick looked around him with a good deal of curiosity. He had never been here before.

The room was one big cube. Walls, floor and ceiling were all alike, flat planes of smooth grey plastic. The only difference was the sprinkler system in the ceiling, what looked like a plastic observation window in one wall, and a set of drain grilles in the floor. In the exact center of the room stood a single piece of equipment. It consisted of three great hoops, mounted with axes at right angles to each other but with a common center. They formed the outer skeleton of a great ball, four meters across. At the center of the ball, attached to the hoops by strong metal struts, sat a chair. It had solid arm rests, foot supports, and a tall back, and loose straps dangled down from it. A short metal ladder led up toward it.

All this, for a test? Rick was walking forward to examine the structure more closely when Tess Shawm came into the room behind him. She was holding a black plastic coverall suit. "You've never had one of these before, I assume?" she said.

Rick shook his head. The hoops looked as though each one could swivel independently of the other two. As each hoop turned, the chair would turn with it. So the chair could face in every direction and at any angle, including upside down.

"Well, it's really pretty simple," Shawm continued. "Put this suit on over your clothes, and zip it up. Those big hoops on the test rig are on what's called *gimbals*, and they're independently driven by motors in the base. There's also a centrifuge effect. You know about that?"

"Sure." Rick knew that he had been told about centrifuges, back in school, but he didn't want to admit that he couldn't remember what they did. He slipped the black plastic suit on, and found that it fitted snugly and zipped all the way up to his neck.

"Good." Tess Shawm checked the top of the zipper. "You hear a lot about freefall, and how it can upset your stomach. It can and it does, but it turns out that almost everybody gets used to it after a while. A week or two in space, and you hardly think about it.

"Anyway, we can't easily test freefall tolerance down here on Earth. What we can test, and what we're going to test today, is tolerance to changes in attitude and acceleration. There's a lot of individual variability in that from one person to another, and in space that actually causes more trouble than freefall. Go ahead, climb up the ladder."

Rick thought he knew what was coming, and it didn't sound like a big deal. He had been on the wildest rides that the city's amusement parks had to offer, and he loved every one. According to Hoss Carlin and Screw Savage, Rick was like a rat. Mr. Hamel had once told them that rats didn't have any way to throw up, and that's why rat poisons worked in the school basement. The rats swallowed the bait, but they couldn't vomit it out.

Poison or no poison, though, the basement always seemed to have plenty of rats left.

He climbed up the short ladder with Tess Shawm right behind. "Put your forearms flat along the supports," she said, "and make yourself comfortable in the seat. When I fasten the straps, let me know if they feel too tight. They have to hold you in for any position of the chair, but they shouldn't be in the slightest bit painful. The head band stretches, so you can move your head forward if you want to."

Rick grinned at her as he leaned back so that she could place a broad band around his forehead. "That all feels fine. Best seat I ever sat in. Like a king on a throne up here."

She gave him a peculiar look, and said, "Uneasy lies the head that wears the crown. Sit tight, your majesty. I'm going down to start the ball rolling. Call out if you want to stop—I'll be able to hear you."

She retreated down the stepladder, picked it up, and carried it out of the room with her. She closed the tight-fitting door. A few seconds later Rick saw her face at the observation window, high on one of the walls. He could not wave, but he gave her a big grin. She nodded back. A few seconds later there was a whine of electric motors and the chair began to tilt backward and to the left.

Gradually, the pace picked up. Rick could see the observation window, floor grilles, and ceiling sprinklers rotating steadily past him. He told himself that this was just another ride, one that he would have paid good money for a few weeks ago.

The walls were going past faster. Another component was adding to the motion. It was a curious, irregular backward-and-forward shift, as though the chair could not only rotate in any direction, but could at the same time be jerked up, forward and sideways away from the center of the hoops. Rick could feel new forces, pulling him every which way. It took a few seconds to realize that this must be the "centrifuge effect" that Tess Shawm had casually mentioned. It took less time than that for Rick to decide that he did not like what he was feeling.

Ceiling, walls and floor were turning into one continuous blur. He was no longer sure which way was up. Rick swallowed hard, and at once felt an urge to belch. He did so, and the sour taste of tomato paste came to his mouth. The vision of the mound of spaghetti that he had eaten swam before his eyes, and he tried desperately to think of something else.

All he had to do was yell, and the test would stop. Tess Shawm had promised it. The only thing that stopped him was the idea of how Vido would gloat next time they met. Someone had warned Valdez, he had *known* not to eat a lot. That wasn't fair.

Fair or not, Rick knew he could not stand much more. He was full of a terrible sense of dizziness, and the chair that held him seemed to swing and turn and veer faster than ever. His stomach felt three times its usual size. It was pressing upward toward his throat.

Stop!

Rick opened his mouth to shout the word. Instead of sound, a great gush of yellow vomit flew out and away. *Stop!* No word came. He leaned forward against the pull of the head band and threw up again, still unable to speak. When he closed his mouth, a sour jet spurted from his nose. When he opened his mouth again, the urge to retch made it impossible to breathe. He closed his eyes and hung against the chair straps in utter misery. As each new spasm hit him, he felt ready to die. And still he could not call out for it to end.

A sudden jolt of cold hit him in the face. He shivered and opened his eyes—and found that he was sitting upright in a chair that was rotating horizontally and steadily slowing. Jets of cold water from the overhead sprinkler system were sluicing down, over him and all over the room. Streaks of yellow and red—his last meal—were steadily disappearing from walls and floor.

He leaned back, welcoming the chill of cold water on his forehead. Although his eyes told him that the chair was stationary now, when he closed them he was sure that he was still turning end over end. He was still dizzy and panting for breath. He had thrown up so hard that his stomach and his throat felt raw and strained. Even so, it was bliss just to sit there and think that, no matter how bad he felt, it was *over.*

He closed his eyes again. This time everything held steady. He did not move until he heard the outer door open and the clatter of the stepladder.

"Still feeling like a king?" Tess Shawm was ascending the ladder beside the chair. There was something different in her expression. He thought at first that she was gloating over his misery, and then he realized that wasn't it. For the first time, she was grinning at him as though he was a human being and not just a test subject. She released his right hand, and he raised it to wipe the wet palm across his mouth.

"I feel like shit."

"But you look like vomit." She freed the other hand, then his head. Last came the bindings on his legs. "Are you still dizzy? If you are, stay right there until it goes away. There's no hurry."

"I'm not dizzy—not any more. But I guess I really blew it."

She was frowning at him in bewilderment. "Blew what?"

"The test. I spewed my ring. Everything I had."

"Naturally. Take a look around you. Take a look at yourself."

Rick did so, first at his dripping coverall, then around the room. Every sign that he had thrown up had vanished.

"Why do you think the room was designed this way?" Tess went on. "And why do you think I put you in that plastic suit? You were *supposed* to throw up. Everybody does, every single person who takes it and passes. You only fail and blow it by shouting for me to stop too soon—for that, you lose all sort of points."

You don't know how close I came. If stomach hadn't beaten brain to it, that's exactly what would have happened.

"So you mean I passed?" Rick tested his balance, and found that it was all right. He stood up and put one foot on the ladder.

"More than passed." She hesitated, as though not sure whether to speak, and then went on, "I might as well tell you this, because given the grapevine in this place you'd know within a day anyway. You lasted longer than anybody else in this whole group. You must have an iron stomach. Congratulations. For this test, you stated it right at the beginning. You're the king."

The king. Sure. Rick didn't feel much like royalty as he stumbled away on legs that were still a little shaky. It would soon be time for the afternoon meal, but he felt not in the least like eating.

He went instead to the dormitory, and was pleased to find it deserted. He lay down on his bed and closed his eyes. When he woke up what felt like two minutes later, he found that nearly an hour had passed and his stomach was empty and growling.

He went along to the dining-room, determined to admit to no one what had happened in the test. That proved to be irrelevant. As he came into the half-filled room, Chick Teazle greeted him with a loud, "Hey, look who's here! The Vomit King."

The grapevine was remarkable—and Tess Shawm must be part of it. No one else could possibly know what Rick had said about feeling like a king.

He nodded at Teazle and took a tray without speaking. If they knew what he said, they must also know that he had done better than any of them. And somehow, even if it killed him, he was now going to eat a normal meal.

The food was a thick beef stew. The first three mouth-fuls tasted sour and greasy, and as Rick swallowed he felt warning twinges in his stomach. Grimly, he kept going. When he was raising the fourth spoonful toward his mouth, Vido Valdez entered the dining-hall.

Vido was walking carefully, on legs that didn't quite seem to meet the ground. His face, always dark, wore an added tinge of greenish-yellow.

Rick raised the spoon of glutinous brown stew toward him in greeting, flourished it in the air, and delivered it carefully to his open mouth. It was gratifying to watch the progression in Vido's facial expressions, as they moved from anger and hatred to alarm and revulsion and nausea. He put his hand to his mouth, turned, and headed for the exit.

Rick chewed steadily. Suddenly, everything tasted a thousand percent better.

Revenge is a dish best served cold. But it was all right to eat it hot, if it was beef stew and every spoonful made your sworn enemy turn a more striking shade of green.

The tests had gone on forever; and then, suddenly, they were over. The unsuccessful trainees vanished one evening, before the final results were announced. No one had a chance to complain, gloat or commiserate. The twenty remaining recruits were simply told the next morning that they would be going to space for additional tests and training.

No official rankings for performance were released, but somehow the word spread. Loudmouth Chick Teazle had done best of all. It was an unpopular result, making him seem even more obnoxious than before. Vido Valdez and Rick

Luban, competing with each other more than with anyone else, had finished absolutely neck and neck. Neither had a chance to crow. Vido's dark face threatened future violence. Alice Klein, looking at the end of the course even thinner, paler and weaker than at the beginning, had somehow squeaked through. Rick couldn't imagine how she had done it—he knew for a fact that she was not half as strong as him, and she didn't seem well-coordinated or fast.

"She must have been screwing one of the testers," said Chick Teazle, standing in front of the electronic board where the list was posted. He brayed with laughter. Alice stared at him with those wide grey eyes, and thought unreadable thoughts.

Once again, the recruits had proof that Vanguard Mining did not waste time. That night there would be a celebration for the successful recruits—"Though what sort of a celebration can you have without drugs and booze?" Valdez grumbled—and the next day they would be on their way.

All twenty would travel together to the White Sands spaceport. Ten of the trainees would ship out first, traveling to a low orbit station on a single-stage-to-orbit vehicle. The other ten would join them forty-eight hours later, after the SSTO had returned to Earth and was ready to make its next ascent.

Dr. Alonzo Bretherton, who all through the tests had said hardly a word, joined them on the last evening and broke what they had begun to think of as his vow of silence.

"You may have questions," he said. "If you do, I'll try to answer them."

So far as Rick was concerned, that was easy. He had learned the rule long ago: The nail that sticks up gets the hammer. Nobody in his right mind drew attention to himself asking questions.

Apparently the other trainees had learned the same lesson, because there was a long silence. It was finally broken by a recruit already pegged by Rick as out of control. She was short and brown and curvy, with enormous brown eyes, and she could never sit still or keep quiet. Her name was Suzie Roy Cruse, but everyone called her Monkey. Word said she had been kicked out of her school for running a professional sex service—inside its walls. She was supposed to be perpetually horny, but Rick had been too stressed out by all the tests even to think of trying her.

"Yes—Suzie?" said Bretherton, as she coughed and fidgeted and held up her hand. Rick was sure he had almost called her Monkey. If the rest of Vanguard Mining was anything like this place, secrets must be impossible.

Having shown that she wanted to speak, Monkey now seemed to be thinking better of it.

"You have a question about Vanguard Mining, and what you are going to be doing in space," Bretherton prompted.

"No." And when everybody laughed, Monkey went on, "I do have a question, but it's not about space. It's about *here.*"

"I'll do my best."

"How come you keep males and females separated at night? And you run a curfew, and you *hit* people. One of the paramedics slugged me yesterday, just 'cause of something I said. That's against the law! I know we signed off on a deal

that says you're like parents, but parents can't do that stuff.
I could sue you, same as I could them."

"Are you planning to?"

"We-e-ell. I dunno. But I *could.*"

"I'll save you the time and effort. You'd lose if you tried."

"I still got my rights. I never signed those away."

"Of course you have, and of course you didn't." Bretherton rubbed at his broken nose, and looked more like an old street bruiser than ever. "But you don't seem to know where you are. Can anyone tell Monkey where she is?"

There was another silence, while everyone stared at each other.

"We're at Vanguard Mining's medical facility, in New Mexico," Chick Teazle said at last. "Least, that's what the sign says outside the front fence."

"And it's telling the truth. But we lease our space from someone else. This land belongs to the Mescalero-Apache Sovereign Nation. You, Monkey, like me and everyone else, are governed by the laws of that nation while we're here. Their laws and civil rights are not the ones you're used to, but we like some of 'em a whole lot better. For instance, parental authority over children. Tess Shawm had every right to pop you one yesterday, when you told her she had great T&A and she'd make a good hooker. You're lucky that's all she did."

Monkey gaped at him. Rick felt that his suspicion was confirmed. Absolutely *no* secrets here, of any kind, and therefore no privacy. There must be hidden monitors all over, too small and sneakily hidden to be found and smashed like the ones at school. This place was like a jail—worse than a jail! Nobody would dare hit a prisoner in a jail, or he'd be up on a dozen charges and have civil liberty lawyers biting his ass before he could turn round. The sooner Rick was out of here, the better.

"Does anyone else have a question?" said Bretherton at last. He had a grin on his battered face. "No questions? And no complaints? Well, then, let's get on with the party. I suspect it's the last one you'll have for quite a while."

He waved his hand toward a long table at the side of the room, loaded down with food and drink, and headed that way himself. Rick estimated the amount of food, counted heads, and made a decision. If he ran out for a quick trip to the head there would be plenty of everything left for him when he got back, and not so many people crowding round the table to get it.

He went in the opposite direction from everyone else, left the room, and headed along the white-walled corridor that led to his dormitory and beyond that to the men's room. When he came out, thirty seconds later, he could already hear laughter from around the corner. The fun hadn't taken long to start. He was hurrying back along the corridor when someone stepped suddenly out of the dormitory. Rick was grabbed by the shoulder, pulled into the dormitory, and spun back against the wall.

"In a hurry?" said a gruff voice.

It was Vido Valdez. Rick dropped into a defensive crouch.

"No fighting while the tests were on," Vido went on. "But that's all over now. Time for you and me to have a little talk, here where it's nice and quiet."

He was standing in front of Rick, hands raised. Rick knew from watching Valdez perform on the tests that he was fast. He was also a couple of inches taller, had a longer reach, and outweighed Rick by thirty or forty pounds. Rick assumed they both had plenty of streetfighting experience.

The only good news was the lack of knives and guns at the Vanguard Mining facility. This was going to be straight hand-to-hand—or foot-to-foot.

As Vido came at him Rick braced himself against the wall and kicked out with his heavy-shod right foot. His target was Vido's testicles, but Vido sidestepped and grabbed for Rick's leg. He almost had it. The only way that Rick could make him miss was to hurl himself forward, using the wall as a push-off point, and slam into Vido's chest. His skull came up under Vido's chin, but it was not a clean hit. He heard a grunt and knew he had done no serious damage. That was confirmed when he was pushed away one-handed and Valdez's other fist came round to swipe him on the side of the head.

Rick jumped out of reach, ear ringing. He now knew for certain what he had suspected before: he could not compete with Vido for raw strength. And he was not sure he could compete on speed.

Valdez was coming in again, crouching to protect his head and testicles. Rick tried a stab with stiffened fingers at the eyes and only managed to hurt himself on Vido's hard skull as the other ducked. An uppercut from Vido missed, but a second later his other fist delivered a swinging roundhouse punch to Rick's other ear. For a second he could not see straight. The only way he could be sure that Vido would not hit him again was to close in and grapple body to body.

He hugged Valdez and tried to butt him and knee him. At the same time Vido was trying to knee Rick in the balls. Their legs tangled together and threw them both off balance.

Clutching each other, they fell to the dormitory floor. Rick's head just missed the solid metal leg of one of the beds, but he landed on top.

He heard the wind whoosh out of Vido. He tried to follow up with a punch to the solar plexus, but they were too close for him to get any real force behind it. And then Vido had him in a bear hug and was squirming around so that Rick was underneath. He fought to get back on top, and they went rolling over and over until they came to the wall.

Rick was the unlucky one. He was on top when they met the wall, but that meant it was his head that smashed into the cement with the momentum from both of them. He lost his hold on Vido and saw stars. The next thing he knew he was flat on his back, wedged in the angle between floor and wall. He could not get his left hand free.

Vido was sprawled on top of him. He gave Rick one solid punch on the left cheek, then skinned his knuckles on the wall trying to hook with his other hand.

He swore and grabbed Rick around the neck. His thumbs dug hard into Rick's throat. Rick bucked and jerked, but Valdez was too heavy and too well positioned. Rick could not dislodge him.

It was impossible to breathe. Rick groaned and gasped. His windpipe was constricted, the air passage cut off. He clawed at Vido's wrists but he could not break the stranglehold. The strength was going from his hands as Vido steadily throttled him. His full weight was pressing on Rick's chest. In another twenty seconds he became just a dark shape above Rick, squeezing ruthlessly.

And then suddenly he was gone. Rick, staring upward bulging-eyed, imagined a second and even bigger form looming over him. As he took in a first long and tortured breath, he saw that Valdez was standing in an uncomfortable crouch, one arm pinned behind his back and lifted toward his neck in a half-nelson hold. Vido was gasping in pain.

"I think that will do," said a cheerful voice. A huge hand came reaching down toward Rick. "Here, grab hold. Are you all right?"

Rick was far from all right—but he was not going to admit that to Doctor Bretherton, and still less to Vido Valdez. "I'm—I'm fine. Bit—short of breath. Guess I'm still not in—top condition." He straightened his clothes.

"Fine." Bretherton had been holding Vido helpless, apparently without effort. Now he released him, and Vido grunted in relief. "So all three of us can get back to the others. One thing, though, for both of you. You've had your fun now, so there'll be no more of this."

"Who told you what was happening?" Vido asked. He was rubbing his chin, where a bruise was already forming. Rick decided it would be all right to massage his own sore throat and ears.

"Nobody told me," Bretherton said. "I saw it coming. I knew you two would be at each other sometime, the first minute I saw you. I'm glad you held off until the tests were over, though. It would have been a shame to kick you out. And I would have. There's no point in having rules if you don't follow them. But do it again here, and you're both history."

"So we don't get—get kicked out?" asked Rick.

"For a little fun? Of course not. What would a party be, without a bit of a fight?" Bretherton headed for the door of the dormitory. "It's time for me to get back there. You, too, but take time to catch your breath. There'll still be plenty of everything when you get there. Remember, though: it's over."

He was gone. Rick and Vido stared at each other warily. Doctor Bretherton was no longer in the dormitory, but his presence seemed to hang over the room.

"Better get back there," Rick muttered at last.

"Yeah. I guess."

They headed for the door at the same time and wedged into it together. Neither one was willing to give way. They turned, so that they were face to face and staring into each other's eyes as they edged through into the corridor.

Vido raised his fist toward Rick, then dropped it to his side. "You got away this time, Luban. He saved your hairy ass, and you know it. I'm not dumb enough to do anything right now, not after what the doc said. But you better remember something, scumball."

His hand came up, to rub at his bloodshot left eye. "This ain't over. It ain't over 'til *I say* it's over."

CHAPTER FIVE

WEEKS of mind-numbing tests, mental and physical, and the discomforts that went with them; they were all converging now, collapsing to a single and final minute.

Rick had been strapped into his seat for more than an hour. Next to him sat Deedee Mao, another of Vanguard Mining's recent recruits. Like him she had been expelled from her school at sixteen, but as he had discovered in the last hour of conversation they had little else in common. She and a dozen other trainees had been flown to the White Sands launch site from an East Coast medical test facility, two thousand miles away, to join Rick and the rest of his group. She was big, loud, and self-confident, just the sort of aggressive female that he hated. She and Rick had found themselves arguing almost from the first sentence. As the single-stage-to-orbit launch vehicle came closer to departure, however, they had both gradually quietened. For the past quarter of an hour neither of them had said a word.

That silence suited Rick. He didn't want to talk to *anybody*. He could not take his eyes from the changing digits of the display. *Sixty-two—sixty-one.* A siren began to wail inside the ship. Only one more minute to lift-off.

He knew, intellectually, that riding the single stage vessel to orbit was not much more dangerous than taking a PV across the city. So why was he gripping the arms of his seat so hard?

There was an odd whirring sound and a vibration of the metal surface beneath Rick's feet. The hatch was moving to its final sealed setting. That meant that the lasers were powered up, waiting for their first discharge. The cover beneath the SSTO would have opened, to reveal the ablative layers.

Rick tried to concentrate on factual matters. The first minute would be the most uncomfortable. That's when he and Deedee and the eighteen other trainees aboard would feel the highest acceleration. After that the ground lasers would be switched off and the onboard nuclear rocket would cut in. The acceleration force on them would drop to two gees.

Thirty-two, thirty-one, thirty . . .

There were voices in the background: the ground crew for the ship, just three people. Their duties had been explained to Rick as part of the "informed consent" briefing.

The moving display in front of him seemed to have slowed, minutes passing between each second. Before he got here, Rick had imagined that travel to and in space would be conducted wearing spacesuits. The first White Sands briefing had taught him that was an idiotic idea, as out-of-date as the notion that aircraft passengers all wore parachutes. Rick was dressed in the same informal uniform of blue shirt and slacks that had become familiar to him since the day he arrived in New Mexico for the medical tests.

Twenty, nineteen, eighteen . . .

Almost as safe as a trip on the PV, the briefings said. But every day the media carried news of PV accidents. The vehicle he was sitting in felt far more vulnerable. Laser power could fail; the nuclear rocket could refuse to cut in; or it could refuse to turn off at the right time and hurtle the passengers away to oblivion. You could sometimes walk away from a PV accident. Had anyone ever walked away from an SSTO failure? There *had* been failures, he knew that for a fact.

Rick tried to steel himself for anything. He failed. It was with total astonishment that he suddenly felt a hand on his thigh.

You were supposed to keep your arms and hands flat on the padded seat support during launch. Rick turned. Deedee Mao was staring straight ahead of her. Her high-cheekboned, yellow face was oddly pale and rigid, but her fingers were squeezing and rubbing his leg.

"Wanna get it on when we're at the transfer station?"

She could only be speaking to him, but he could hardly hear her or see her lips moving. "Y'know, in freefall. I hear it's somethin' special."

It was the worst possible time for a sexual proposition. Even if he had known Deedee well, even if had *liked* her, Rick was far too nervous to feel horny.

But he wasn't going to admit to her or anyone else just how he *did* feel.

"Sure." His voice sounded like an old man's. He cleared his throat. "Sure." Then he couldn't say any more.

Twelve, eleven, ten . . .

"I'll be in c-cabin t-t—." Deedee's fingers on his thigh were trembling. "Cabin t-t-twenty-eight."

Five, four, three—

"Oh, sweet Lord—"

Her hand was trembling worse. With fear, not passion. Rick felt an unexpected sympathy. Deedee was seeking distraction, anything to help her through the first seconds of launch.

"She's tracking," a crewman's voice said.

"Mirror's free."

Two, one . . .

Anything to help. And he needed distraction as much as she did.

Zero.

"Up ship."

As the final digit flickered into sight, Rick broke the rules, too. He lifted his arm from the padded support, placed his hand on top of Deedee's, and patted it.

Within half a second he knew that he had made the mistake of the century. Lift had begun. Deedee's hand and his own were suddenly welded together, pressed down by more than five gees of acceleration. His leg was tilted slightly upward and their joined hands inched up his thigh toward his groin.

Rick gasped with pain. If that monster weight kept moving up his body, it would turn him into a eunuch. He tried to lift his hand and arm and found them sheathed in lead. He could not raise *his* hand, let alone Deedee's. All he could do, with one desperate jerk, was push their hands a couple of inches away along his leg and hold them there.

The pain and pressure was excruciating. Deedee's whole forearm lay across his thigh. He could feel bruises forming there in real-time. He sat silent and sweating, pushing and pushing forever, until without warning all weight vanished completely. His stomach at once came free of its moorings and started to float up into his throat, but before he had time to gag he was again pressed back into his seat. This time the force was endurable. It had to be the two gees of the nuclear drive, but compared with the laser-boosted liftoff it felt like nothing.

Rick lifted his hand away from Deedee's, closed his eyes, and relaxed. After a few moments he felt her hand leave his thigh.

"Luban. That your name?"

"Yeah?" He opened his eyes and glanced across at her. Deedee Mao's smooth face was still pale but now it bore its old belligerent expression.

"Don't get no funny ideas, Luban."

"Like what?"

"I mean, about what I might have said back there at liftoff."

"I won't."

"I mean, I was just making conversation."

Rick couldn't let that pass. "Like hell! You were scared white. You should change your name from Deedee to pee-pee. You were ready to pee in your pants."

"Making love to you appeals less than screwing a swamp toad."

"I guess you've tried that. Tough on the toad."

She reached over and grabbed his arm. "Listen, if you want to have this out when we get to the station that's fine by me. I've eaten smart-ass jerks like you—"

She paused. The steady roar beneath them had ended. Suddenly they were in freefall, gliding upward in dead silence. Rick once more felt his stomach start to move up his throat.

"—eaten them for breakf—" Deedee couldn't complete the word. Her brown eyes bulged and her mouth clamped shut. She turned away from Rick, reaching forward and trying to hold off long enough to get her suction mask into position.

Rick clenched his own teeth and closed his eyes again. He wished he could close his ears, too. Any smart-ass jerks that Deedee had eaten for breakfast were coming up again, along with everything else; and from the sound of it Deedee was just getting into her stride. Rick didn't want to watch.

Sex in freefall—or, fighting, or anything else with the possible exception of dying—didn't seem to be in Rick and Deedee Mao's immediate future.

Rick had been told quite a few things about Vanguard Mining's operations, but he lacked the glue to put the pieces together. For instance, he knew from the short briefings at the medical facility and at White Sands that franchises for commercial mining of the Belt had bogged down in endless debate within the Council of Nations. That deadlock had continued until the Council's own international (and multilingual) mining effort had ended in disaster, with the loss of all equipment and personnel.

At that point, business interests were suddenly permitted to mine the asteroid belt—and welcome to it. The Council had decided that there was no profit to be made there, although they were more than ready to accept franchise fees. They were astonished when Vanguard Mining's prototype mine and refinery turned out to be profitable. In the subsequent sixteen years the company had established commercial mining and refining operations on thirty-eight different asteroids out in the Belt.

Rick knew all that. He had also been told, at the time of his first tests by Vanguard, that the woman speaking to him was located on some place called CM-2, in translunar orbit. But in school, astronomy had been of no interest. He didn't know the difference between LEO and GEO, or cislunar and translunar. He was more interested in chastity belts than asteroid belts.

It never occurred to Rick to connect the things he had been told until the translunar transfer vehicle carrying him and thirty-one other trainees up from the holding station in low earth orbit was close enough for Rick to actually *see* CM-2.

He had been expecting some sleek, clean-lined structure. Instead he found their vehicle was closing on a vast irregular lump of dark rock.

"That thing?" Rick spoke to Deedee, who was standing

between him and Jigger Tait, a Vanguard miner who was
hitching a ride back from Earth with the trainees. "That can't
be the training center."

In the two days since first lift-off, Rick and Deedee had
been observing a sort of armed truce. Their ship, station, and
dining-area seat assignments had forced them to be together
most of the time, but neither one was sure enough of either
knowledge or stomach stability to risk an assertion of superiority. So it was Jigger, big-boned, iron-stomached, unaf-
fected by freefall, and apparently totally self-confident in
every way, who raised his pale eyebrows, sniffed disdainfully,
and said, "Don't you guys know *anything?* That's CM-2 out
there—commercial mine number two."

"But I thought the mines were all out in the Belt."

"They are. But this one has been worked out commer-
cially. When the iron and siderophiles—that's nickel and
platinum and iridium—were all gone they attached low-
thrust engines and moved it to translunar, so now it's the
headquarters for the Vanguard training school."

"I don't remember that from any briefings." Rick looked
questioningly at Deedee, who shook her head.

"Me neither."

"Then you didn't use the browse feature on your
reader."

"We weren't told we had to."

Jigger sniffed again. "I'm sure you weren't. But I'll give
you some free advice that I had to learn the hard way when
I was a trainee: If you only do what you're *told* to do, you'll
soon be in trouble at Vanguard Mining." Jigger lifted from
his seat, moving effortlessly in the zero-gee environment.
"Okay kids. Better get your act together and strap in. We'll

be docking in a few more minutes. But before you sit down, take a quick look at that."

He pointed outside, away from CM-2. At first Rick saw nothing but bright unwinking stars. He stared hard, and finally noticed something like a tiny feather of sparkling blue-white where Jigger Tait had pointed.

"What is it?" asked Deedee. "A comet?"

"No such luck. That, friends, is the competition. Take a good look, and hope you won't be seeing a lot like it."

"That's a *ship*," Rick exclaimed. "Isn't it?"

"It is. But it's not one of ours, you can tell that from the drive. They use pulsed fusion, we use continuous fusion. So their ships don't show a continuous exhaust. If you want to travel rough, ride one of those babies—an acceleration that varies between zero and two gees and back, every ten seconds."

"What do you mean, not one of *ours?*" asked Deedee.

"What I said. That's part of the fleet of Avant Mining and Refining."

"Who?"

"God! Don't they tell you guys *anything?*" Jigger glared at them. "Avant Mining and Refining. Founded seven years after Vanguard. They're aggressive, expanding fast. That one's on its way back from the Belt. Did you think we had a damned *monopoly* out here?"

"Nobody ever mentioned Avant Mining," said Deedee defensively, and looked at Rick for confirmation. He nodded.

"Well, they will," Tait said. "Maybe you shouldn't hear this from me, but you're going to find it out sooner or later. Avant make our management real nervous. They've had a couple of big successes in the Belt, places where they got to

a rich asteroid and staked their claim on it before we did—
even though we thought our prospectors had found it first,
and we had the inside track. Believe me, Avant is *tough*. Pa-
cific Rim financing, and they play real hardball. You'll see."

He floated away toward the rear of the ship. Rick and
Deedee lingered at the screen for a few seconds longer, staring at the insignificant mote of Vanguard's competition. But
then their attention turned again to their destination. CM-2
seemed much more important to their immediate future than
Avant Mining.

Now that they were closer they could see the true size
of the training asteroid. Each of the wart-like bubbles that
covered the surface of the planetoid was actually the exit
point for a mine shaft, three to ten meters across. The whole
object must be riddled with tunnels. CM-2 seemed more like
a whole world than a training facility.

The now-familiar warning siren began to wail. Thrust
was coming in sixty seconds. Rick led the way back to their
seats, striving to mimic the easy free-space motion of Jigger
Tait. He couldn't do it. After a few seconds of aimless drifting he was forced to pull himself along using seat backs as
handholds. Convinced that Deedee was watching him and
laughing, he turned his head. She had just bounced off a wall
and was turning end-over-end with a bewildered expression
on her face. He went back and helped her to reach her seat.

One thing about freefall, Rick thought as they reached
CM-2 and went through docking, pressurization, and dis-
embarkation: it made you a lot less likely to laugh at somebody else—because you never knew how soon your turn
would come to look like an idiot.

As he left the pressurized dock he turned and caught a

glimpse of Earth through the transparent overhead dome. It hung above him, about twice as big as a full moon.

He halted and stared up at it for a long time. Somewhere on that globe was his school, with Screw and Hoss and Juanita and Jackie, with Mr. Hamel and Mr. Preebane and Principal Rigden. Somewhere were his mother and Mick, living it up on what they had been paid by Vanguard Mining—unless it was already all spent. Somewhere were Doctor Bretherton and Tess Shawm, taking in the next batch of recruits and testing them to the point of collapse.

They were all on that far-off blue-grey ball, all invisible, close to each other in space but seven hundred thousand kilometers away from him.

It felt more like seven hundred million.

CHAPTER SIX

L **ET** me introduce myself." The man was plump and balding, with fleshy cheeks and drooping jowls. "I'm Turkey Gossage, chief of the training program on CM-2. You can think of me as the principal here—the head teacher. You don't know it yet, but I'm the best thing that ever happened to you."

Rick had taken a position near the back. He craned for a better look. The man in front of the group was dressed in a black tanktop and jeans rather than the standard jacket and slacks. He scowled aggressively as he stared at them, but his blue eyes were sparkling. There had been a low general mutter from the group, and he was reacting to it.

"You heard me, sweethearts? The *best* thing. So if you got something to say, get it off your chest now."

No one spoke.

"You, sweetheart." Gossage pointed a finger at a woman in the front row. "I see your mouth moving, but I don't hear you. Don't whisper. Tell all of us."

"Don't you call me sweetheart!" It was Deedee, not much to Rick's surprise. "You can't do that."

"I can't, eh?" Gossage was grinning, but his neck and jowls turned red as turkey wattles. It was suddenly obvious how he got his nickname. "Why not?"

"Because it's degrading, and it's insulting. It's also sexually discriminatory. Do it one more time, and I'll take you to court." Deedee paused.

"You mean you'll sue me?" Gossage grinned again, but now it was unexpectedly friendly. "Sweetheart, that word is music to my ears. It proves we've got innocent new blood out here on CM-2, and it leads me straight in to what I have to say to all of you. Let's get a few things out of the way right now. First, forget the sexual discrimination talk. I call *every-one* sweetheart. You, and bluebeard standing next to you"— that was Chick Teazle—"and the one at the back with the shitface grin on his chops."

Gossage was looking right at Rick. Rick stopped smiling. He saw Vido Valdez in front of him turning to smirk. Next to Vido, Alice Klein stared at and right through Rick.

"Far as I'm concerned," Gossage went on, "you're *all*

sweethearts 'til you prove otherwise. As for suing me, good luck to you. You're not on sue-'em-all Earth now. We got exactly two lawyers out beyond the Moon, and they're up to their asses in mineral depletion allowances and tax codes. If you can afford their time, you don't belong here. And if you did manage to sue, you'd lose for reasons that I'll go into in a minute. So tell me what else is on your mind. You were angry before I ever called you sweetheart."

Deedee shook her head. It was another youth in the second row, one of the East Coast additions to Rick's group, who spoke up.

"What's this *teacher* bullshit? I done with school two month ago. Nuthin' 'bout school in anythin' anybody said to me."

"I see. What's your name?"

"Cokie Mulligan."

"All right, Cokie Mulligan. Nothing about school in anything anybody said to you. Right. You *read* your contract, did you? The one that you and your parents or guardians signed."

"Sure I did."

"The whole thing?—including the fine print."

Mulligan hesitated. "Yes."

"Then you noticed the place where it says that Vanguard Mining, and in particular its authorized instructors—people like me—are *in loco parentis* to you for the duration of your contract."

"Don't know what that means."

"*In loco parentis* means *in place of your parents.*" Turkey Gossage smiled horribly at Mulligan. "So now I'm like your daddy and your mommy, all rolled up into one. And I'm going to take better care of you than they ever did."

Mulligan shook his head. "Maybe. But I don't want no teacher, an' I'm not goin' to no dumb school. I hate school and I'm done school. I never signed up for that."

There was a general mutter of agreement from everyone in the group.

"I see." Turkey Gossage turned, floated across to a chair facing the front of the room, and straddled it with his forearms folded along the back. "What we have here, I suspect, is a simple failure to communicate. It's that hated word, *school*, isn't it? It suggests the wrong thing to all of you, and I shouldn't have used it.

"So let's agree that this isn't a school. Let's say it's a survival course for off-Earth mining operations. The Belt is a dangerous place. You can screw up bigtime out there, eat vacuum, OD on radiation, blow yourself up, get flattened by an ore crusher, get stranded and starve to death. No legal liability for Vanguard Mining—read your contract. But Vanguard doesn't want you dead, because we already have an investment in you. You think all those tests you took don't cost money? So it's my job to make sure that by the time you leave here you know how to *avoid* killing yourself. That means learning a few new rules. Anybody object to the idea of *surviving?*"

Rick shook his head and glanced around at the others. Everyone was doing the same.

"Good." The smile never left Turkey Gossage's face. "Now we get down to details. I'm going to give you assignments that have to be completed before bedtime. But before we talk about them I want to talk about *you*. I'm sure you all think you're hot-shot and special and smarter than most people. And maybe you actually are—otherwise you wouldn't be here at all. But smart or not, at the moment you're still zeros. No skills means no value.

"Before we're through here, that will change. You'll have skills. You'll have value. You'll have a *reason* to think you're hot-shot and special. And it all starts with the assignments. Today it will be reading. All right?"

Nods all around.

"Just one thing." Turkey Gossage was deliberately casual. "I said *reading*, and I meant reading. By you. Not with a reading machine. There will be times out in the Belt where a knowledge of complex instructions is vital and no electronic readers are available. So you have to be able to read. I'll let you into a big secret, something you'd never be told in an Earth school: reading is easy! Practically everyone can learn to read with a bit of effort. All of you can, or you wouldn't be here. And we won't go too fast at first. Short words, easy sentences."

There was a stir at the back of the class. A short-haired and overweight blond girl was moving toward the door.

"Now where are you going?" Gossage did not raise his voice. "Leaving us already?"

She turned angrily at the doorway. "Yes, I am."

"What's your name?"

"I'm Gladys de Witt. I didn't read none when I was in school, and I'm damned if I'm going to start now I'm out of it. Go screw yourself, Gossage. You think you're the boss, but you're not. You can't stop me leaving. I seen the contract. I don't have to stay. It says you can't use violence on me, neither."

"That's quite true. I can't prevent any one of you from leaving. I can't be violent with you—though we might disagree on what constitutes violence. And I can't make you complete your assignments." Gossage nodded slowly. "Very true. All I can do, Gladys de Witt, is explain these to you." He held up a handful of small pink cards. "They are meal vouchers. You need one to obtain food from the cafeteria service system. When you complete your assignment satisfactorily—by this evening, or tomorrow morning, or tomorrow midday, or whenever—you will receive one voucher. But if you fail to complete your assignment to my satisfaction, you will not."

"You can't do that to me!"

"I'm afraid I can. Read your contract. Vanguard Mining, *in loco parentis*, decides the manner and extent of trainee nutrition. Now, Gladys. Are you going to leave? Or would you like to stay here with the rest of the trainees while I explain today's assignment? Dinner is lasagna with mushrooms, peppers, and garlic bread. The choice is yours."

Turkey Gossage could smile and coax with the best of them, but he was one tough son of a bitch. His language would have horrified Mr. Hamel, and he hadn't been kidding about the food voucher policy. After a few missed meals and a taste of CM-2 gruel, even the toughest and most ornery—and hungriest—trainee came into angry line.

Rick observed closely, then put Turkey Gossage into his "handle with care" category. What he couldn't understand, though, was how Gossage had found himself such a pleasant, easygoing—and droolingly sexy—assistant.

Gina Styan was a graduate trainee from three years back, returned for two months to work with Gossage on CM-2 before she went to her post on the newest of the thirty-eight Belt mines. She had a figure that made Juanita Cesaro and Monkey Cruse look like boys, clear dark skin, and short-cropped black hair that emphasized delicate bone structure and high cheekbones. Those, plus what Rick read as an unmistakable interest in her brown eyes whenever she looked at him, bristled the hair on the back of his neck. The sight of her made him catch his breath.

She had the hots for him. He was sure of it. All it would take was a quiet place and an opportunity.

Which seemed to be exactly what CM-2 was designed not to provide. It was just as well that Deedee Mao's liftoff invitation to Cabin Twenty-Eight had been bogus, because it now proved to be impossible. She shared her tiny cabin with three other trainees, including Monkey Cruse. Rick would love to have heard the conversations in there, but when it came to accommodation he was no better off. His cabin had five recruits in it, including Cokie Mulligan, who snored like a saw in freefall though he swore he hadn't when he was back on Earth.

Vido Valdez, thank goodness, was two cabins along, bunked with Chick Teazle and a couple of East Coasters. Vido and Rick still glared at each other whenever they met, but apparently Valdez was willing to see their feud damped down—at least for the time being.

Privacy was no better during work periods. The recruits were never out of each other's sight, except when they were busy on work assignments. Then they were permitted the privacy of a single small cubicle. After the first week Rick suspected Turkey Gossage of doing that on purpose. When the only way to be alone was to sit in a little room by yourself and pretend to study, you found yourself actually studying part of the time out of sheer boredom. Almost against his will, Rick found himself starting to read. He still wasn't good, and he resented every word, but within a couple of weeks he'd have beaten everybody in his old class and most of his fellow trainees. He was in no hurry to rush on ahead. After reading, Turkey Gossage threatened pure and applied mathematics— "the queen of the sciences, the high spot of all your training," as he put it, without convincing anyone. And before they could graduate, every one of them had to write a letter home.

"What the hell for?" Chick Teazle protested. "My mother hates my guts—and anyway, she can't read."

"I'm sure she loves you dearly." The smile never left Turkey's face. "She'll find a reader, or get somebody else to read it to her. But even if she doesn't, even if she tears it up and throws it straight down the chute, that doesn't let you off the hook. You still have to write—and I have to be able to read it."

Rick had started a letter three times in the first two weeks, and scrapped the result after a couple of sentences. What was he supposed to say? That he preferred it out here to being with his mother and Mick? Even if that was true, Rick suspected that Turkey Gossage wouldn't let a letter go out that way. The problem of *what* to write was going to be as difficult as the writing itself.

Rick crumpled up his fourth shot at writing, threw it away, and stared at the cubicle wall. Never mind letters to his mother. They wouldn't make him feel any less horny. The big problem now was Gina Styan. How was he ever going to make out with her if they were never alone?

A possible answer came in the third week, when the pure theory of space operations gave way to practical experience. All the trainees had become accustomed to freefall, so nausea was a thing of the past. But manual work in space was another matter. That took lots of practice.

And practice they were going to get, in assignments that Turkey Gossage described as "Manual coordination and control in a weightless environment." A euphemism, as Rick soon discovered, for unpaid hard labor.

Weightless environment. Moving things around in space, where an object didn't weigh anything, sounded easy as breathing. Nothing to it. Jigger Tait, staying a while on CM-2 with Turkey Gossage before shipping to the Belt again, assured Rick as much. Then he and Rick went together to the deep interior of CM-2 to clear one of the chambers. They moved massive pilings and metal I-beams and irregular chunks of rock.

After four hours of that Rick ached in every bone. His burdens might have no weight, but they still possessed *inertia*. And inertia was *worse* than weight. In fact, it was twice as bad. Back on Earth, once you had lifted something you could just let it drop and gravity would do the rest. Here you had to work to start a rock moving, then put in just as much labor to stop it.

But Jigger had not been lying. He did the work effortlessly. It *was* easy as breathing—for him.

Rick wondered how many other half-truths and hidden catches were tucked away in the Vanguard Mining training program. Turkey Gossage was sticking to his policy on the meal vouchers. After two bowls of cold and sticky oatmeal, Rick had finally handed in his last assignment. He had been handed a meal ticket just before he left with Jigger. It sat burning a hole in his pocket while his stomach growled in protest. He could hardly wait for the word to quit.

But when Jigger Tait told him they were done for the day, Rick still had enough energy and curiosity to notice something when they emerged through the airlock from the planetoid's stony interior. It was a different lock from their entry point, and next to it sat another small chamber. It was like no other structure that Rick had seen. There were flat, solid, windowless walls and a massive close-fitting door.

Rick's question about it produced no more than a shrug and a dismissive "Historical interest only" from Jigger. Tait would have continued back around the planetoid toward the training facility quarters, but Rick stopped in front of him and swung open the heavy door.

"Hey! Padded floor and walls. What's the deal?"

"Bolt-hole." Jigger followed him inside. The interior lights had come on automatically. "Before the mining work produced the deep interior tunnels, the miners always faced a radiation danger. Our suits aren't enough to protect us."

"Solar flares?"

"Yeah." Jigger stared at Rick. "I thought you couldn't read."

"Videos. Show it as a standard hazard for space travel."

"Well, for once they got it right. If you're out on the surface of an asteroid and a big flare hits, you have three choices: you can move to the interior tunnels, if there are any, or you can head for a special shielded chamber like this one. Me, I'll take this any day. Your own air, see, the interior fills by itself when the door is locked. And there's plenty of reserves of food and drink. Stay here for a week if you had to."

"But there's no airlock."

"There is on the inside. That was put in later. When they built this they figured anyone coming in from space might be in one hell of a hurry."

"You said there are three choices?"

"Sure." Jigger was already moving back through the thick door. "You can stay outside and fry if you want to. Freedom of choice. Isn't that what people back on Earth are all so proud of?"

"Freedom to *die?*"

"Sure. Most basic right of all." Jigger started around the planetoid, swinging easily along on the fixed network of cables. "Hell, you should be free to die when you want, where you want, how you want. If you're not, your body and your life don't belong to you at all. They belong to your keepers."

"You can die any way you want to?"

"Sure I can. Anyone works for Vanguard Mining has that right. But dying is a right, no more. It's not an *obligation.* So watch your step, Rick. Space is more dangerous than you think."

CHAPTER SEVEN

RICK remembered Jigger Tait's words about the dangers of space, more or less. But what he thought about a lot more in the next few days was that shielded chamber. Radiation-proof—and soundproof. He visited it a couple more times when he had no other duties. Thick walls, padded floor, and tight-fitting door. Total privacy. Just what he needed.

It took four days before he could trade with Monkey

Cruse for her next one-on-one training session with Gina Styan in the interior of CM-2. Fortunately Monkey had her own hot ideas about Jigger Tait. She didn't tell Rick what this particular training was for, and Rick didn't ask. He'd be willing to move a lot of rocks for a chance at Gina.

This time his job turned out to be both easier and harder than manual labor. Rick had to learn to operate remote-controlled cutting equipment, and Gina proved to be a hell of a tough teacher. She ran him through scores of operating steps again and again, watching him with that slightly mocking, sexy and intimate look on her face whenever he messed up a sequence.

"There's a lot to this." Rick felt obliged to defend himself when the session ended with the cutter under his control waltzing wildly sideways to gouge a hole in the tunnel side wall. "How long did it take *you* to remember all the variations?"

"I'm not sure I ever did."

"You have a pictorial prompt in your suit helmet? Then why in hell didn't you give me one?"

"No prompt." Gina waved a small red book at Rick. "The control steps are in here, along with a lot of other stuff. But it's all in words and formulas. Once you can read well—"

"This is really dumb. A few simple pictures, that's all it would take."

"You think so? Listen to this, then you tell me how you would put it into pictures. 'Pressure equalization between old and new drilling is best achieved by releasing stored air into the evacuated chamber. The cutting equipment normally produces a straight cylindrical cavity three meters in diameter, so the volume to be filled is simply $2.25 \cdot \pi \cdot L$ cubic meters, where L is the length of the new drilled tunnel in meters.' You know what π is?"

"I think so. I'm not sure." Rick was actually quite sure. Sure he didn't.

"It's a mathematical constant. Draw me a picture of *that* if you can. Do you know its value?"

Rick shook his head. This wasn't going the way he had imagined it, but he'd bide his time. Let Gina feel superior for the moment. She would find out soon enough who was the real boss.

"Why should I bother to know any of that math stuff? If I ever need it I'll pull it up on a calculator."

"π is equal to 3.14159." She didn't seem to have heard him. "That's to six significant figures. It's as accurate as you'll probably ever need unless you get into orbit work, then you'll want it to twelve. You'll have the value of π engraved on your brain stem and your butt before you leave CM-2, along with a lot of other numbers you've never heard of yet. And while we're at it, let me tell you what happens to a calculator or an electronic prompter during a blow-out or a big radiation storm: they die, or they become totally unreliable. But this"—Gina held up the red book—"it can stand more radiation, heat, and cold than you can. By the time a book like this became unusable, you or I would be long dead."

She tucked the book into a pocket on her suit. "You'll learn, Ricky boy. Let's go."

Rick had learned, at least some things. He had spent most of his few free hours studying and committing to memory the network of passages and chambers that criss-crossed the interior of CM-2. Without saying anything to Gina he headed for the surface along a particular set of passages. He emerged, just as planned, right beside the shielded chamber. The door was as he had left it, slightly ajar.

He stopped when he came to it, and led the way inside. "You ever been in one of these?"

"Ages ago. This, or one just like it." Gina had followed him and was glancing around her with no particular interest. "I don't know why they keep this place in working order. It has no uses since the interior was excavated."

"It does." Rick swung the heavy door into position and pressed the sealing button. Interior lights came on at once and there was a hiss of released air. He went across and checked that the inner door was also sealed.

"Not needed for radiation protection," he went on, "but it has other uses." He took off his suit helmet and gestured to Gina to do the same.

"You're wasting air." But Gina did not sound much concerned by that, and she followed Rick's lead and removed her own helmet. "Other uses? Like what?"

"Like this." Rick had been sizing up their positions and rehearsing his own next action. He knew the moves and he was pretty experienced, but that had been back on Earth. He had to do things differently in freefall.

The smart thing was to make a first move that he knew he could manage. He was close to the chamber wall. He kicked off from it, drove hard across the room, and pinned Gina against the opposite wall. He had to use both arms and legs to hold her there, but they finished face to face.

"Gina." He spoke in a whisper, though he could have screamed and no one else would have heard a thing. "Gina, you're really something special. Let's get out of these dumb suits and have some fun."

He tried to kiss her, but she turned her head away.

"Dammit, Rick, that's enough fooling. And it's not funny. Let me go."

He almost did. Then he remembered Screw Savage's advice to him and Hoss. "*No* never means no with a woman. They say it because they like to play hard to get, but they really want it bad as you do. You gotta ignore what they *say* and keep chargin'. Go for the gold!"

Rick moved his left arm quickly to turn Gina's head back toward him, pressed his mouth to hers, and started to give her a French kiss. His right hand felt at the same time for her breast.

It was as though he had pressed a starter button. As his fingers met her left nipple through the resilient material of the suit, her right knee pistoned up between his legs. It hit him squarely in the crotch like a bony hammer.

Rick gasped and curled up into a ball, hanging in midair. He was sure that the blow had burst his testicles and driven them right back inside his body. He vaguely heard Gina speak through his fog of pain.

"You little shit! *Nobody* does that to me, *ever*. Apologize." She had him by the ear, pulling it off his head. "Apologize, right now, or I'll really hurt you."

Rick was curled up, forehead close to his knees. He could hardly breathe, and he certainly couldn't apologize. But if he didn't she might do the same thing to him again.

"Sorry!" It was more a gasp than a word. "Sorry."

"I don't know what made you think I'd be interested in a semiliterate oaf like you, but here's news: I'm not."

She let go of his ear, then clapped his helmet back onto

his head hard enough to make his ears ring. While he hung dizzy and helpless, she flipped his suit seals into position.

"You can find your own way back, dummy, or you can die trying. I don't much care which."

Rick heard the inner door slam shut and the airlock cycling. He tried to lift his head to see if Gina had gone, until a worse worry took over. Nausea swept through him. He felt ready to vomit—inside his suit.

He swallowed hard, closed his eyes, and fought the urge. The spasm slowly faded. By the time it was over his forehead was beaded with cold sweat and the sickness had been replaced by an agonizing throbbing in his belly and groin.

Fifteen minutes passed before he felt strong enough to leave the chamber. Then it was a miserable splay-legged crawl back to the training facilities. He paused before entering.

What had Gina told Turkey Gossage? Surely, the whole horrible episode. Rick was done for. He was going to be kicked out of this place, just as he had been kicked out of school. And where could he go now? Back to join the Pool on Earth?

Might as well get it over with. He couldn't hang around outside forever, and there was no way he could avoid the rage of Turkey Gossage.

Rick eased his way out of his suit and limped to Turkey's office. He didn't see anyone on the way, and he almost changed his mind when he was right at the entrance. But Gossage had already seen him on the threshold and waved him in.

"You took your time." Gossage nodded to Rick and at once returned his attention to the screen in front of him. "I didn't think you'd make it before I closed for the day. Help yourself to a meal voucher."

Rick, tensed and ready for a storm of anger, stared at Gossage open-mouthed. "What did Gina say?"

Turkey really looked at Rick for the first time. "Say? Why, what do you think she said? She said you did well. I know you rammed the wall with the cutter at the end, but Gina said that the test she gave you was harder than anything in the standard course. So you passed. Now, go and eat before I change my mind."

Rick grabbed the voucher and left before Gossage could ask him anything. But he didn't feel in the least like eating, and still less like going into the cafeteria where he might have to face Gina. He was sore, exhausted, and bewildered. He started for his cabin, knowing that he needed rest. Then he visualized Cokie Mulligan and the other trainees, watching him limp in and starting with their questions.

He couldn't stand that, either. Where could he go? The study cubicles were always crowded at this time of day.

The only place he could think of was the gym. It was a bit of a mystery why CM-2 even had a gym, because so far as he knew no one ever went there. But the region had light centrifugal gravity, and there were showers. He could examine and bathe his bruised and tender balls, stretch out on a couch, and not move until it was time to wake up and use his meal voucher for breakfast.

He dragged his way toward the outer circle of the station where the gym was located, thankful that it was a time when few people were about. Safe inside the bath-house, he removed all his clothes and took a warm bath. He examined himself closely. So far as he could tell everything down there was perfectly normal. He didn't even seem to be swollen, though it felt that way from the inside. Finally he went into the shower, set the water temperature as hot as he could stand, and simply let the stream run over his head and back for a long time.

By the time he dried himself and put on a change of clothing he was feeling human again. He emerged from the shower area and stopped. The gym was no longer deserted. Jigger Tait was running laps, round and round the inside of the big high-gee wheel. He must have been there for a while, because his blue tee-shirt was stained with sweat.

He nodded down at Rick when he caught sight of him and ran around the hoop of the track toward him. "Want to join me?"

Rick shook his head and started toward the exit. But he couldn't help moving in an awkward bow-legged fashion.

"You all right?" Jigger stepped closer.

"Yeah. I'm all right."

"You sure don't look it. That's a John Wayne walk—like you got a bad case of hemorrhoids, or you just took a dump in your pants. What happened?"

"I just—" Rick paused. He didn't have a lie in his head. Anyway, Jigger would find out soon enough, along with everybody else. He sighed. "I just did something really dumb."

And then, when Jigger said not a word, it all came spilling out. It seemed even worse in retelling than in reality. Jigger stood and listened in silence, the sweat cooling on his moon face and steam rising from his damp tee-shirt. It was only after Rick told how he had made his move on Gina, and she had kneed him in the testicles, that Jigger shook his head and said, "Wish I'd been there."

"You'd have stopped her?"

"No. I'd have broken you in two." Jigger grabbed Rick by the arm and led him to a pair of rowing machines, the only place where the two of them could sit down facing each other. "How old are you, kid?"

"Sixteen."

"Thought so. Know how old Gina is?"

"Nineteen?"

"She's twenty-two. You're like a baby to her. Hell, you *are* a baby. Back in school you probably felt like a real big shot—I know I did. I'd had girls, I'd busted teachers, the whole bit. But to Gina a kid from Earth is still in diapers. I'd say each year in space, 'specially in the Belt, is like three on Earth. You were a little kid making a pass at a grown-up."

"But she didn't report it to Gossage. And she *passed* me on the test I took."

"Sure she did, if you did well on it. Why wouldn't she? You didn't really upset her. How'd you feel if a ten-year-old girl came on strong to you? You'd think it was ludicrous. And you were being tested for proficiency, not maturity. Anyway, believe it or not, Gina likes you. If she didn't she'd have ripped your balls off and stuffed them down your throat. She'd have got away with it, too. What ever made you think for one second that she might be interested in you?"

"She looked at me like she was really fond of me."

"Yeah. Know why? Because you remind her of her kid brother. He's back on Earth and going nowhere, just the way she was before she tripped up and was sent out here. Gina admits it, she used to be a real tearaway. Her parents couldn't do a damn thing with her. But her brother's less of a rebel, and she's afraid he'll just stick in school to the end and finish up in the Pool."

"You don't think she'll tell anyone about what I did?"

"Don't see why she should. But I'll talk to her and make sure."

"Will she listen to you?"

"I think so." Jigger stared at Rick for a second, his head to one side. "You're not too observant, are you? I mean, you've never noticed that Gina and me are an item, have been for a year and a half. That's why I came to CM-2 instead of heading right out for the Belt. That's why I know about her, and what a hellcat she used to be, and all about her kid brother."

Rick gazed at Jigger in horror. He had just remembered what Jigger said about breaking him in two. "I didn't know— I didn't notice. I'm sorry. I mean, if I'd had any idea that you two—"

"You know now. Nothing wrong with feeling horny, either—it means you're physically adjusting to space. But stick to trainees. And don't forget one other thing. California where you came from has the strongest laws in the known universe against sexual harassment and rape, but they still don't work worth a damn. Out here we do things differently. A woman is taught a few tricks so she can look after herself. Deedee and Monkey and Gladys are getting special training you'll never hear about. All the girls are being taught how to look after themselves. Remember that, if you want to keep your balls." Jigger stood up from the rowing machine, came across, and patted Rick on the shoulder. "And while your jewels are still sore, use what happened with Gina to remind you of one other thing: If you want to survive in space, it's not enough to be able to read and write and calculate. You have to learn to *notice things*—the sort of stuff you won't find in any book."

*   *   *

Rick skulked for a week. He hid away in the privacy of the study cubicles, until finally and inevitably he had the dreaded face-to-face meeting with Gina. She came into the cafeteria with a group of trainees while he was taking a hurried meal.

Rick froze. But her casual greeting suggested that nothing unusual had ever happened between them. Rick breathed a prayer of thanks and decided that he could return to the normal harassed life of a trainee on CM-2.

It didn't work out that way. He didn't hide away any more from Gina, but soon he had even less free time than usual, as two new things happened in quick succession.

The first came when he ran into Jigger Tait, and the big man was again on his way for a session in the gym.

"Every day," said Jigger in answer to Rick's question. "So does Gina, and so does Turkey Gossage."

"But why? None of you is fat or anything."

"No. But we're in space, in a low-gee environment. Regular exercise is absolutely essential, otherwise you suffer calcium loss. Keep that up for a while and your bones get weak. When that happens it's a real bugger to get back to normal."

"But nobody's making *us* exercise."

"Give it another week and they will. You've only been excused because Turkey likes trainees to get their space legs before he lets them loose in the gym. Otherwise they run into walls or fall over things or tear muscles using the exercise equipment." Jigger studied Rick as they moved along side by side. "You seem to handle space pretty good. Take a bit of advice from me. Get a head start right now, and use the gym regular. The sooner you do, the less chance you'll have of long-term space problems."

Rick nodded, but he might have ignored Jigger if he hadn't run into Vido Valdez half an hour later. They converged in the quiet study area. Exactly one cubicle was vacant.

They stood together in front of the sliding door, with Rick a few inches in front. "Guess we could take turns," he said. "You—"

He didn't finish the sentence. Vido sideswiped him from behind. Rick went sprawling forward into the wall, and before he could get up Vido was inside and had closed the door.

"Bastard!" Rick tugged at the handle, then hammered hard on the panel. "Open up!"

"Go screw yourself."

"I was here first." When Vido did not answer, Rick hammered on the door again. "Let me in."

There was a chorus of complaints from the neighboring cubicles. "Get the hell out of here!" "Shut the racket!" "Hey, this is a *quiet area.*" And then, from a piercing female voice that Rick recognized as Gladys de Witt's: "Stop your screaming, Luban, and bugger off—or we'll call Turkey Gossage."

Rick tugged one more time at the door. It did not budge. In an absolute fury he banged again, then hurried away to another series of complaints and abuse.

It ain't over 'til I say it's over.

It wasn't over between him and Vido, far from it. Rick rubbed at his shoulder. Valdez was strong, and the blow from that muscular arm had *hurt.* If another fight was coming—and it seemed to be—Rick would get creamed again. Unless he could somehow change the odds.

He recalled Jigger's advice. Though it was the last thing in the world—or out of it—that he felt like doing, he headed for the region where the gym was located. He couldn't make himself bigger and heavier than Vido, but maybe he could make himself harder and fitter.

He changed into shorts and a tee-shirt and went through to the hooped track with its centrifugal gravity. Someone was already there, running with an easy, floating style that appeared totally effortless. He halted. If that was Gina, and she misunderstood . . .

But it wasn't. It was Alice Klein, dressed in a black singlet and the briefest of black shorts. Rick waited until she came past where he was standing, then accelerated to the point where he could step onto the moving track. He ran until he was at her side.

"Mind if I join you?"

She turned her head and gave him that smile that never got above her mouth. Rick took it as an OK, and matched his stride to hers. Within a minute he realized there might be another reason for that smile. She was moving *fast*—and not even breathing hard. Low gee must suit her, she seemed to float along as though this was her natural element. Out here her thin limbs looked graceful, even beautiful.

Well, he wasn't going to put up with another fiasco, like the one on the treadmill. Instead of trying for more conversation, he looked straight ahead, lengthened his stride to one more natural to his height and the reduced gravity, and concentrated all his attention on running. The track was about a hundred meters long, forming a hoop that rotated at constant speed about its center. Centrifugal force produced an effective gravity maybe a third of Earth's. As you ran, the path ahead seemed to rise all the time in front of you; yet you always felt as though you were on level ground.

A blue strip across the floor of the hoop marked the beginning of each lap. After the first two, Rick began to look for the line of blue and count as they passed it. Three, four, five . . .

When the count reached twenty laps, he wondered how long he would be able to keep it up. He stole a sideways glance at Alice, trying to look nonchalant—and found that she had turned her head at the same moment.

"That's it for me," she said, and slowed her pace. "But you don't have to stop on my account."

She was laughing at him, Rick felt sure of it. There was a sly, satisfied tone in her voice. He slowed too, trying not to gasp for air. Still she did not seem to be out of breath.

"How long have you been doing this?" he wheezed, as they stepped together off the rotating track.

"This? You mean running? Since the third day after we got here." And then, as though reading his mind, "You'll find it gets easier fast, once you do it regularly. I had real trouble the first few days."

Instead of setting a course for the showers she was heading to the equipment room. Rick followed her. The rowing machines that he and Jigger Tait had used were right near the door, and Rick hadn't even taken a good look at the rest of the place. He watched as Alice Klein sat down on a padded seat and strapped herself in. She reached up to a horizontal bar and pulled it down with some effort to chest level. Rick had seen similar work-out equipment back on Earth, but here there were differences. On Earth, a machine like this made use of gravity. You pulled down, and a cable ran up from the bar, over a pulley, and raised a set of weights. As you allowed the bar to go back up, the weights were lowered.

Here, though, in negligible gravity, weights would not do the trick (Turkey Gossage didn't even want the trainees to use the word *weight;* he said the right term to use in space was *mass).* This exercise machine had an arrangement of multiple springs, so that as you pulled the bar it exerted a constant upward pressure all the way down for you to work against.

"You don't get fit watching," said Alice, after half a dozen pull-downs. She did not look at him, but Rick moved forward to sit at the next machine. Then there was another twenty minutes of silence, as he learned that his upper body was even more in need of conditioning than his legs and lungs.

Finally Alice allowed her bar to go all the way up to its rest position and came to stand next to Rick. She studied the settings on his machine and shook her head.

"I can't match you there. You have twice my muscle power, and you always will."

"And you'll always be able to run me into the ground."

"Could be. That's life. Horses for courses."

She nodded at Rick and headed for the showers, leaving him to wonder what on Earth she meant by that last remark. In his whole life he had never even *seen* a live horse. Where Alice Klein came from, in the Dakota Black Hills, life must be very different from a southern California big city.

What had *she* done, to get herself kicked out of school and sent up here with Vanguard Mining?

He doubted that he was going to find out any time soon. Alice Klein was not the sort of person you could easily ask a question like that.

CHAPTER EIGHT

RICK did not exactly *avoid* Vido Valdez for the next two weeks. He preferred to think that he was so impossibly busy that they did not run into each other. With the increasing difficulty of the assignments set by Turkey Gossage and Rick's self-imposed work-out schedule, there was no time to do more than study, exercise, and collapse exhausted into bed.

On the other hand, Rick knew that he was not going any

place where he was likely to run into Vido. That made him secretly uncomfortable with himself.

He kept exercising, but he didn't feel either fitter or stronger. He was surprised when after ten days he went to the gym and again found Alice Klein there, and they ran thirty silent laps side by side with Rick hardly aware of either his legs or his breathing. Apparently physical fitness crept up on you.

After they had showered they walked back to the school area together, discussing the latest horror that Turkey Gossage was trying to inflict on them: *algebra*. It produced the greatest outburst of eloquence that Rick had ever seen in Alice.

"Useless!" she said. "Why does he make us learn it? I'll never get the hang of all his a's and b's and x's. It's not as though you would ever run into a situation where you might want to use it."

Rick was not quite so sure. Certainly, he could see zero value in the equations that Turkey made them set up and solve. But Turkey Gossage did not strike Rick as someone likely to make anybody learn things just for the sake of learning. Every activity on CM-2 seemed to have a defined goal.

"It's like the ladder thing this morning," Alice went on. "He told us how long it was and how far the end was from the wall, and he asked us to find how high up you could reach with it. I don't know how to do that, but it doesn't matter. Out here you don't need a ladder. You just jump!"

She was trying to justify the fact that she didn't know how to solve the problem. Rick was pretty sure that he did. It raised a real question: Should he explain to her what she had to do to get an answer? Just as in the physical tests back in New Mexico, the trainees were in competition with each other. Some were going to fail. If Rick helped Alice Klein, or anyone else, might he be ruining his own chances?

On the other hand, Alice had encouraged him to run and to work out with the exercise equipment. She didn't have to do that.

Rick sighed. "The ladder isn't really the point," he said. "Turkey put it that way, but really it's just an equation we have to set up and solve. All you need is that formula we did the other day about the sides of triangles with a right angle. See, think of the ladder as the long side of the triangle. . . ."

Alice listened in silence as Rick explained and they walked to the study cubicles. "You're right," she said at last. "That does it. But it doesn't change my basic point. You can solve dumb problems with algebra, but it isn't something anybody needs in the real world. Thanks anyway."

She left, leaving Rick to go on into one of the cubicles, close the door, and wonder. He also couldn't see any practical use for what they were being taught. But Vanguard Mining was not an organization to waste money. More importantly, you did what you were told on CM-2 if you wanted to eat and rest.

He bent over the day's assignments. His own trouble spot wasn't the math, it was the reading. He was sure he was falling behind. Why wasn't anything written the way it sounded? Why were words that were *spelled* almost the same and ought to *sound* almost the same completely different when you spoke them?

bough	*cough*	*rough*	*though*	*thought*	*through*
cow	*off*	*stuff*	*owe*	*taut*	*few*

Rick, hard at work, heard the cubicle door slide open behind him. He turned, suddenly nervous, then relaxed. It was only Monkey. She had lost a few pounds since arriving on CM-2, and it suited her. The uniform showed off her new and slimmer figure, and with her thinner face her brown eyes looked gigantic.

She slid the door closed behind her. Rick wasn't worried—but he was puzzled. Perpetually horny or not, Monkey had shown not the slightest interest in him. It went both ways. He knew she was attractive, but she didn't light his fires the way a couple of the other trainees did. Attraction between the sexes was a total mystery, but it was a definite reality.

Which left the mystery of what Monkey was doing in Rick's cubicle. Study cubicles were supposed to be *private*, not the place for social chit-chat.

Monkey answered that at once, by setting the printout sheet she was holding down on the working surface in front of Rick. It showed an array of blank squares, with writing alongside. She touched the sheet. "I got no idea what any of this means."

"Yeah? Well what the hell has that got to do with—"

"Alice says you're real good at explaining math stuff. She says you just helped her."

"So what if I did? What you think I am, some free service center? I got my own work and my own problems."

"If you'd help me, I'd pay you back." Monkey saw the look on Rick's face, and shook her head. "I'm not talking about anything like *that*. I'd help you with your assignments."

"What makes you think I need any help?"

"I got a look at your history paper. You trying to tell me

you *don't* need help?" Monkey smiled. "I like that stuff, and I know it. I can show you. So what do you say?"

Rick had already taken a look at the sheet that she had placed in front of him. It was one of Turkey Gossage's damnable math crossword puzzles. You had clues for across and down, but the answers were all numbers. There was enough information provided to fill in the whole thing—just—but to do that you had to work enough logical connections between the clues to pin down unique digital values for each square.

Rick wasn't about to admit it, to Monkey or anyone else, but he *liked* doing this stuff. It wasn't hard to nod grudgingly and say, "Sit next to me, where we can both see the sheet. I'm not going to do this for you. But I'll show you how to do it for yourself."

"That's what I need. I won't be sitting where I can ask you during the tests." Monkey squeezed onto the seat next to Rick. The cubicles were intended for solo study, and it was a tight fit. Rick felt a warm hip press against his. When he moved his right hand to the sheet, his elbow brushed her breast.

"Sorry. Couldn't help it."

"That's all right. The pleasure's mine." Monkey's reply sounded like a come-on, but there was no flirtation in her voice. Her attention was on the clue that Rick was pointing to.

"Now, you can certainly do this one," he said. "It's straight arithmetic. All you have to do is add the two numbers, and that's the answer to D Across."

"Yeah. Wish we had a calculator."

"Wish on. You know Turkey." Rick controlled his impatience as Monkey took pencil and paper and slowly and patiently worked out the answer. "Good. Now you do F Across the same way, and that will give you some of the numbers you need for getting a handle on E Down."

"Right." She started to calculate again. Slowly, at glacial speed, answers came and were transferred to the crossword sheet. After fifteen minutes, fewer than half the numbers of the square had been filled in. Monkey seemed pleased. Rick wasn't. He knew from experience that the tougher half lay ahead.

They were puzzling over one of the clues, heads close and bodies touching all the way from hips to shoulders, when a sound came from the door behind them. Rick was concentrating and didn't move. It wasn't just that Monkey's proposed answer was *wrong*. It was more like totally baffling. How could anybody produce such a weird result and somehow dream it might be right? So when the door opened he merely said, "Yeah? What you want?"

There were no words at first, just a gasp of disbelief. And then, "Deedee said you was in here. I was sure she was lying."

Rick swung his body as far as he could, but he was jammed too close to Monkey. He craned his head around. It was Vido Valdez, his face twisted with shock.

"Vido." Monkey squirmed against Rick, struggling to get up and off the seat. "You don't understand. You've got it all wrong."

"I understand what I see. You in here, wriggling and rubbing your tits all over him. What you think I am, a dummy?" Vido lifted his arm as though he would strike Monkey, then lowered it. He looked ready to cry. "Just get out of here," he said in a quiet, dead voice. "You bitch, after all you said to me. I don't even want to talk to you."

"Vido, we weren't—"

Valdez was not listening. He had moved forward to stand in front of Rick and was glaring down at him. "You're too scared to fight, so you thought you'd get back at me some other way."

"Monkey came here asking me to help her. We didn't do anything."

"You been avoiding me, I know that. You're too much of a coward to face me. Well, you get to face me now." Vido reached out and hauled Rick backward off the seat. "You think you're good with women, let's see how you do with men."

The cubicle was small and cramped. Rick knew one thing for certain: if he and Vido started a fight in here, he was doomed. There would be no space to dodge and weave, and Valdez was far stronger. As Vido reached forward, Rick ducked low and dived for the cubicle door. He landed on all fours in the narrow corridor and started to scramble away along it.

"No you don't." Vido was rushing after him. Rick rose to his feet and turned to face the blind charge. He got in one good punch on the side of Vido's head, enough to divert the other's forward momentum away from him, then he ran away as fast as he could in the other direction. He had been lucky with that first punch, but the corridor was too narrow to maneuver. If he was to stand any chance at all against Vido he needed lots more space.

Doors were opening on both sides of the corridor as Rick zoomed along it. Other trainees were coming out to see what the noise was. With any luck they would slow Vido's progress.

When Rick came to the gym it was deserted. He wasn't sure whether that made him glad or sad. Jigger Tait might have halted Vido and stopped the fight, but that would have solved nothing. Vido was so mad he would just wait and jump Rick the next chance he got.

Locking Vido out would be no better. It had to be here and now.

Rick turned. Vido was running toward him. Unlike on his first rush, his hands were up to protect himself. As he came close he reached out to grab Rick in a bear hug.

Rather than dodging to the left or right, Rick jumped straight up. He rose about fifteen feet to the ceiling, reached his target of one of the exercise brackets, and grabbed it to check his movement. He hung easily, supporting himself with two fingers of one hand. Suddenly he realized that the dynamics of a fight in low gee were completely different—and to his advantage. He had weeks of experience with the exercise equipment, and he was pretty sure that Vido had none.

He looked down. "You want me, dum-dum? Then come up and get me."

Valdez produced a choked grunt of rage, crouched, and jumped at Rick. It was exactly what Rick wanted him to do. Once his feet left the ground he could do nothing to change his direction. He came floating upward.

Rick waited, bracing his back against the ceiling. When Vido was within reach, flailing his arms and legs helplessly, Rick kicked out hard with both feet. The heel of his right foot caught Vido on the jaw, while his left foot set the other's body spinning. Vido crashed shoulder-first against the hard ceiling, rebounded, and floated slowly back down. His raised arms and head smacked into the padded floor. Then he did not move.

Was he unconscious, or just faking it?

Rick could not tell. Rather than repeating Vido's mistake and finding himself helpless in mid-air, he crabbed along ceiling and wall using the exercise brackets. Within a few seconds he reached the floor and could walk warily over to where Vido was still lying face-down.

Unconsciousness could be faked. Blood could not. Rick saw the stream of red oozing from Vido's scalp and nose and suddenly felt scared. He had meant to put his enemy out of action, not kill him. He bent to turn Vido over, wondering what to do next.

He did not have to make that decision. Gina Styan suddenly appeared at his side. "Get back to your dorm," she said curtly. "You've done enough for one day."

"I didn't—" Rick began. But he went unheard, because Monkey came into the gym, screamed, and ran across to cradle Vido's head in her arms.

"You've killed him." She was glaring up at Rick, her brown face flushed darker with blood. "He's dead."

"He's not dead." Rick had seen Vido blink and move his feet. But Monkey screamed again. "You've killed him!"

Gina caught Rick's eye and jerked her head. "Out of here. This will be easier on everybody if you're not around."

Easier on Rick, that was for sure. He saw a dozen other trainees crowding into the gym. They were all staring at Vido's bloodied head, then frowning accusingly at Rick.

He pushed his way through them without a word and

headed for the dorm. His daily assignments were not finished, but there was no way he could work on them now. He was too agitated.

Back at his empty dorm he threw himself onto his bed. If he had just told Alice Klein to go take a jump instead of explaining her problem to her, none of this would have happened. He would be quietly at work on his study tasks. And now look at him. Vido was sure he had been screwing around with Monkey, when he hadn't laid a finger on her. Everybody else believed he had knocked the shit out of Vido, when actually all he had been doing was defending himself. And because he wasn't getting his work done, he would be forcing down lumpy oatmeal tomorrow.

So much for trying to help people. Rick closed his eyes. Next time he would know better.

CHAPTER NINE

EARLY next morning before classes began, Rick was summoned to Turkey Gossage's office. Sure that he was in trouble, he was in no hurry to get there yet afraid of being late. He finally arrived a few minutes ahead of time.

Gossage nodded him to a seat on the other side of the circular table that he used as a desk. He went on studying a monitor, invisible to Rick. He was muttering to himself, until at last he looked up.

"I guess you think you're a real hot-shot."

"I never meant to hurt him." When Turkey looked blank, Rick blundered on. "I didn't. I really didn't want to fight at all."

"Oh, *that.*" Turkey waved his hand in a dismissive gesture. "I wasn't talking about that. I had a meeting with Valdez last night, and he says the whole thing was his fault."

"*His* fault!"

"You got hearing problems? Your physical didn't show it. You heard me, his fault. He says he came across a situation, misinterpreted it, and blew his lid. You were just defending yourself. You want to disagree with that?"

"Well, no. But I'm surprised." Suddenly Rick felt like a coward.

"That's permitted. Thank him when you see him. Now let's start over." But Turkey had to pause, because there was another knock on the door. "Come in."

It was Deedee Mao, arriving to the appointed second. Turkey waved her to a chair next to Rick. "I'll ask you the same thing I just tried to ask Luban," he said. "I guess you think you're a real hot-shot?"

"No." Deedee glanced at Rick, convinced that he must have said something about her, but he shook his head.

"So you don't know, either?" Turkey went on.

Rick looked at Deedee. She seemed just as puzzled as he was. "I don't," she said.

"Then I guess I'll have to tell you." Gossage was studying their faces. "The pair of you are sitting near the top of the trainee heap, along with a couple of others. You and Chick Teazle and Gladys de Witt are all doing well. Keep going this way, and you'll graduate."

Rick's pleasure at that surprising news didn't last too long, because Turkey hadn't finished and he had a diabolical look of glee on his face.

"Naturally," he said, "since you're such hot-shots we want you to have a specially good chance to make a mess of things. So for the pair of you, the training course just moved beyond supervised instruction. Tomorrow morning you'll be partners on a practical exercise in space ore mining. And I promise you, it won't be easy. I suggest you spend the rest of today studying the problem. You have until the close of the work day tomorrow to complete the assignment."

Rick and Deedee exchanged grimaces. They had pretty much avoided each other since their first liftoff into orbit. Now they were supposed to cooperate—even *depend* on each other.

"Studying *together*." Gossage had read their faces. "The more you know about each other's strengths and weaknesses, the better. And remember something else: in the real world you don't always get assigned to projects with your best buddies. Go get to work. The universe doesn't care how much people like each other."

The "practical exercise" that Gossage and his staff had prepared did not sound too hard. Rick and Deedee would load a five-hundred-ton ore carrier with low-grade tailings, controlling a semismart mining robot to do all the heavy work. They would fly the carrier to CM-2's refinery, drop off the ore, and return to the mine area on the empty carrier. Their own safe return through CM-2's interior would mark the end of the exercise.

But as Deedee remarked, the devil was in the details. Smartness in a mining robot was a mixed blessing, and the instructions given to it must limit its initiative. That meant learning the interaction manual and understanding the robot's powers and limitations. The ore carrier was no better. Examining its flight path and fuel needs, Rick and Deedee learned that the fuel supply provided for the round trip was barely enough. One mistake, even a small one, would leave them drifting helplessly away from CM-2 and calling for help from an empty carrier. Turkey Gossage, obviously by intention, had provided no precomputed flight trajectory.

Finally there was a hidden variable mentioned nowhere in the project description: according to training course rumor and legend, Gossage always threw in some extra problem on a practical test, a zinger that could not be predicted ahead of time. You found out about it when it hit you in the face.

Working with Deedee, Rick grudgingly had to admit that she was *smart*. She seemed less cocky and belligerent than he remembered her, and she caught on to new ideas at least as fast as he did. He suspected that in a pinch she could read and remember better. And she never seemed to get tired. The cocky statements from Chick Teazle and others of the New Mexico training group, that the East Coasters were all butt-head weirdos, hardly applied to Deedee Mao.

Rick tried to match her. He drove himself harder than ever before, until late at night they found themselves sitting side-by-side and staring helplessly at a set of schematics. The lines on the screen seemed to blur and curve as Rick watched. The circuit had to be completed correctly before the display would advance, but nothing seemed to work.

"It *can't* be that hard," Rick muttered at last.

"It isn't." Deedee sighed and reached forward to turn off the display. "It's us. We've saturated. At least, I have. How about you?"

"An hour ago. I just didn't want to admit it." Rick stood and reached up to rub at his stiffened neck muscles. "Better get some sleep. We've got a big day ahead."

"Yeah." Deedee stretched. "I'm in Cabin Twenty-Eight. Wanna get it on? Y'know, in freefall. I hear it's somethin' special."

Her tone of voice was casual and she wasn't looking at Rick. But she was smiling.

He shook his head. "Better with a swamp toad. God. That was us. Only a few weeks ago, and it seems like ten years."

"It *was* ten years. Ten real years." Deedee headed for the exit. "Who said that time proceeds at a uniform rate? Whoever it was, he was crazy."

"Or she was."

"Fair enough. Good night, Rick."

" 'Night, Deedee. Sleep well."

Maybe she did. Rick certainly didn't. He woke long before he needed to, the details of the project swarming through his mind. After half an hour of tossing and turning, he rose, dressed, and headed for the cafeteria. It was deserted, as it usually was at such an early hour. He was ordering a meal when Deedee wandered in. Her face was calm but a little pale.

She came straight up to him. "Anything in the rules that says we can't start early?"

"Nothing I know of."

"Right. Let's get going."

"No." Rick gestured to the place opposite him. "First you eat."

"Hunger sharpens the brain."

"And low blood sugar turns it off." Rick keyed in a huge meal for her, then felt obliged to increase his own order. "We eat. Then we go."

They chewed doggedly, without enjoyment, watching each other's plate until both were empty. By the time they had finished it was close to official breakfast time. Unwilling to talk to other trainees they hurried out and headed for the lock that led to the interior of CM-2.

The hardest thing of all was to avoid rushing. They put their suits on carefully and checked each other's seals. No little surprises there from Turkey Gossage. But as Deedee pointed out, he was not likely to do anything so obvious.

"Which means if he *did* do something obvious," Rick pointed out, "it *would* surprise us. No assumptions."

"Agreed. No assumptions."

They drifted together through the deep interior of CM-2, heading for the side of the planetoid opposite to the main training facilities. The corridor by now seemed as familiar as home. They did not need to consult map or tracers. The ore carrier and the mining robot, as promised, were waiting in the main loading chamber. The tailings had already been sintered to form oddly-shaped but identical solid blocks, each weighing half a ton. In a pinch, Rick and Deedee could load each one themselves; but that was a sure way to flunk the exercise.

They put the mining robot through its paces on a dummy run, checking that each movement corresponded exactly to that pictured. Finally, and gingerly, Deedee directed the machine to begin loading. She watched the pick-up stage, while Rick counted blocks and monitored their stowing aboard the ore carrier. There were still a hundred more to go when he came out and told Deedee to stop.

"Why? The robot's doing fine."

"Maybe. But we have a problem. The carrier is nearly full. It won't take more than another couple of dozen and we've only loaded nine hundred."

"That can't be right. The carrier is rated for at least five hundred tons cargo mass. Maybe the blocks are heavier than they're supposed to be? Or maybe they're less dense and bigger."

They checked the mass of a sintered block. It was half a ton exactly. Its density was as it should be. Then they crouched in the loading chamber, helmet to helmet, and pored over the electronic and printed manuals. At last Rick sighed. "I get it. I'm a dummy. I should have realized it as soon as the loading started."

Deedee was still staring at the electronic layout diagram of the carrier. "Well, I don't. Everything looks just fine."

"The carrier's fine. The ore blocks are fine, too."

"So what's the problem?"

"It's the *shape* of the blocks. I noticed they looked odd when we first came in. They have the right mass and density but they don't pack tight. There's too much space left between them."

"So what do we do?"

"We look for a better packing arrangement, one that fits the blocks together more tightly."

Ten minutes of useless brainstorming was enough to

prove that they would never find the answer by abstract thought. Under Deedee's direction the mining robot began to fit blocks one on another, turning them every way to seek the best fit of the irregular faces. The right answer, when they finally reached it, seemed absolutely obvious. With one particular arrangement the sintered blocks keyed in together tightly and seamlessly.

Then the carrier had to be unloaded, and the whole operation begun over. This time the five hundred tons fitted with room to spare. Deedee came over to watch the last block go in. She ordered the mining robot in on top of it before she closed the hatch.

"Think that was the Gossage surprise?" she said as she followed Rick into the ore carrier's control room.

"The first one, maybe. Nobody said he keeps it to one. There could be another right here."

They examined the carrier's status indicators one by one with enormous care, until at last Deedee shrugged. "We can't stay here forever just *looking*. Do it, Luban."

Under Rick's nervous control the carrier crept forward out of the loading chamber and into open space. By all Belt standards the journey was a trivial one: a couple of hundred kilometers through unobstructed vacuum, to rendezvous with another body having negligible velocity relative to CM-2. The training facility's refinery was in an essentially identical orbit around the Earth-Moon system.

That fact did not offer Rick any sense of security. He was keyed tighter than he had ever been until at last the carrier was snugly into the refinery's dock. Then it was Deedee's turn. She unloaded the robot and it carried the sintered ore blocks one by one to the refinery's gigantic hopper.

They stared at each other as the final block went in.

"Smooth," Deedee said at last.

"Too smooth?"

"There's no such thing."

"You know what I mean." Rick stared at the distant bulk of CM-2, its outside lights clearly visible from the refinery. "Let's get back. If there are surprises here I don't want to hang around and wait for them to find us."

He checked the fuel as he switched on the drive. More than enough. He could cut off power after a couple of minutes, coast all the rest of the way to CM-2, and finish with a little fuel to spare. And even with the delay in loading they had plenty of time to complete the assignment before the end of the work period. Maybe the only Gossage surprise was the sintered block shape.

That comforting thought was still in his head when he realized that the star field outside was slowly rotating. Instead of heading straight for CM-2 the ore carrier was yawing, turning its blunt prow farther and farther away from the planned heading.

Rick slapped at the controls and turned all thrust power off.

"What's wrong?" Although he had not said a word, Deedee caught the urgency of his movement.

"Drive. We're crabbing." Rick was already calling up onto the control display the rear perspective layout of the carrier, to show the six independent but balanced units that provided the ship's drive. "Something's wrong with one of the modules. We're getting no thrust from it."

Deedee was watching the changing starscape in the front port, noting the exact direction of rotation of the ship.

"We're tilting to the right and down." She touched her gloved hand to the display, one finger on the stylized image of a module. "If it's a problem with just one thruster, it has to be this one. Any of the others would turn us in a different direction."

"Agreed."

"So turn off the *opposite* one of the six, directly across from the bad one. Do it, Rick! That will balance us again."

"I can't." Rick gestured at the control panel. "The thrust modules are not separately controllable. It's all or nothing."

"So what do we do?"

Rick did not answer. He had called up a section of the ship's manual onto the display. More than anything he had ever wanted in his life, he wanted to read that manual. And he couldn't. The words were too long and unfamiliar, the sentences seemed too complex. He strained to understand, *willing* the words to make sense. And still he couldn't read them. The ship was drifting along, but CM-2 was not directly ahead. Their present course would miss the planetoid.

"Help me, Deedee." Rick was sweating inside his suit. "Help me to figure this out. The manual will tell us what to do. It has to. Help me to read. You read better than me."

"I don't. You know I don't." But Deedee was following Rick's lead, reading each word on the screen aloud, stumbling over the hard ones.

They struggled on, reading in unison, cursing unknown words, correcting each other. Until finally Deedee cried out and pointed at the display, "Att-it-ude. That's what that word is. *Attitude control.* This is the part we want. Come on, Rick. Read it!"

Rick was certainly trying; but he had already discovered

that simple need and urgency didn't let you read any faster. They ground on together, word by word, through the next three paragraphs. And at a certain point, groaned in unison.

"It's *obvious!*" Rick slapped his knee with his gloved hand.

"And we're idiots." Deedee repeated the important sentences, gabbling them on the second time through. " 'In the event of thrust module imbalance, the carrier must be returned to the main maintenance facility.'—Yeah. Thanks a lot.—'However, should a thrust module fail and a temporary course adjustment be necessary in space, this can easily be performed by the use of minor lateral control jets. These can be used to spin the ship about its long-it-ud-in-al'—hell of a word—'axis, so that the mean thrust is maintained in the desired direction. The same elementary technique can be used to make general direction adjustments, by halting longitudinal rotation after any suitable angle.' Do it, Rick!"

"I *am* doing it." Rick was already using the lateral thrusters, turning the ship about its main axis to bring the failed thruster module onto the opposite side. "I'm going to have to juggle this. If I thrust too long in the other direction we'll swing too far and miss the base on the other side."

"Do it in—little bits." The main thrusters fired, this time in a pattern as jerky as Deedee's speech. "We still have plenty of time. Go easy. You can afford to go easy."

"I will go easy. Trust me."

Rick was eyeing CM-2 as it swung back into view in the forward port. Under his control the drive was stuttering uneasily on and off while the ship rotated unevenly about its main axis. He knew exactly where he wanted to go—into the hard-edged aperture that sat like a bullet hole in the planetoid's rugged side. But getting there, exactly there, was another matter. It was another half hour before Rick could turn off all power, shiver in released tension, lift his hands from the controls, and wait for the magnetic arrest system to guide the carrier to a berth within CM-2.

Before the grapple was complete Deedee was out of her seat and heading for the lock. "Come on. We have to go."

"What's the hurry?" Rick was moving more slowly, stretching cramped hands as he eased himself from the pilot's chair. "You said we had plenty of time."

"I lied." Deedee was already in the lock, waiting impatiently. "I didn't want you worrying about time when you were flying the carrier. But it's going to be touch and go."

Rick took a glance at his helmet chronometer and leaped for the lock. "We only have twenty-three minutes left!"

"I know." The lock was cycling. "We can do it, though—so long as we don't meet any more snags."

They flew side-by-side from the docking berth to the mine entry point to CM-2. "Say, two minutes each end." Rick hit the entry combination. "Twelve minutes to get through the tunnels—that's about as fast as we can go. But we still have a seven minute cushion." He keyed in the entry combination again. "What's wrong with this thing? It shouldn't take this long."

"The power has been turned off." Deedee pointed to the telltale set in the great door. "And it's too heavy for manual operation."

"Turkey. The bastard. He's screwed us. We can't get in."

"Then we'll have to go around. Or use one of the side tunnels?"

"No good. They all lead outside, not to the training facility."

"That's our answer." Deedee had turned. "We can go right around the outside. Don't waste time with that door, Rick. *Come on!* We're down to twenty-one minutes."

She led the way, zooming at maximum suit speed for the open entrance of the mine loading chamber. Rick, close behind, did the calculation. They had to make their way right around CM-2 to almost the opposite side of the planetoid. Say, three kilometers. If they could average ten per hour, they would do it. If not . . .

All Rick could think of was that early this morning he had made Deedee sit down and eat breakfast when she was hyped up and raring to go. If they were too late now, it was his fault.

They came to the edge of the loading chamber and burst out from the darkness. As Deedee, still ahead of Rick, emerged into full sunlight she reversed suit jets and came to an abrupt dead halt.

"Keep going, Dee. I'm right behind you."

But she was not moving. "Listen to your dosimeter, Rick."

He became aware of a tinny rattle in the background. It was his suit's radiation monitor, operating well above the danger level.

"Back inside." And when he hesitated, "We have to, Rick. *Right now.*" She had him by the arm of his suit, towing him. "It must be a solar burst, a sudden one and a big one. We're safe enough as soon as we get some rock shielding around us."

They were already out of sight of the Sun. Safe enough. And *failed.* Rick glanced at his chronometer. Eighteen and a half minutes.

"Deedee, we wouldn't be outside for very long. I'll

bet the integrated dose would be small enough, it wouldn't harm us."

"Maybe. But are you *sure?*"

He wasn't. Worse than that, he didn't know how to make sure. The calculation couldn't be very difficult, no more than a formula and a few simple summations. Jigger would probably have done it in his head. But Rick didn't know how to do it at all. He groaned.

"We're safe enough here." Deedee had misunderstood the reason for his misery. "Rock is a perfect shield."

"I know. I don't *want* a shield. I want to beat that god-damn deadline."

"We can't possibly. A solar storm could last for days, and we have only seventeen minutes left."

Rock is a perfect shield.

"Dee, we still have a chance. The sun is shining almost directly into the loading chamber. The training facility is on the opposite side. We can go through a side tunnel to a point where we're out of direct sunlight, then jet the rest of the way outside shielded by CM-2 itself."

"Sixteen minutes. We'll never do it in time." But she was following Rick as he plunged back into the dark interior. He picked one side tunnel and went into it without hesitating. Fortunately Deedee didn't ask why Rick knew so well the net-work of passages and chambers that criss-crossed the interior of CM-2. He certainly wasn't going to mention it or the di-sastrous episode it had led to with Gina.

The passageways had been designed for mining rather than rapid travel through them. The trip through the inte-rior seemed to take forever. At last Rick and Deedee were at the surface again, about a quarter of the way around the planetoid, but they were running out of time. Five minutes left. A kilometer and a half to go on the outside, hugging close to CM-2 to avoid the solar flare. It didn't sound far. But it meant averaging eighteen kilometers an hour. You couldn't do that. Not in a suit, zooming around the irregular exterior of a planetoid.

Rick knew it. Deedee probably knew it, too. Neither said a word as the final minute flashed past and the deadline was missed. They kept going, bitterly, all the way to the lock that would lead them into the training facility.

As the lock opened, Rick halted. "No good. Six minutes late. Sorry."

"I know." Deedee came to his side, put an arm around him, and hugged him. She leaned her helmet against his as they moved into the lock together. "We gave it our best shot. Nobody can take that away from us."

The lock pressure equalized. They reached up to remove their helmets as the inner door opened—and found themselves staring at the anxious face of Turkey Gossage. Turkey glanced at once at his watch.

"Don't say it." Rick moved out of the lock. "Six minutes late."

"I wasn't going to. Did you come around the outside?"

"Part of the way." Deedee came to stand at Rick's side.

"Let me see your dosimeters so—"

"No problem. We did the first part in the interior, and we only came outside when CM-2 was shielding us from the Sun."

"Smart move." Gossage relaxed visibly. "Of course, even in the Sun the dose you'd have received in the short time you were there would have been tolerable."

"We weren't sure." Rick was suddenly more tired than he had ever been. "We didn't know how to calculate it."

"I can show you that in five minutes."

"I'm sure you can. But not today, sir, if you don't mind." Rick slumped against the chamber wall and allowed his arms and legs to go limp. "We did our best, we really did."

"And we came so close." Deedee flopped down by Rick's side. "If there had been one less problem to solve—just one."

"I see. Would you agree with that, Luban?" Turkey seemed more amused than sympathetic.

"Yes. But I don't see why it matters."

"It matters very much. To me, at least." Gossage squatted down so that he was facing the two of them. "You see, it's not every day that people mistake me for a deity." And, when Rick and Deedee stared at him with dull and exhausted eyes, "I gave you a test that I thought would stretch you right to your limits. If you did everything right, and fast, and clean, you could make it back before the deadline—just. I rigged the shape of the sintered blocks. I fixed the drive so it would go wonky on the return trip. I turned off the power on the main entry door so you couldn't get back inside and would have to come around the outside. But if there's one thing that even Turkey Gossage can't do, it's to arrange a solar flare for his special convenience. I'd have to be God Almighty to do that. The flare wasn't in my plans, any more than it was in yours."

He reached out, taking Deedee and Rick's right hands in his. "If it hadn't been for the flare you'd have beaten your deadline with time to spare. That's good enough for me. You did well, better than I expected. You've passed. Now, don't go to sleep on me!"

Rick and Deedee had simultaneously closed their eyes. They showed no sign of opening them again.

"All right." Gossage stood up. He was still holding their hands and his movement lifted them to their feet. "You've passed the practical test, the pair of you, but you don't seem to care. Eat and rest, rest and eat. We'll talk later." He released them, turned, and headed for the tunnel. As he reached it he added, without turning his head, "Just don't get cocky. You still have theory finals—and I guarantee they'll be tough. You won't have things this nice and easy all the time."

CHAPTER TEN

TURKEY Gossage was as good as his word and better. The theory final was more than tough. It was murderous. Rick staggered out of a private cubicle—no chance to "borrow" your answers on CM-2—and saw his own despair mirrored on everyone's face. They had been asked questions far beyond anything taught in class. Jigger Tait's early warning had been right: if you didn't learn how to browse all around a subject, you were in trouble at Vanguard Mining.

Give the formula for the velocity, v, *achieved by a ship accelerating with acceleration* a *for a time* t.

That was fair. Turkey had pounded the simple formula, $v = at$, into their heads a dozen times. He said they had to remember it for the rest of their lives.

But then came the zinger: *State circumstances when the formula that you have just given does not apply.*

That had definitely *not* been mentioned anywhere, in any lesson. Rick had a vague feeling that things went wrong if you kept on accelerating until the calculated velocity was near the speed of light. He knew for sure that the formula couldn't work if the answer you got was *more* than the speed of light, because nothing could go faster than that. But he had absolutely no idea what the right relation between speed and acceleration would be in such a case.

Stating all those thoughts, clearly and precisely, was just about impossible. Rick decided that he had waffled. Whoever listened to his spoken answer would know it. It all came back to what Mr. Hamel had said on the far-off day Rick had been kicked out of school: it's a lot easier to be exact when you *write* something than if you try to *speak* it.

The good news was that the tests were finally over. The one he had just taken was the last. Now came the wait to learn how badly he had done. Turkey Gossage knew they would all be in agony until the final results were tallied. He had promised not to keep them hanging longer than one day.

What Turkey could not guarantee was the subjective length of twenty-four hours. As Deedee had said, time didn't proceed at a uniform rate. When you were having fun, it flew by. When you were waiting for something, every minute dragged.

Like now.

The exam had finished at midday. Afternoon had been occupied in chores just tricky enough to keep a person from brooding over other things. The makework tasks were all done by dinnertime, and no activities had been set for later. Some instinct for solitude took over. The usual evening group session in the cafeteria, where people met to talk about the events of the day, never happened. Tonight everyone quietly picked up cartons of carry-out food and left at once.

Rick sought out his own private place, an abandoned outer chamber of CM-2 where he could sit and watch the stately rotation of the starfield. He was not sure he could stand the idea of going back to the dorm at all until tomorrow morning.

The asteroid training station made one revolution every twenty minutes, too slow to notice unless you were looking outside. As Rick was eating he idly took his drinking straw and released it. The straw drifted steadily downward, to land on the glassy floor of the observation room. There should be a way to calculate the effective gravity in which the straw fell, using the size of CM-2 and the time it took for the planetoid to turn on its axis. Jigger Tait or Gina Styan would rattle off a formula, but Rick did not know it.

The steady turn of the station was bringing Earth into view on the left. He watched it mindlessly, all the way until it slowly vanished from sight on the right. Then he realized that his mind had not been blank at all. He was thinking again about that damned theory exam, mentally reviewing his answers—and revising them, even though there was no way to change anything! It was a sure way to go crazy.

Rick left the observation room. He went wandering around the exterior paths of CM-2, until he came to the radiation-proof chamber where he had once tried to jump Gina Styan. He paused outside the door. He might have flunked the training course, but he'd learned at least one thing since he came to Vanguard Mining. He felt his testicles draw upward in his scrotum, his body's reminder of the agony he had felt when Gina showed who was really the boss. It would be a long time before he tried anything like that again.

The door to the shielded chamber was open. Someone was sitting inside with the lights off. Apparently Rick was not the only one who didn't want company. He was all set to retreat when a voice said, "Come on in. I felt sure you were heading this way. Don't put the light on if you don't want to."

To Rick's astonishment he knew that voice. It was Turkey Gossage. Rick peered into the dark interior.

"You knew where I was?"

"Of course. Many's the night I've done the same thing myself. There's no better place than the outer ring observation ports to feel the size and majesty of the universe, and know there's more in it than you'll ever see or understand. And I knew just when you left there."

"You've been watching me?"

"Not just you. Everybody." Turkey gestured to Rick to come in and raised the level of the lights. "We learned the hard way not to let any trainee go off alone and unmonitored the night after finals. Sit down and take it easy. Are you feeling upset?"

"I don't know if that's the right word. I can't stop thinking about the exam."

"I'm sure. That's why I'm here—to end the suspense." Turkey thrust out his hand. He had a big grin on his face.

"It's over, Luban. Congratulations. You passed the final. You'll be heading on to the next stage of training."

Rick gaped at him. "Passed? But you said that *tomorrow*—"

"That was my time cushion, a margin for error. We finished the final comparison and collating of results four hours ago. I've been doing the rounds since, telling people. You're the last."

Rick finally did as Turkey had suggested, and flopped down onto the padded floor. *He had passed!* He would be leaving CM-2 and going out to the Belt. But it had come so soon and so suddenly—it did not feel real.

"When? When will I go?"

"Soon. A day or two."

"So—what happens now?"

"You mean, right this minute? Well, I don't imagine you feel much like sleeping."

"Never!"

"Good. There's a celebration party in the senior mess, and it should be swinging along nicely by now. So I suggest you head over there."

"Are you coming, too?"

"Eventually. But not for a while." Turkey's voice became heavier and all the humor went out of it. "You see, Luban, this training station isn't Happy House. It's not like your school back on Earth, where everybody has to do well and everyone must graduate with honors, otherwise their precious self-esteem would be ruined. Nearly a fourth of the people on the training course have failed. They won't be going to any party, and they need me tonight a lot more than you do. So maybe I'll see you later. But if not—you'll understand why."

"Who—who failed?" And, when Gossage did not answer, "Vido Valdez, and Deedee Mao, and—"

"I prefer not to talk about individuals. Why don't you get along to the party? There will be a complete list posted there later." Turkey nodded. "Go now."

It was an order, in a tone of voice that the trainees had learned not to argue with. Turkey would accept no more questions. Rick swallowed, rose to his feet, and stumbled out.

His path to the senior mess, normally off-limits to lowly trainees, took him past the dormitories. All the lights were on in spite of the late hour, but the corridors and rooms were eerily deserted like ghosts of their usual selves. Rick hurried past his own dorm and the open doors of the next two along. He glanced inside each, not expecting anyone, and was surprised to see a heavyset form at the far end of the second dorm, sitting on a bunk with his back to the door.

It was Vido. Rick paused. The two of them had hardly spoken a word since their last fight. He should go on. But the other's hunched shoulders spoke of total misery.

Rick moved forward hesitantly to Vido's side. "I'm really sorry," he began, then could add nothing more.

Vido turned to stare up at him, his broad black face stony with grief. "It was my fault. All my fault."

Rick reached out his hand intending to pat Vido's shoulder, then drew it back. "You did your best. We all did. I'm really sorry that you—that it didn't work out for you." He could not bring himself to say that awful word, *failed*.

"For me?" Vido stared in confusion.

"That you didn't pass."

"But I did! You thought—"

"But you said—"

"Not *me. Monkey!* She failed, and it was all my fault."

Vido put his head down and stared at nothing. "She came to you for help, an' I hated it. I asked her not to do that no more. And she didn't, for my sake. But you could have helped her. It was the math, you see, she could handle the rest of it but she couldn't handle that. An' you're a real good math teacher, Alice an' Deedee both say so. If only I'd been less selfish, if only I just hadn't *stopped* her."

Rick hesitated again. He wasn't sure what he wanted to say next would please Vido, but he knew that he had to say it. "Vido, it wasn't you. I talked to Monkey for a long time that day before you came along. When it comes to math, she just doesn't get it. Not at all. I could have taught her every day, so could you, and it wouldn't have made any difference. She'd never have passed that theory final in a hundred years. She just didn't seem able to get the basic ideas. You know her a lot better than me. Surely you saw that?"

"I thought it was me. I thought I wasn't explaining right."

"It wasn't you. It was Monkey. I'm really sorry, Vido." Rick finally reached out and patted the other's shoulder, knowing it was something that no sixteen-year-old male did to another male in his old school without risking mockery. But the hell with that, things were different in space. "I'm really glad you passed. Honest. Congratulations."

Vido looked startled. "I never asked. You?—"

"I passed, too. We'll both be going to the Belt."

"Yeah. Guess so. The Belt." Vido took a deep breath, then stood up and held out his hand. "Congratulations. But you're not at the party!"

"I'm on my way. You should go, too. It's terrible about Monkey, but there's nothing you can do about it. Let's go."

"I won't be able to enjoy the party without her. Shit, I'll probably take a swipe at Gossage the minute I see him, for flunking her."

"I don't think so. He won't be there." Rick repeated what Turkey had told him. "He's got the toughest job of all tonight. You owe it to him to go and at least try to have a good time."

"Yeah. Maybe I do." Vido sighed. "To hell with it. To hell with everything. I thought this was goin' to be the best day of my life, or it was goin' to be the worst. An' here it is both."

He sniffed and rubbed his eyes. For a change, both of them were bloodshot. "Let's go, Luban. Before people start sayin' I'm getting soft."

For the rest of the way, Rick wondered about Deedee Mao. He knew she was really smart, but she might not be good at taking tests. Suppose that she, like Monkey, had flunked? It was a huge relief to enter the crowded senior mess, and see her almost at once. She had been watching the door with an anxious expression, and the moment she saw him come in her face lit up and she gave him a double thumbs-up sign from across the room.

She came pushing across to his side. "I'd really started to wonder about you." She had to put her face close to his and shout because of the noise.

"Hell, Deedee, if somebody like *you* could pass, I— ouch!" Rick grunted as she poked him in the ribs. "What's going on over there? I thought this was supposed to be a party."

A line of trainees was forming at the other side of the room, facing Jigger Tait.

"Not just a party. This is graduation. First you graduate, *then* you party."

"You did?"

"Graduate? No. I was waiting for you."

"And that's it? The whole thing?" Rick had dreaded and half-expected the pomp and circumstance of a high school graduation ceremony, with robes and pictures and diplomas and celebrities, and boring windbag speeches *ad nauseam*. What people seemed to be getting was one quick handshake from an overall-clad Jigger Tait, "standing in for Turkey Gossage the one and only," as he put it.

"What about my certificate?" Chick Teazle called out from halfway along the line.

"What would you do with a certificate if you had one?" Jigger was beaming. "You can't hang it on the wall where you're going—none of you will have a wall. You'll be lucky if you get food and air."

"We'd treasure your signature, sir." Gladys de Witt was still wearing a cast and performed a southpaw handshake with Jigger. A sprung cable had broken her right arm on the final stage of her practical test, but she had finished, flying the ship home to base one-handed. Now she waved her white cast in the air. "You can sign this for me instead."

Jigger did so, to enormous applause. The ones closest to them hooted at what he had written, while Gladys turned pink and held her arm against her body.

The line moved along slowly. Deedee and Rick were at the very end. "Thank God!" Jigger said, when they finally reached him. "How do politicians stand it? The only good part must be kissing babies—once they reach the right age." He bent over and gave Deedee a hug and kiss instead of a handshake, producing cries of "No fair!" and "Do one, you do us all!" from the other girls who saw it happen.

"You can come and see me in private," Jigger called back. "That's my quota for tonight." He winked at Rick, the last in the line. "Not a word to Gina, all right? She'll be here a bit later, she can't resist a dance."

Music was beginning, loud and with a foot-tapping bass. A few couples came out to move awkwardly in time to it. Walking and running in low gravity was something that they had all practiced. Dancing was another matter. It was the first time that most trainees had tried it on CM-2. Rick, standing at the edge of the area cleared for dancing, was in even worse shape. He and his friends at school had always sneered at dancing and he had no idea how to do it.

He stared around the room. He had not seen the list that Turkey had mentioned, but he didn't need it. He knew every trainee by name.

Vido of course had made it. Rick wondered if the two of them had again achieved near-identical scores. There was Chick Teazle, no surprise, and Gladys and Deedee next to him. At the edge of the dance floor, standing by herself and staring blank-eyed at the dancers, was Alice Klein. Rick was not surprised by that, either. In spite of her troubles with math, Alice had a way of scraping through. So did Goggles Landau, standing next to her. He wasn't wearing glasses and he must have taken out his contacts, because he was squinting his eyes at everyone, probably wondering who they were.

So who was missing? Monkey, of course. So far as Vido was concerned she was the only one who mattered. Who else?

There was no sign of Cokie Mulligan. He had sworn at the beginning that he was done with school forever, and now it looked like he was right. Rick also couldn't see Henrik Voelker, the "Carolina Kid" that the other East Coasters all swore was a mad genius. He had probably aced the hardest theory questions, but screwed up totally on anything that needed a bit of common sense. A handful of others had been no-hopers after their failed efforts on the practical test. They had been given a chance to make it up somehow on the theory, but apparently none of them had.

All the same, it looked like the class as a whole had beaten the odds. From a total of forty trainees starting out, thirty or so were here in the room. Rick started to count. He had reached seventeen when he became aware of Jigger Tait at his side.

"Not dancing?"

Rick shook his head. "Not yet. I was just counting how many of us there are left."

"You'll have plenty of time for that on the way out to the Belt. You shouldn't do it now. You've done enough work for one day, and you ought to make the most of tonight. Tomorrow the honeymoon's over. No more spoon-feeding. Things get tough, and you learn what *real* work is like. Come on."

He grabbed Rick by the arm and led him puzzled around the dance floor. They were heading for the place from which Gladys de Witt had now vanished, leaving Deedee standing alone.

"After the first dance you're on your own. For this one you get no choice." Jigger beckoned Deedee onto the floor, faced her and Rick toward each other, and walked briskly away.

There was a long, awkward moment. Finally Deedee shrugged, stuck her tongue out after Jigger, and began to move her shoulders and arms in time to the music. "You hear what the man said."

"I'm a lousy dancer." An understatement if ever there was one.

"So what? You're not here for prizes." And, when Rick still stood rooted to the spot, "Look, Luban, I know you got no more rhythm than a fire hydrant. You want *everybody* to know that as well as me? Watch what I do, and move them big feet."

They were standing out on the dance floor. He would be even more conspicuous not dancing than dancing badly. Rick began to move, trying to follow what Deedee was doing. After the first minute he realized that no one but Deedee would notice whatever dumb moves he made. They were all too wrapped up in their own efforts.

He began to relax. Deedee was grinning at him, yet he knew she wasn't grinning *at* him. She was just enjoying herself. And she could dance like a professional. Rick tried to mimic that supple, limber action. He knew he was failing, but she didn't seem to mind.

Tomorrow the honeymoon's over. No more spoon-feeding. Things get tough, and you learn what real work is like.

What was it going to be like, out there in the Belt? That thought flashed into Rick's mind, and was followed at once by the sudden memory of an answer he had given on the theory test. It was the wrong answer, and now he knew the right one. But—*it didn't matter.*

He smiled at Deedee, and was rewarded by a flash of white teeth and a graceful sexy pirouette that was offered for him alone.

He caught her as she finished the turn and moved her body against him. She put her mouth to his ear and whispered, "Hey! That's more like it."

Unbelievably, the tests were over. They had passed, and Jigger Tait was right. They had done enough work for one day. For tonight at least they had earned some fun.

CHAPTER ELEVEN

THE change predicted by Jigger came sooner and harder than expected.

The trainees had partied all night and collapsed into their bunks at dawn. They were still settling into exhausted sleep when a fist hammered on the door and a loud female voice shouted from the corridor: "Ten minutes to get to the main assembly hall. If you're not there, you won't be going anywhere."

It wasn't Gina Styan or Coral Wogan. In fact, it wasn't anyone who Rick recognized when he stumbled, still yawning and stretching, into the main hall with the rest of the groaning trainees. The woman waiting for them was tall and big-shouldered. She had black hair and bright blue eyes, and she might have been pretty but for her oddly lopsided face.

She counted, and nodded. "You don't know me—yet. And I've seen your names but not your faces. So let's begin with that. I'm Barney French. Start there at the right." She pointed at Chick Teazle, who had been first into the hall. "Each of you state your last name."

As the roll-call proceeded she hardly seemed to be listening. But at the end of it she pointed to Vido Valdez. "You. Valdez. You came close to flunking geography on your test. That won't do. You'll be given special assignments to bring you up to speed.

"You, Klein." She pointed at Alice. "Your mathematics is a disgrace. We'll do something to take care of that—or rather, you will. Beverly Landau—"

"It's Goggles, ma'am." Goggles blushed and wriggled, while the others stared at him. "Goggles Landau."

"Isn't your real name Beverly?"

"Yes. But I never use it."

"Why not?"

"Well, it's—Beverly is a girl's name."

"I see." She glared at him. "You mean, it's a girl's name just like Barney is a boy's name?"

Goggles was smart enough not to answer, and she went on, "Well, *Beverly* Landau, I'll call you what I want to. Your parents certainly did. And, *Beverly* Landau, if your test results are anything to go by, the amount you understand about atomic structure could be written on the small point on the top of your head. That's going to change. Agreed."

"Yes, sir—ma'am."

"Very good. Actually, I prefer sir. Now, Mao." She turned to Deedee. "Is there any special name *you'd* like me to call you by?"

"No, sir."

"Good. So let's talk about history. You stated on your general knowledge quiz that Rome was founded in the year 753 AD. Would you be interested in revising that opinion?"

There was a long silence, as Deedee opened her mouth and then closed it. Finally she said tentatively, "753 BC?"

"Correct. A mere difference of fifteen hundred years, but what's that between friends? Bravo. Or is someone else to be congratulated? Was there a little help from a person behind you? You—Luban. Did you tell Mao the right answer?"

"No, sir." Rick had been trying to be totally inconspicuous behind Deedee and Vido Valdez.

"Do you know who did?"

"No, sir." Rick felt his gut tighten. He had just told a direct lie. He had heard Gladys de Witt, on his immediate left, whisper the answer.

"I don't believe you." Barney French studied his face. "But I will let it pass. You are in enough trouble already. For the past two months you have been in a position to look at Earth anytime you chose. Did you do so?"

"Yes, sir. Many times."

"And yet you cheerfully asserted on your final test, despite the evidence of your own eyes, that seventy percent of Earth is land area, while only thirty percent is covered by water."

"I said it backwards." Rick cringed at his own stupidity. "I meant it the other way round, seventy percent water."

"Really? How very reassuring. I suppose you consider it all right to remove oxygen from your suit when you intend to add it. Or perhaps to accelerate your ship when successful rendezvous requires you to decelerate?

"Now listen, all of you." To Rick's relief she turned away from him to address the whole group. "You may be thinking, what the hell is all the fuss about? Barney French is nitpicking on things that don't make a damn of difference. Well if you think that, you're wrong. No matter how much fudging you got away with on Earth, or even here on CM-2, that ends today. I'm not like Turkey Gossage, willing to blow your nose and change your diaper. When you leave CM-2 you leave kindergarten. Accuracy and precision *do* make a difference when you're out in the Belt. The details *matter*. You have to get things *right*. If you don't believe me, take a look."

She walked along the line of trainees, turning so that they could get a good view of her misshapen face.

"See the scars? See the bone grafts, and the facial reconstruction? Take a close-up. You're seeing me *after* thirty-seven operations and the best plastic surgery that money can buy. My body is in worse shape than my face—I have more metal than bone in my shoulders. And I'm one of the lucky ones. Four people died in the accident that did this. And do you know what caused it? One lousy plus sign that should have been a minus, in one small subroutine that controlled one phase of a continuous casting operation on CM-24. The man who made the error paid for it. You probably saw plenty of horror videos when you were back on Earth. But you've never known real horror, until you see what a pressure jet of molten steel does when it hits a human body in low-gee."

She stared at and through the hushed group of trainees. "You will see simulations of accidents just like the one I was involved in—but not today. So you can go now. Pick up your assignments as you leave. Each of you will find your name on one of the packets. I want all the work done in the next three days. What each of you is required to do reflects your individual weaknesses, plus one additional question that you must all try to answer. Cooperate as much as you like—but remember, you get no credit if you spend your time helping somebody else, and then screw up on your own work. You're not trainees any more. You're *apprentices*. Earn that title.

"Oh, yes, and one other thing. I don't think you want to open those assignments right now, because we'll be lifting from CM-2 in four hours. Pack your bags, and say your fond farewells. Anyone who wants to go to the Belt should be at the main port by eleven hundred hours."

CM-2, so alien two months ago, felt like home now. Rick had his few belongings packed in ten minutes, spent another hour wandering the familiar exercise rooms, dining-hall, and dormitories, and then fifteen minutes on his bunk examining the packet that he had been given by Barney French.

He stared in dismay at the contents. He was tired out, nervous, and about to enter the new environment of a ship heading for the Belt. But somehow he was supposed to tackle these assignments and finish them in the next three days.

Your knowledge of Earth geography is inadequate. Read the following—pages of references. Tons of reading, for someone who still had to mouth out most words of more than two syllables.

Your lack of knowledge of the Belt and the solar system is de-

plorable. Learn the following by heart. Sheet after sheet of data about the planets, asteroids, rings and moons of the solar system, endless names and numbers and lists and computer file references.

Back in school he had never been forced to learn things by heart. That was dismissed by the powers-that-be in the Earth education system as "rote learning," old-fashioned and restrictive and undesirable. It didn't leave a student with what Principal Rigden always called "time for smelling the roses."

Rick didn't recall smelling many roses. He did know he had spent a lot of time watching the tube.

Not any more, though. No tubes, except as video outlets for education and training modules. He suspected he was going to see plenty of those.

He puzzled over the final question, the one given to all the apprentices: *Estimate your ship's travel time to the Belt. Tables of the coordinates of the destination, CM-26, as a function of time, together with an initial position of the starting point, CM-2, will be found in this packet. You may assume that there will be continuous acceleration and deceleration on the journey at one quarter of a standard Earth gravity. Answers within ten percent are acceptable.*

Rick groaned to himself. Absolutely baffling—he didn't know how to do orbital mechanics. Hell, he couldn't even spell the words.

Just yesterday he had been on top of the world, now it was back to the same old grind only worse. He would force down some breakfast—he still believed what he had told Deedee, an active brain needed food—then he would head for the main launch port.

Jigger was right. The honeymoon, if it had ever started, was over.

With an hour or more to go to eleven, the main port was already crowded when Rick got there. He had seen ships come and go from CM-2, and as part of the practical course the trainees had been given a guided tour around one of them; but he had never examined any ship the way that he studied the *Vantage*, waiting now for its passengers and crew.

The ship was huge, ten times the size of the transfer vehicle that had carried the trainees from low Earth orbit out to CM-2. Most of it, though, was the drive. The living quarters would be a tight fit for the forty passengers and crew. Rick walked over to the point of closest approach to the main engines of the *Vantage*, and stood staring up at them. They were Diabelli Omnivores, a linked ring of a dozen blue cylinders, each about four meters across and forty meters long. Within them, deuterium and helium-3 would be fused. The heat produced by that raised the main propellant, hydrogen, to a temperature of more than a million degrees.

Naturally, the Omnivores were never used close to any other object. Smaller ion rockets surrounding the main drive ring provided for maneuvering and docking. The main engines were called *omnivores* because with some modification they could fuse any of the lighter elements up to neon. It meant that the *Vantage*, like her sister ships *Vanquish* and *Vanity*, could find suitable fuel anywhere in the solar system.

It also meant that in the hottest fusion mode the internal temperature would reach a billion degrees.

"Close your mouth, Rick." Deedee's voice came from

right next to him. "You're an apprentice now, not a trainee. You're not supposed to gape."

He turned. Apparently two hours sleep agreed with Deedee. She was bright-eyed and full of bounce. Rather than look at her he pointed up at the Omnivores. "We'll be sitting right on top of those monsters. If something goes wrong with the drive, we'll never even know it. Might as well be in the middle of a supernova. How come you're not as worried as I am?"

"Maybe I am. Maybe women just know how to fake things."

"Yeah. But you never gave me a chance to find out about that."

Although Rick kept his tone light, there was a hidden bitterness in him. Apparently Deedee thought nothing unusual had happened the previous night. But it had. After a couple of hours of dancing, Rick had suggested that he and Deedee go off together, just the two of them, and find someplace quiet. He spoke casually, as though it was no big deal, which was the way you handled these things. That didn't mean it was, though.

And she had declined.

"Not tonight, Rick. Tonight I want to dance 'til I drop. But if I did go with anybody, you're the one I would want to go with."

She had known very well what he was suggesting, but she had hauled him back onto the dance floor. Her answer left him horny and restless. The way she had put it he was not supposed to feel rejected. He did. But he wasn't going to let her know it, then or now.

There was a stir among the people at the far end of the

chamber. Looking that way, Rick saw that an entry port to the front part of the *Vantage* was opening. A light ladder was scrolling out and reaching down to ground level, though in such low gravity it was hardly necessary. Every one of the apprentices could jump to hit the port blindfold. Some of them were already moving forward toward the ladder.

"Wait for it!" Barney French's roar came from the entrance to the chamber. "Didn't you lot ever hear of discipline? Apprentices stay there. I have to be first up so I can assign quarters—unless you all want to sleep on top of each other."

She came soaring over their heads and went through the port dead center. Just behind her flew Jigger Tait and Gina Styan. It was news to Rick that those two were taking a ride out to the Belt on the *Vantage*, but he was delighted to see them.

"All right!" Barney reappeared in the port. "Come on. All aboard that's going aboard. Girls first!"

Her last words were lost in a burst of laughter. Chick Teazle, too impatient to wait for her to finish, had jumped before she got to "girls first."

Once you were launched in low gee there was no way to stop yourself. Chick floated upward, waving his arms and legs uselessly. Barney waited until he reached the port, then reached down to grab his foot and boosted. He went spinning away right over the top of the ship, to Barney's raucous, "There you go, Miss Teazle."

It was new proof that the trainee group still had tricks to learn in space. Rick waited his turn, right after Goggles Landau, then bent his knees and jumped. It was a point of pride to hit the exact center of the port, and he did it.

Barney French didn't seem to notice. "Luban, 24-C," she said. "To the right. Keep moving."

To the right meant toward the front of the ship. Rick floated his way along a cramped corridor with bare metal walls. He had expected that 24-C would be a dorm, and was surprised to find that he had a tiny private room. It held a terminal, a small cabinet up near the ceiling, one chair, and a bed that could be opened all the way only when the chair was folded up into a recess in the wall.

Rick took from his bag the picture of his mother. He had sneaked it out when he left home, and been ashamed to show it back in the dorms of New Mexico or CM-2. Now he placed it on top of the data terminal. Everything else in the bag went into the cabinet. After that there was nothing to do.

Barney French had told him to come to 24-C, but she had not ordered him to stay there. He went back into the corridor. Vido Valdez was heading toward him. He did not seem nearly as unhappy as he had been yesterday, when he learned that Monkey had failed. And Rick had seen him close-dancing late in the evening with Gladys de Witt.

So much for undying love.

Since people were still coming aboard the *Vantage*, Rick headed the other way, toward the bows of the ship. The corridor ended in what looked like a food service area, with little tables that could be folded out of the walls. It would seat no more than eight people. Beyond it was another corridor, even narrower. Rick eased his way along it, and found himself at last in a tiny round chamber with a curved and bulging transparent wall.

He was in the very front of the ship, staring out at the blank metal facade of the main port floor and wall. As he watched, he heard a series of clanging sounds from behind him followed by the slow rotation of the ship. The port floor was deserted. Rick decided that the ship must now be sealed, and the external pressure would be dropping toward zero so that the docking facility could be opened to space.

And he was still here, sitting in the bows. Shouldn't he be somewhere else, safely strapped in before the *Vantage* began to move?

Then he realized that the ship *was* moving, so gently that he had not noticed it. He was looking out at the starscape beyond CM-2.

He leaned back, overwhelmed by two thoughts. First, he realized the enormous difference between moving *to* space when you left Earth, and moving *through* space, which is what they were doing now. To get into space called for powerful thrusters and high accelerations, and you were wise to strap yourself in. But once you were here, even the gentlest acceleration was enough to move you around and no special precautions were needed when you started.

Second was the sudden knowledge: *they were on the way.* Earth was visible over on the right-hand side of the transparent bubble. When he had first looked at it from CM-2 it had seemed so far away. But in the next few days it would shrink from a whole round world to a tiny pale dot, no brighter in the sky than Venus or Jupiter. Hundreds of thousands of kilometers of distance would gradually turn to hundreds of millions.

Rick stared at the little blue-grey marble, and made a decision that surprised him completely. He had been pleased to leave Earth, and he couldn't wait to get to the Belt.

But one day, some day, he would come back.

CHAPTER TWELVE

THE training course on CM-2 had been tough. It was hard for Rick to believe that anything could be worse. During the first horrendous days of travel to the Belt, he learned that he was wrong.

The difference, in one word, was "yourself." Where Turkey had listened patiently to questions and provided answers, Barney French did no such thing.

"What do you think I am, your bloody nursemaid?" she

said, when Rick went to her with an innocent question about silicaceous asteroids. "That's what data banks and computers and hypermedia systems are for. They know a thousand times as much about planetary compositions as I do. Look the damn thing up for *yourself*. And while you're at it, check out siderophilic ore refinement. You're going to need that, too."

Instead of an answer, Rick found himself thrown out with an additional assignment. It was hard to avoid Barney French in the ship's cramped interior, but he quickly learned to do it. Sarcasm was her favorite mode of expression, and each time you met her she loaded another task on top of your heap.

DIY—Do It Yourself. Within twenty-four hours it became the motto of the apprentices. One of the first things that Rick had done for himself was to look up the word "apprentice," which he had heard of only vaguely back in school. He found it defined as a "person under a legal agreement to work for a master craftsman in return for instruction and support."

Nothing there about working at a terminal until your eyes popped out of your head and your brain was ready to turn to watery gruel and trickle out through your nose. All the same, he liked the sound of "master craftsman." The suggestion was that you could eventually be one yourself.

Rick hid away in his cramped cabin and buckled down to his assignments. After the first few hours of stately recession from the Earth-Moon system there was little to see from the *Vantage*'s observation ports, and nothing to do inside but eat, sleep, and work.

He realized very quickly that there was no possible way he could complete all his assignments in the time available. Two months ago he would have thrown up his hands in despair, turned his back on the whole thing, and guaranteed his own failure. But he was learning. Nobody in the universe could know everything. Therefore, everyone made choices. Success might be no more than the right choice—plus a little bit of luck.

He examined the list of what he was supposed to do, and decided that the geography of Earth would be invaluable—to someone about to go there. He was heading in the opposite direction. The most important things for him to know were about the Belt. After that he could tackle other planets and moons, and if there happened to be any time left over he would worry about the rest. Not only was it logical to start with the Belt, but he knew from experience how much easier it was to learn about something in which you had a personal interest. Back in school, even the dullest idler had no trouble following the lessons about masturbation and sexual foreplay.

And what about the other problem they had been set, to estimate the travel time of the ship to the Belt? On the face of it, that was absolutely impossible. He would have to learn all sorts of orbital mechanics, for a body moving under the gravitational influence of the Sun and the Earth and who knew what else. And yet it was totally out of character for a question to be asked that a trainee had no chance of answering. . . .

Rick put the problem to one side. Instead, he tracked computer references and pulled up the Belt databases. He found that this piece of the assignment was actually fairly interesting. He had heard the word "Belt" thrown around many times since he signed up, and it brought to mind a tidy construct of sizeable planetoids orbiting the Sun in some well-defined and neat region of space. But the reality was more like a disorganized swarm of objects, some bodies dipping in their motions closer to the Sun than the Earth, some as they moved around the Sun also rotating about each other like miniature Earth-Moon systems. The main region of the Belt, between Mars and Jupiter, occupied a trillion trillion cubic kilometers of space. The bodies ranged in size from whole worlds like Ceres, a fifth as big across as the Moon, down to small pebbles and grains of sand.

From the point of view of Vanguard Mining, neither the very small nor the very large were apparently of interest, except to be avoided. The big ones did not permit Vanguard's secret mining methods, which would be revealed to the apprentices when they were out in the Belt; the smallest ones were simple navigation hazards. The payoff lay in medium-sized bodies between half a kilometer and two kilometers across.

Even there, composition was important. Some asteroids were ninety-nine percent silicon oxides; in other words, they were just lumps of rock. But others were mostly metals, valuable iron and nickel and platinum and iridium. If a body was really high in metals, mining it was relatively easy—compared with *finding* it in the first place. You couldn't send a prospecting ship to one little body after another, until you found the one that you wanted by taking material samples from it. That would be too slow and expensive. Instead, the exploration technique called for instrument surveys in which a body's reflected light was measured from a distance in many different parts of the spectrum, then matched with predicted reflectance curves for different mixtures of metals and rocks. Only after that work was all done on the computers did it make sense to send a ship to a promising asteroid and stake a claim.

For the first time, Rick understood what Jigger Tait had been talking about when he grumbled about Avant Mining. Recently, the Vanguard staff had found, again and again, that when they sent a ship to an asteroid Avant Mining had beaten them to it and already staked a claim.

Just how did Avant or Vanguard mine an asteroid, once they had mining rights? Rick was all set to follow the data bank pointers and try to find an answer when he halted in mid-command. He had just been told that the Vanguard mining method was proprietary. Chasing information about it would be a pure waste of time. And time to waste was one thing he surely did not have.

Rick sighed, erased his query, and turned to the next piece of his assignment: learning the names of the major bodies in the Belt, together with their size and composition.

Within a few minutes he realized that the new task was mind-bogglingly boring. It was a relief to be interrupted by a soft tap on his door. He half-expected it to be Deedee, and he was all set to treat her with the coldness that he felt she deserved. But to his surprise it was Alice Klein.

"Mind if I come in?" She still had that shy little girl voice, but he noticed that she did not wait for his answer before she entered.

"What do you want?" He remembered Barney French's warning: Help someone else with their problem if you like, but don't think for one moment that it will get you off the hook with your own assignment. "I don't have time to talk, I'm really busy."

"That makes two of us." He had the only seat, so she

moved to sit on the edge of his folded bunk, as languid and graceful as ever. "I'm not here to pick your brains, Rick. At least, not just for that. I want to suggest that we work together on a problem."

"Which one?" Rick knew from what Barney French had said that Alice still had problems with math. He didn't, at least so far, which meant that working with her would be a one-way street.

"The problem we all have. The time it will take us to get to CM-26, out in the Belt. Have you looked at that yet?"

"Not yet." Rick's skepticism increased. To tell the truth, he had mentally given up on the problem. It didn't just call for straight learning of facts. You had to understand loads of math and orbital equations, which even Gina Styan admitted was a job for specialists. He wasn't sure where to start. "Do you know how to do it?"

It was a question designed to get rid of her. He was convinced that Alice would have no idea. She would admit her ignorance, and then he'd ask her to go away. But she was pursing up her mouth and wrinkling her nose.

"I don't know." The grey, wide eyes focused on Rick— for the first time, she seemed to be looking *at* him and not *through* him. "Back when we were studying for our theory test, Turkey Gossage told me something that he said I ought to keep in mind for future reference. I have, but I don't know what to do with it. That's why I came to you. You're smart, you can see through things."

She was praising him, buttering him up. Rick knew that, but still he was pleased. Flattery, even when you recognized it, made you feel good. Maybe because it showed somebody thought you were *worth* flattering.

"What did Turkey tell you?"

"He said that the Sun's gravity controls the movements of every body in the solar system."

"Big deal. We all know that."

"Yes. But he went on to say that the real surprise was how *small* the Sun's gravitational force is. For instance, he told me that if you work out the acceleration on an object at Earth's distance from the Sun, you find that it's less than a thousandth of a gee. And when you get out to the Belt, it's less than one ten-thousandth of a gee."

"So?" But Rick already had the conviction that Alice was on to something.

"Well, we were told to assume that this ship is accelerating at a quarter of a gee."

"I believe that, it certainly feels about right."

"But that means once we get well away from Earth, the gravity forces from Earth and Sun and every other planet are nothing, compared with the ship's own acceleration. I feel sure this is relevant to the problem—only I don't see how to use it."

"But I think I do! Give me a minute." Rick sat staring at nothing. If all other accelerations on the ship were hundreds of times smaller than the ship's *own* acceleration—

"Alice, we don't need to know a whole slew of orbital theory. Our own ship's acceleration is so high, we can get a good value for our travel time by assuming that we travel in a straight line and ignoring everything else. All we need is our own acceleration, and the distance we have to go."

"But we don't know the distance—CM-26 keeps moving."

"Sure it does." The boredom and frustration had been

swept away by excitement and certainty. Rick suddenly had a clear mental picture in his head. "See, here's what we do. We make two tables. The first has two columns. It shows times, say, every hour from the time we started, in the left column. The right column shows the distance from CM-2, where we started, to CM-26 for the corresponding time. It has to be a table, because CM-26 keeps moving. The information to make that distance table comes right out of the co-ordinates given to us in the problem packet."

"But we don't know the travel time—that's what we're supposed to find out!"

"I know. Let me finish. Now, we make another table. This one also has two columns. The left column is the same list of times, in hours. The right column says how far the ship goes in that much time, assuming that we accelerate for half the time, and decelerate for the other half. We already had the formula in class for the distance traveled in a given time with a given constant acceleration. It's just half the time mul-tiplied by the final speed."

"But we don't *know* the final speed!"

"Yes we do—at least, we know the formula for it. We had it on a test, it's just the acceleration multiplied by the time."

"If you say so. But I *still* don't know what we do next."

"We're almost finished. We have two time/distance ta-bles, right? Now we plot them both as curves on one graph. The first curve is the distance to CM-26, hour by hour. The second curve shows the ship's distance traveled, also hour by hour. Those two curves cross somewhere—they have to, or we'd never be able to reach CM-26. And the time where they cross is the travel time—our answer. It's the time when the ship will have gone just far enough to reach the position of CM-26. An approximation, but I bet it will be closer than ten percent."

Alice was shaking her head. "You'll have to go through all that again. You went too fast for me. Say it one more time."

"I'll do more than say it—we'll do it, together. You make the table for the distance to CM-26. I'll make the table for ship's distance traveled. Then we compare and make the graph. Here's a calculator for you."

While Alice began to work out distances to CM-26, Rick began to make the table for ship's distance. The result made him whistle in astonishment. A quarter of a gee didn't sound like much of an acceleration, compared with the five gees and more that they had briefly endured on the way up to low Earth orbit. But keep it going, and the results were amazing. After an hour of accelerating and another of decelerating, you had traveled over thirty thousand kilometers. No big deal. Increase that to two days, though, and you were eighteen *million* kilometers away from your starting point. And in eight days . . .

"Alice, I want you to check this and see if I'm screwing up somewhere."

"What's wrong?" She had been working steadily, sitting on the folded bunk and biting her lip in concentration. Now she paused and smiled at Rick. For a change, the smile involved her whole face. Looking at her it was hard to believe that she usually seemed remote and uninvolved.

Rick held out his calculation. "According to this, if we travel for eight days we'll have gone almost three hundred million kilometers. We'd be out in the Belt!"

"Let me look." And, as she quietly did her own calculation. "You know, nobody *said* the trip out would take weeks and weeks—we just assumed it. Maybe that's the point of the problem we were all given."

"You mean, they want to see if we can figure out for ourselves that we're going to be there sooner than we thought?"

"That's right. You know what Turkey told us. The zingers wouldn't stop when we left him." She studied the final number on her calculator. "I get a different answer—twice as big as what you said."

"Let me take a look." Rick studied what she had done. "You weren't listening to me. You've accelerated the ship for the whole eight days. You can't do that. Look at your final speed, it's nearly seventeen hundred kilometers a second. You'd go right through the Belt like—" Rick paused; *like shit on skates* was what he had been about to say, but he couldn't see that expression pleasing Alice. "—like lightning," he finished weakly. "You have to *accelerate* for half the time, then *decelerate* the other half, so you're not going fast when you get there."

"Let me do it again." She repeated the calculation, slowly and carefully, and nodded. "I agree with you now. Four days accelerating at a quarter of a gee, then four days decelerating, takes you about two hundred and ninety million kilometers."

"That could be more than enough to get you to Ceres." Rick decided he sounded a bit know-it-all, and added, "I was just learning the asteroid distances when you came in."

Instead of replying, Alice got up from the bunk, went across to the door, and locked it. She came back and stood directly in front of Rick. "You've finished the problem, everything but comparing the two tables."

"You did it, too. I had no idea where to start. You brought me the key information."

"But I'd never have figured out how to use it without you. You provided the brain power, not me. My question is, what now?"

"I don't know what you mean."

"Do we keep this to ourselves?"

Rick hadn't thought about that, but it didn't take long to reach a decision. "Of course we do! Barney French said we *could* cooperate, but she didn't say we had to. I don't know about you, but I need all the extra credits I can get. There's no reason to share what we've done with everybody else."

"With *anybody* else?"

"With anybody else."

"Good." Alice motioned for Rick to stand up, and quietly folded his chair into its niche in the wall. "It's a deal, then. Our big secret, just the two of us. I like that." She studied his face, alive with excitement at the work they had just done together. "And I like you, Rick. I watched you dance the other night, and I wished that you were dancing with me."

"I didn't realize that."

"No reason you should. I didn't have the sense to come over and ask you, did I? That won't happen again."

The months since he left school had been filled with surprises, but there had been nothing as surprising or exciting as Alice. To think that he had known her since the first bus trip from Albuquerque airport, and not really known her at all. He had never suspected that her face could flush so vividly, and those wide, grey eyes could look at him with such excitement.

A soft chime over the ship's central communication system brought him out of his reverie. It meant that first mess was beginning, and if he wanted to eat at second sitting he had just twenty minutes to get up, dress, and make his way to the little food service area. When he had first seen it, he had never imagined that it might be the only place to eat on the whole ship. But it was. The apprentices ate there in relays.

He dressed slowly and folded away his bunk, then paused for another look at the time/distance tables that he and Alice had generated to solve the problem of travel to CM-26. After dinner he would go over their work again, but he was not worried. What they had done had the right feeling to it, the feeling that you couldn't describe but also couldn't mistake. Once you hit on the right method, a problem suddenly became ridiculously easy. It seemed like a general truth: what you knew was easy; what you didn't know was hard.

Rick wandered slowly along the narrow corridor to the mess area. He had never felt so good in his whole life. He arrived just as the first sitting apprentices were getting ready to leave and dumping their plates and cups in the hopper to be vacuum cleaned. Alice was at the table nearest to Rick. He walked over to her.

She stood up, turned toward him—and hurried past him as though he did not exist. Before he could think of what to say she was out of the room. He took two steps after her, then paused. Deedee Mao was entering, blocking the way, walking right up to Rick and smiling at him.

"The first person here again. You got a tapeworm, or just hollow legs?" She frowned at him. "What's wrong, Rick? Are you feeling all right?"

"Yeah—I guess." Rick slumped down bewildered at one of the tables. What was going on with Alice? Why had she cut him cold like that, after what had happened between them? "Yes, I'm fine."

"Well, let's see what tonight's mystery is. I'm getting fed up with squid pie." Deedee sat down right opposite Rick. The people assigned to different sittings changed all the time, but they all went through the same ritual. You were served an anonymous lump of something for the main course, and you guessed what it might be. The winner was the one who came up with the most imaginative—usually rude—suggestion.

Tonight, though, Rick didn't feel in the least like playing the game. He didn't even want to talk, although it was obvious that Deedee was in a chatty mood. He did his best to reply normally but she started to look at him strangely across the table, her smiles changing to frowns. It was a huge relief when somebody else bustled in, sat down next to Rick and said, "All right if I join the two of you?"

The kid was someone Rick had never seen before, although up to this point he had thought he knew every apprentice on board the *Vantage*. Somebody must have been added at the last moment. The skinny newcomer had a tousled mop of curly light brown hair and a fresh, ruddy complexion, as though he had just come in from a brisk walk in the open air. He grinned at Rick and Deedee, stared down at the plates that were appearing from the server, and said "Deviled dingo dong again, I see."

Rick just stared. It was Deedee who stuck out her hand

across the table and said, "Hi. We've never met before. I'm Deedee Mao."

"Tom Garcia." The kid smiled at her and turned expectantly to Rick.

"Rick Luban." Rick held out his hand in turn, and then, with no idea what to say next, added, "How are you doing with your assignment?"

It sounded inane, and felt even more so when Garcia put his head to one side, pursed his lips, and said, "Dunno. I guess if we get to CM-26 in one piece I'm doing all right."

"Huh?" Deedee's face reflected Rick's own confusion.

"Maybe I should have been more informative during the introductions." Tom Garcia waved his arm around him. "You see, it's my job to fly this thing."

"You mean the ship?" asked Deedee. "You're the *Vantage*'s *pilot*?"

"I'm afraid so. I hope it's not too big a disappointment for you. Actually, I'm one of two. The other is Marlene Kotite, and she's holding the fort right now while I'm here feeding my face."

"But you look younger than I do!"

"So they tell me." Garcia shrugged. "I'm sorry, but what can I do? Wait twenty years, I suppose, and it will take care of itself."

"But the seniority system—" Deedee began, then stopped herself. "I guess everything out in the Belt is so new, there aren't any really senior people."

"That's partly true. More to the point, it's not like the transportation system back on Earth, set in stone. Out here, people who are best at the jobs get them." Garcia shook his head. "I'm sorry, that sounds like I'm boasting. I didn't mean to."

"You have every right to boast. You're in charge of this whole ship!" Deedee's attention was no longer on Rick, and he didn't mind that at all. "Would you mind if I asked you some questions," she went on. "About the ship, I mean."

"Ask away. Only two conditions. First, you've got to give me time to eat. Second, I won't tell you anything that might give you an advantage over the other apprentices on the travel time question that Barney French set all of you."

"No problem. That's completely impossible anyway. Everybody agrees, no one will get an answer." Fortunately all Deedee's attention was on Tom Garcia, otherwise Rick's face might have given him away.

"If the Diabelli Omnivores can fuse any element lighter than neon," she went on, "Why do you use a deuterium/helium-3 mixture? Turkey Gossage told us those are rare materials, hard to obtain in large quantities."

"Quite true. Two reasons. First, all the fusion products except for neutrinos are charged particles, so the Omnivores can direct them all in the same direction by using electromagnetic fields. That gives a very efficient drive. If I need to, I can accelerate the *Vantage* at a couple of gees. If we fused carbon or oxygen, we'd be down to a fifth of a gee or less. Second, fusing heavier elements requires much higher temperatures, up in the billion degree range. That means more wear and tear on the engines, and much more frequent maintenance. For a working ship, the fraction of time in service is one of the most important variables."

Rick listened to everything that the pilot said, but half his mind was all the time somewhere else. He could not get

Alice's strange behavior out of his head. As soon as the meal was over he slipped away, leaving Deedee still fascinated by what Tom Garcia had to tell her.

He was not sure where he would find Alice, but he went wandering aft toward the women's quarters. He received odd looks from half a dozen female apprentices as he went, but at last he located her where he might have expected—in the tiny exercise room, running doggedly on the treadmill.

"Alice!"

"What?" She gradually slowed the pace to zero, and stood there with her chest heaving.

"You ignored me back there. I wondered why. I mean, I didn't do anything."

She glanced across at the door. "Not here. We can't talk here."

"Why not?"

"I'll explain later. Go back to your room."

"But I want to—"

"I'll see you there in fifteen minutes. Now *go*—this second."

Rick retreated along the corridor to his room. He unfolded his bunk and sat down on it. When Alice arrived at last she closed the door and locked it.

"Rick, we should have talked before I left for dinner. Do you want a job with Vanguard Mining, or would you rather be kicked out and sent back to Earth?"

"That's a dumb question. You know the answer. What does it have to do with you and me?"

"Everything. Vanguard has a very simple operating philosophy: The company comes first. One sure way to fail is to put emotions and personal feelings ahead of the company and your job. There's a very easy way, however, to have the best of both worlds: Do what you like, but *don't let it show*. Do you have any idea how many people were getting close to each other in the New Mexico training camp, or on CM-2?"

"Jigger and Gina—"

"Did you realize they were partners, until the party on the final night?"

Rick shook his head. He had known, but he didn't want to tell Alice just *how* he knew.

"I wasn't going to say anything or do anything in the mess hall," he protested. "I was just going to talk to you."

"Yeah, sure. Talk to me. You didn't see your face. You big simpleton." She hugged him close, to take the edge of what she was saying. "Anyone who saw you looking at me would know in a minute how things were between us. You couldn't have made it any clearer if you'd written my name on your forehead."

"I can't help the way I feel."

"Nor can I. But we have to be *discreet*. We can't afford to moon around looking lovesick. So don't expect me to be anything but cold and distant when we're in public. Getting bounced from the program is one chance neither of us can take."

"What about in private?" Rick wasn't being rejected, but he felt like it.

"That's a different matter." She smiled at him and touched her finger to his lips. "In private, what we do is your business and mine."

CHAPTER THIRTEEN

RICK was convinced that no one else would solve the problem of the ship's travel time. It was a shock when at the end of the third day Barney French announced that a total of six people had obtained the right answer.

She did not, however, provide the names.

"You know who you are," she said to the assembled group. "This isn't a school. My job isn't to give out prizes."

Which left Rick to stare around and wonder who was so smart. Chick Teazle? Gladys de Witt? Vido? Not Deedee, if what she had told Tom Garcia was the truth. Had a whole group of them cooperated, without telling the rest? Not judging from their expressions. It seemed to him that everyone was staring round at everybody else.

Barney also offered no public comment as to how people had managed on their individual assignments. She simply called them in later, one at a time, asked a few questions and made barbed comments on the answers, and piled on the work load.

"You'll need this, and this, and this," she said calmly to Rick. He didn't argue, but he knew that each item she dropped on him meant four or five hours hard work. It made him wonder why he had been so keen to succeed when he was on CM-2.

He carried his assignments back to his cabin and started the grind. The next couple of days were endless labor, broken only by food, sleep, and stolen hours with Alice. Barney French had dumped on her even harder than Rick. Alice had only just squeaked through the finals on CM-2, and still she was barely making the grade. Rick felt almost guilty at the time they spent together—but he never suggested that they might stop seeing each other. Amid all the work, Alice provided the bright spot in a sea of drudgery.

Halfway point came and went, a few minutes of weightlessness while the *Vantage* turned end-over-end. Deceleration began. Four and a half more days, and they would be at their destination in the Belt.

Seventy-two hours after turnover Rick, wandering along to the dining area dazed by an excess of studying, found him-

self sitting opposite Deedee. She stared at him in a sad-eyed
and accusing way, but all she said was, "How you doing,
Rick?"

"Fine." Did she know? How could she know? He had
not spoken a word to anyone, and after the first day he had
been careful not even to look at Alice in public.

He pulled out of his trance and made a big effort. "I'm
fine," he repeated. "How are you doing?"

"Busy. Working hard. Thinking a lot. About a lot of
things."

Their food had not yet appeared, but she stood up and
went to another table. Rick felt uncomfortable, though he
told himself that he had not certainly not done anything to
Deedee. She kept looking at him from where she was sitting
at the other table.

He wolfed his food down as fast as he could and returned
at once to his cabin. It was late, and Alice had told him that
she didn't think she would be able to make it until the next
day, but he really wanted to see her and touch her and talk
to her.

He was lying on his bunk, supposed to be learning the
table of the elements but actually drifting and dreaming,
when it happened.

An urgent voice spoke over the general announcement
channel. "Emergency. Please return at once to your cabin and
secure all movable objects. Lie on your bunk and strap yourself down. In five minutes we will perform a major course
change and move to high acceleration. Repeat, this is an
emergency."

Rick glanced around the little cabin. The chair was
tucked away in the wall. He went across to the terminal,

grabbed the picture of his mother, and locked it away in the high cabinet. As the announcement was repeated—this time he recognized Tom Garcia's voice, nothing like as casual as usual—he went back to the bunk, lay down, and secured the straps across his body and legs.

Now what? The terminal came on without his touching it, something he had not realized could be done. Barney French's image appeared on the ceiling above Rick. He realized for the first time that the terminal could also serve as a backlit projector, throwing an image onto the flat plane of the white ceiling.

"To repeat what our pilots told you," Barney said quietly, "we have an emergency situation. Let me assure you that this is not what you apprentices refer to as a 'zinger,' part of a planned test. Since Tom Garcia and Marlene Kotite are otherwise occupied, I have agreed to tell you what we know so far. Fifteen minutes ago we received word from Headquarters of a major accident on one of our advanced mining facilities, Company Mine 31. There are casualties. We don't know yet how many. After the initial message from CM-31 there has been no communication of any kind. Because of the changing geometry of our mines in the Belt, the *Vantage* happens to have the best location and velocity vector of all our vessels to reach CM-31 in minimum time. We will shortly change direction and go to our maximum acceleration of a little more than two gees. That will be maintained for four and a half hours, after which we will perform turnover and decelerate with equal force for six hours. We anticipate that accommodation changes on board the *Vantage* will be necessary upon our arrival at CM-31, but I cannot yet inform you of what those might be.

"I know that each of you has experienced much higher accelerations than two gees, but only in physical tests or for the short period of an ascent to orbit. Do not experiment. As soon as our thrust pattern has stabilized, I and others familiar with high-gee shipboard activity will come to each cabin in turn and instruct you on safe operations until we reach CM-31. Meanwhile, remain in your bunks."

The screen went blank. Rick lay back and waited. There had been no sign of the usual sarcasm in Barney French's voice, but also no room for compromise on her face. Anyone who left his bunk, that look said, would be in major trouble. Something terrible must have happened on CM-31, though Rick could not imagine what.

Ten minutes ago he had been brooding over Alice's absence. Now he was glad that she had not been able to come to him. Were other apprentices struggling right now into their clothes, and scrambling back to their own cabins?

The drive turned off. There was the usual moment of disorientation as his stomach came up to meet his throat, and then the giddiness of a rotation and realignment of the ship in inertial space. Before that could become uncomfortable he was pressed back hard into his bunk. Wrinkles in the mattress and blanket that he had never noticed before made their mark on his back.

He had been told not to move from his bunk, but he was free to move within it. A set of controls for the terminal lay on the bunk's right-hand edge, so that if you wanted to you could work the data banks while you were lying in bed. Rick keyed it now, with difficulty, adjusting to the use of fingers that suddenly did not want to lift from keys.

COMPANY MINE 31—at last it came—ONE OF THE

NEWEST OF VANGUARD MINING'S ASSETS, THE BASE ASTEROID FOR CM-31 HAD AN ORIGINAL FORM CLOSE TO A TRIAXIAL EL-LIPSOID WITH SEMI-MAJOR AXES 0.9, 0.7, AND 0.5 KILOME-TERS. . . . What was that supposed to mean? Nothing at all, so far as Rick was concerned. He plowed on, word after un-familiar word. . . . ALTHOUGH SMALL COMPARED WITH OTHER MINES SUCH AS CM-8 AND CM-20, CM-31 IS UNUSU-ALLY VALUABLE BECAUSE OF ITS HIGH CONTENT OF SIDEROPHILES. . . .

Siderophiles. Rick swore. That term again, the one Barney French had told him to check out—and he hadn't done it.

He could hear sounds from outside his door, but no one came in. He had to be quick. He moved to the word-search data bank, and the definition appeared on the screen.

SIDEROPHILE: LITERALLY, IRON-LOVING. IN MINING OP-ERATIONS THE TERM REFERS TO A GROUP OF ELEMENTS THAT COMMONLY OCCUR IN THE PRESENCE OF IRON AND ARE PREF-ERENTIALLY REMOVED WITH IRON DURING AN EXTRACTION PROCESS. THE MOST IMPORTANT OF THESE FOR COMMERCIAL PURPOSES ARE NICKEL, IRIDIUM, AND PLATINUM.

So CM-31 was a potential gold mine—or at least, a plat-inum mine. Rick switched back to his other data file.

. . . CM-31 FORMS A TEST SITE FOR NEW LARGE-SCALE CENTRIFUGE AND ZONE MELTING METHODS. IT IS BEING USED IN PROOF-OF-CONCEPT MODE FOR SUCH MINING TECH-NIQUES. . . .

Centrifuge was what they had done to him during the physical tests, spinning him around on the end of a long arm with a balance weight at the other end, faster and faster, until he blacked out. He didn't see how you could put a whole asteroid on the end of anything.

Zone melting made even less sense. It was another phrase that meant nothing. He went again to his online dictionary and this time met with less success. The database defined what he wanted as a method of purifying certain metals, but after that it quickly became gibberish: "The zone melting process relies on the fact that many impurities prefer to remain in the liquid phase rather than freeze out into the solid phase. A melted section propagating along an otherwise solid body will collect impurities in the moving melted section. They will be swept along and concentrated at one end."

Rick puzzled out the message, word by painful word, and was as mystified when he finished as when he started. *Concentrated at one end.* One end of what? An asteroid didn't have ends, the ones he had seen were all irregular roundish lumps.

. . . IN VIEW OF THE HIGH METAL FRACTION OF CM-31, A RECORD 99 PERCENT OF THE TOTAL MASS (ROUGHLY 8 BILLION TONS) CAN BE EXTRACTED. IT WILL BE TRANSFERRED TO CISLUNAR SPACE EMPLOYING A SMALL PART OF THE DROSS AS REACTION MASS FOR LOW-THRUST ION PROPULSION UNITS.

Dross. Rick swore again. What the devil was dross? The trouble with learning was that the more you learned, the more you realized how much you didn't know. Once you started you were on a never-ending treadmill and you couldn't get off.

The opening door ended his frustration. It was Barney French herself, panting hard. "Luban? Up out of the bunk." She caught sight of the screen display. "Good choice—let's hope you don't need that for a while. Don't rush getting up. Slow is smart, first time you do it."

Not just the best way—the only way. Rick came gingerly to his feet and stood there swaying. Tom Garcia had said two gee, but it felt more like ten.

"You'll get used to it." Barney was reading his mind. "All of you have been spoiled the past couple of months by low-gee environments. This is nothing. Think yourself lucky you didn't sign with Avant Mining and have to live with pulsed fusion. Their high-acceleration mode takes them from two and a half gees to zero and back every few seconds, all day long. You ever try to eat dinner bouncing on a pogo stick?"

She moved to the door without waiting for an answer, and Rick followed her out of the cabin. He paused on the threshold. The passageway, along which he had often zoomed with so little effort, had become a deep vertical well. Handholds and footholds that he had never noticed before were placed every foot along it.

"This is the seventh time I've done this," Barney complained. She looped a thick soft rope around her waist, tied the other end around Rick under his armpits, and motioned for him to start down. "Make me an old woman before my time, it will. Go on, start down. I'll be right behind you. And *go slow*. You use both hands and both feet, and three of those must work to support your weight at all times. Did you ever go rock climbing back on Earth?"

"No. No rocks where I lived."

"That figures."

"I did a few night climbs, though. Up and down the outside of buildings." Rick still shivered when he remembered the jump from the roof of the Lafferty apartments to a balcony on the building next door. Only eight feet, but when you stood in the dark waiting, ten stories up, eight seemed more like eighty.

"Dumb ass." Barney sniffed, a few feet above him. "Risking your neck for nothing. Trying to impress some girl, I bet."

"No." Rick was climbing down the shaft, slowly and carefully, a boulder strapped to each arm and to his back. If he fell, Barney was supposed to hold him until he could grab another handhold. But could she do it? She'd have to hold up four times her own weight. "I was just trying to prove I was brave," he panted.

"And did you?"

"I don't think so. I proved I was scared." Rick had no more breath for talking. He could see now why Barney had been struggling for breath when she came into his cabin. But he was almost there, reaching the solid floor of the little dining area.

"Take your time," said Barney. "You won't need to do much of this unless we have an emergency, but you have to know how ahead of time—just in case."

Rick nodded a head made of solid lead. He turned, making sure that his feet landed in the correct place—and found himself staring into Deedee's anxious face. Goggles Landau was next to her.

"Message from the flight deck," said Goggles at once. He was talking not to Rick but to Barney French, now on the last step of her own descent. "Pilots Garcia and Kotite want you there as soon as possible. They have more news."

"Shoot. I've got one more still to do. Anybody know where Teazle's cabin is?"

"I do," said Rick and Deedee simultaneously. They

stared at each other. Her cheeks darkened with a blush, and she glared defiantly at Rick.

"Good." If Barney noticed, she did not care. "Landau, you come with me. I have a job for you. Mao and Luban, I showed you how to climb. Now you go and show Teazle—I want *all three* of you roped together when you do it. Understand?"

"Yes, sir."

"I'm putting a lot of trust in all of you, more than I should in an apprentice. Don't let me down."

"We won't." Rick and Deedee stared at each other as Barney and Goggles left the dining area for the lower level between passenger quarters and drive units, where the flight deck was located.

"What do you think happened on CM-31?" Deedee asked.

Rick jumped at the chance of a neutral subject. He was forced to put his arms around her to tie the rope, and it was the closest they had been since the night of the dance. He couldn't help brushing against her.

"I'll make a guess," he said. "They were using new mining methods. Something went wrong while they were melting and separating the different metals. CM-31 is mostly metal, iron and nickel and platinum."

She didn't ask how he knew, merely nodded and started to climb. He followed close behind. Going up was harder work than going down, but it was also easier. You could see just where your hands had to go, instead of groping around with your feet.

"Do you know what centrifuge melting is?" he asked, after they had climbed about five meters.

"Sure." She was breathing heavily, but moving up steadily. "It's a confusing term—two different things in one. It means melting, plus centrifuge separation. You take a cylinder filled with different materials, and you melt them. At the same time you spin the cylinder around on its axis. That gives you like a gravity gradient, but of course it's not gravity, its centrifugal force. The denser liquids go to the outside, farthest from the axis. The light ones stay close to the middle, sort of floating on the heavy ones. So you've separated them out from each other. The dross floats at the very center."

"Dross?"

"Scum. You know, the light useless stuff."

The long speech had taken all her breath, and she paused in her climb. Rick, focused on the placement of his own hands and feet, took an upward step and ran the top of his head into something soft.

"Oof! Do you mind?" Deedee sounded exasperated. "That's my rear end you're poking. It's off limits."

"Sorry. Not the first time you've called me a butt-head, though." Rick waited, until she began to move upward again. "What happens if you don't have a cylinder available?"

"Then you can't do centrifuge melting, can you? Why are you asking?"

"The data bank says CM-31 was testing centrifuge melting methods. That's why I said I guessed that something went wrong when they were trying to do it."

They had finally reached Chick Teazle's cabin, tucked away up near the very front of the *Vantage*. Deedee knocked and went in without pausing.

"Hey there!" Rick heard Chick, loud and self-confident

as usual. "This is an unexpected treat. Let's get"—Chick saw Rick at the door, and his voice changed on the final word—"friendly."

"Barney French sent us." Deedee sounded abrupt and unnatural. "Get up from your bunk. We have to show you how to climb down to lower ship levels."

"Why you two?" Chick stared at Rick.

"We happened to be there with Barney." Rick held up the thick rope. "We have to be all tied together, just in case."

"I don't need no damn rope." But Chick took the end that Rick handed him, looped the rope around under his arms, and tied a deft knot. "All right, go ahead. I'll follow you down."

"No." Rick put his arm on Deedee's, just as she was about to start the descent. "You go first, Chick. That way if you fall, we'll be above you and have a chance to brace ourselves. If you were above us you could knock us with you."

"I'm not going to fall, you dummy." Chick glared at Rick, but he moved forward. "What happens if you fall on me?"

"You cushion my landing." Rick watched as Chick started down. He was long-limbed and powerful, and he moved with a speed and confidence that Rick envied. Deedee followed, saying what Rick was thinking: "Slow down a bit, Chick, or you'll pull us off-balance."

Chick grunted, but he did as she asked. The three descended steadily, to find Barney French waiting for them back at the dining level.

"Good," she said. "Everyone has been through the drill. Now you do it without the rope. I want each of you back in your own cabin, and on your own bunk until we get to CM-31."

It seemed such an anticlimax that they all stared at her instead of jumping at once to do what she said.

"Can't you tell us more about what happened?" asked Deedee.

"I propose to do exactly that. But I'm not going to go round telling you one at a time. Get to your bunk, or you'll miss the beginning."

It was incentive enough. Chick went swinging away up the vertical passage like a monkey, while Deedee started downward.

Rick, about to follow right behind Chick, felt Barney's hand on his arm.

"Give him a few seconds," she said. "If he does goof, I assume you don't want two hundred pounds plummeting down on you under two gees."

Rick waited impatiently, staring up but ready to jump out of the way, until Chick vanished into his cabin. Then he made his own ascent, trying to strike the balance between speed and caution. Barney was right. Practice made all the difference. Already it felt easier than the first time.

He lay down on his bunk, fixed the straps into position, and waited impatiently for something to happen. What had Chick meant when he said, "Let's get friendly"? And why had Deedee suddenly turned all stiff and weird?

Rick could guess, but before he had time to brood on it Barney's image was again projected on the ceiling.

"I told you during our very first session that when you came aboard the *Vantage* all the babying ended," she said. "Well, I lied. This phase of your training is supposed to place you in what we call a Level Three environment. Unfortunately, the situation at CM-31 represents a Level Five environment—the highest level of danger and uncertainty that fully-trained staff ever expect to meet. You are not ready for that, but needless to say this was not from choice. Head-quarters have again confirmed that every other ship in the fleet will need at least thirty-six hours more than the *Vantage* to reach Company Mine 31. That time could be the differ-ence between life and death. Therefore you, the apprentices, must assist in operations. When we reach CM-31 you will supplement six experienced staff members: myself, Tait, and Styan; Garcia and Kotite, our pilots; and Skipios, our engi-neer.

"Meanwhile, in the nine hours remaining until our ar-rival at CM-31, you are all to remain in your bunks. If you can sleep, do so. First, however, I am going to give you back-ground on where we are going and what we will find there."

It was far into the usual rest cycle and Rick was tired out, but the idea of sleep while in a two-gee field sounded like pure fantasy. The slightest movement made you aware of your body. Even breathing was an effort.

"Here is CM-31," Barney went on, "as it was when our original prospecting team arrived and confirmed the nature of the find." Her face vanished, and was replaced by the image of an irregular and pock-marked lump of rock. Rick knew that the Belt held billions of similar mountain-sized boulders. Without knowing this one's composition there was no hint that it might have unusual value.

"Now for a few basics," went on Barney. "Gravity is the force that defines the whole shape and movement of the solar system—the galaxy, too, if it comes to that—but for objects the size of the one you are looking at now, gravity is a very weak force. It is just strong enough to pull small particles of material into contact with each other, but if gravity was all that held CM-31 together, you'd be able to mine it and the other asteroids with a spoon. But when the dust and grains of sand and pebbles meet, a different form of bonding takes over. The little particles *sinter*, which means that they all stick together to form a single mass. And that mass doesn't come apart easily. You can think of CM-31 as we discovered it as a ball of iron, with some rock and small fractions of other metals. It's solid, and it's hard, and if you want to break a bit off you have to do it with a chisel.

"It's strong enough that it would still hold together if you started to rotate it around its principal axis of inertia, which is the most stable way to make it spin."

The lumpy surface of CM-31 now showed dozens of bright points of light all around it. They were drive units. Rick could not tell if this was a simulation or the real thing, but the body began to turn, slowly at first and then gradually faster.

"You can rotate it pretty fast, and the body will still hold in one piece," Barney's voice said. "But that's not true if you also *heat* it. We use electric induction, which will produce internal currents to heat the body all the way through. If you did that until CM-31 melted, and it was also spinning, it would just fly apart."

The image on the screen showed the dark planetoid beginning to glow a dull red. It slowly deformed to the shape of a thick plastic disk, then suddenly disintegrated and was gone, parts flying away in all directions.

"Obviously, that's no way to mine an asteroid. You'd lose the asteroid itself, and you'd lose valuable drive units. It's also not what people imagine, when they think of the word 'mining.' You might ask, what's the point of heating and spinning a body, when you could just as well mine CM-31 the way most of the mines, like CM-2, were done? Remember the tunnels in CM-2? Mining machines made those, dug ore, and brought it out from the interior.

"The answer to my question, in one word, is economics. It's far less expensive if you can melt and refine and process a whole asteroid, in one swoop.

"And you can. Here's how.

"First, you place a cylinder in position around the whole body."

CM-31 reappeared, just as it had been at the time of discovery. Now a huge silvery cylinder appeared from nowhere and gradually swallowed the whole asteroid into its open end. When the body was totally engulfed, the open end of the cylinder irised shut.

"There's a couple of things to notice about that cylinder," said Barney. "First, if you look very closely you'll see drive units spaced at intervals around the curved part. On the cylinder, *not* on the asteroid. They will make it spin around its central axis. Second, you can't see them but there are also hundreds of induction field generators on the cylinder. They will heat anything inside by induced eddy currents. They will also, if the cylinder is rotating, make the asteroid inside start to rotate through an electromagnetic dragging effect. Keep that up long enough, and the material inside will melt. When it melts, it will be thrown outward to the wall of the cylinder.

"One other thing, and this you can't see: the cylinder is made of the strongest material we know, dislocation-free carbon filaments. It remains strong at high temperatures. It will contain the materials inside it, even when everything is spinning around the cylinder main axis at high speed."

Rick could see what was coming next, he had known it the moment that the cylinder appeared. The fact that he really owed his knowledge to Deedee did nothing to lessen his pleasure. He could imagine her, tucked away in her own bunk, hugging herself in satisfaction. She had got it exactly right.

"I assume you can all see what's coming next," said Barney's voice, taking away Rick's sense of superiority. "As everything rotates, the liquid metals press outward on the cylinder wall, the heavier ones toward the outside and forcing the lighter ones closer to the axis of rotation. Actually, it's not quite as simple as that, because some metals form eutectic alloys that don't separate by centrifuging, but the general principle is valid. The heaviest metals are tapped first, from spigots on the outer circle of the circular ends of the cylinder. Then we run out the lighter ones. Finally all that's left behind is a low-density layer of melted rock and sand. With a really high metal content asteroid, that's not much more than a froth. We empty that, too, and leave it behind in space, all that remains of the original asteroid. At that point, the empty cylinder—after a bit of scrubbing and servicing—is ready to move on and tackle the next mine.

"I'm sure you're asking, what went wrong in processing CM-31? If I could answer that, I would tell you. But I don't know. We're moving closer as fast as we can, and a few hours from now we'll be able to take a look. Until then I suggest that you all rest, even if you don't think you can sleep."

Barney French stopped speaking. The projection unit remained alive, throwing onto the ceiling an image of the cylinder, drive units flaring, spinning hypnotically. Rick watched and watched, until at last he slipped into a half-trance. He was neither asleep nor fully awake. He was aware of a time of freefall, when the *Vantage* turned end-over-end and began its deceleration, but he could not have given an estimate as to how long it lasted. It seemed long after that when the thought came into his head that it should not be necessary to watch a simulation. By now it might be possible to see the real CM-31.

He roused himself and tapped the code for Barney French's cabin. There was a risk that she was sleeping, but somehow he doubted it.

"Yes?" The answer came at once.

"This is Luban."

"I know. I can see your call ID. Why aren't you sleeping?"

"I can't. I want to ask your permission to climb up to the front of the ship and use the scope there to look for CM-31."

"You may not be sleeping, but your brain is turned off. We passed turnover a while ago, so we are now *decelerating*—which means that the front of the *Vantage* is pointed directly *away* from our destination. You'd see nothing." And, while Rick was feeling like a prize buffoon, "You are the fourth person to call and ask me that, so I suppose it's a general concern. There is no observation port down toward the stern, but there are imaging sensors. Stay where you are. I'm going to hook the output of the rear-pointing sensors into the terminal display. You'll have a chance to see CM-31 at the same moment as the pilots. Don't expect anything for a while."

The projection on the ceiling above Rick flickered through a kaleidoscope of random color swirls, then settled to show a stationary star field. A blue icon at the upper left of the image blinked "target zoom." There was an impression of impossibly fast motion as stars moved toward the scene edge and disappeared. The image became increasingly grainy, until at last the words "maximum magnification" replaced the first icon.

Rick peered, and saw nothing but fuzzy points of starlight. The scene was steady now, but as minute followed minute he noticed that one point of light at the outside edge of the image area was creeping slowly across the screen. That was not a zoom effect. The moving point had to be a substantial asteroid. It was close to the *Vantage* compared with everything else, but it could not be CM-31. The ship's telescope would surely be aimed to place the mine at the center of the field of view.

He focused his attention on that middle area, and was finally rewarded by the sight of a central point of light that came and went at random. The sensitive detectors of the ship's imaging system must be picking up and displaying single photons. It was their first sight of the target mine.

Rick settled again into a near-trance. He did not think that he slept, but he did close his eyes occasionally. Each time he opened them there was a little more to see. Over minutes and hours the vagrant point of light gradually steadied, to become a pale silver dot, and then a blurry round disk. Soon the ship's optics made an adjustment, trading magnification for contrast. It was possible to discern that the disk had a slight asymmetry, longer top to bottom than it was side to side.

Fifteen minutes more, and there was no doubt. Rick was looking at an oblong shape, longer than it was wide. It must be the mining cylinder enclosing the ore body of CM-31. But it was not the smoothly spinning regular figure shown in the simulations. There was a definite slow wobble to its motion, and part of the curved surface seemed darker than the rest.

"We have established contact with a maintenance module associated with CM-31." Tom Garcia's voice brought Rick's attention away from the growing image. "Signals indicate two survivors on board the module. We have no indication of survivors on the main mining habitat. The module is running very low on air. The *Vantage* will end deceleration and achieve rendezvous in fourteen minutes. Personnel stand ready for emergency stations."

"You heard that." The distorted cylinder of CM-31 vanished and was replaced by Barney French's impassive face. "Over the next ten minutes I will assign an emergency station to each apprentice. Do not—repeat, *do not* go to those stations until I tell you to do so. In thirteen minutes we will change from our present deceleration to a near-freefall environment. Remain in your bunk until that time. Once we are in freefall, unstrap yourself, make sure that you are dressed in regulation fashion, and remain in your cabin. Be prepared to move at once when I tell you to do so. Do not worry if you hear nothing more from me for the next few minutes. I will be addressing each one of you individually."

CM-31 appeared again, close enough for a clear image to fill the projection screen. Rick was looking at a distorted shell, wobbling slowly around an off-center axis. A long split ran almost from end to end, revealing a dark interior. It looked as though the cylinder had burst, buckling outward. Where were the billions of tons of metallic ores that had been inside it? Where was the maintenance module, with its sur-

vivors? He could see no sign of it—no sign of anything re-
sembling a ship or a life-support habitat. What had happened to the rest of the miners on CM-31?

"Luban," Barney's voice said suddenly over the intercom.

"Yes, sir."

"Do you know the location of Port A-3?"

"Yes, sir."

"You will go there when we move to freefall, without
waiting for further instructions. Put on a suit, and take your
subsequent orders from Tait or Styan. Understood?"

"Yes, sir."

"Any questions?"

"No, sir." Rick had a thousand, but this was no time to
ask them.

"Very good."

The intercom fell silent, leaving Rick in a ferment of
nervousness and speculation. He had been in a suit often
enough, that was not a problem. Some other fear—of dying,
of failure, of loss of nerve—was tying his guts into a knot.

The image was still on the screen but he took little notice. He was mentally rehearsing, over and over—unstrap-
ping himself, hurrying out of his cabin, swinging his way
down to Port A-3. *The module is running very low on air.* That
part of Tom Garcia's message didn't need explanation. The
speed with which the crew of the *Vantage* acted could be the
difference between life and death.

Freefall—sooner than expected. Rick was off his bunk
and out of his cabin in seconds. He realized at once that his
mental rehearsal was totally useless. He had missed the obvious—that a score of other apprentices would be scram-

bling through the same narrow passageways, all heading for different destinations.

He eased past Goggles Landau, past Skip Chung, past Lafe Eklund, all heading in the opposite direction. Chick Teazle, by some miracle, zipped past Rick going in the *same* direction. Deedee Mao and Alice Klein were standing together in the dining area, obviously waiting for somebody. Rick nodded at them and zoomed on, down to the lower ship level where Port A-3 was located. Vido Valdez was already there, working his way into a suit. Rick was oddly pleased to see him—he trusted Vido, maybe more than any other trainee. Rick put on his own suit, and they went through the thirty-six point sequence together, checking suit seals and functions.

Before they were done, Jigger Tait arrived. He was already in his own vacuum suit, complete with mobility pack.

"Radios on?" he said. And at their nods, "Good. I don't expect you'll be going outside, but if I need help I'll holler. Here." He handed each of them two squat oxygen cylinders. "Hang on to these, and stand by for cycling."

They were clearly in emergency mode. The air pressure dropped three times as fast as usual, and even before vacuum was established the outer lock was opening. The remaining air puffed away. Rick, floating with the security of an anchor line, realized that he was at the very edge of open space. The deformed cylinder of CM-31 hung in front of him, huge and somehow ominous.

"There they are," Jigger said. "Spitting distance. Hats off to Tom Garcia and Marlene Kotite. Be ready with the oxygen and wait here."

Without another word he was away, jetting toward a

small crab-shaped vessel poised in space no more than two hundred meters from the *Vantage*. Rick and Vido stood and stared. Five more suited figures were leaving the ship from some other exit lock. They all wore mobility packs. One of them was heading for the maintenance module, the other four were jetting off in the direction of CM-31's cylindrical hulk. It was impossible to make individual identification, but everyone moved in space with the confidence and economy of long space experience.

Jigger and one other person had reached the crab-like maintenance module and were entering on its under side. Within seconds they had reappeared, each holding a suited figure. They jetted at once toward the *Vantage*. If they had said one word to each other, it was on a frequency not received by Rick and Vido.

They reached the lock, and Rick saw that the other person was Gina Styan. Still without a word, she and Jigger grabbed oxygen cylinders. They attached them to the suits of the two new arrivals. Jigger peered in through the visors. The eyes of the occupants, both women, were flickering open.

"All right," said Jigger. "We sure cut it fine. I'm going to cycle the lock so we can flush carbon dioxide, but there's no rush on that now."

One of the women was giving him a weak thumbs-up sign.

"I'd better get back out there and secure the module," Gina said. "Then I'll see if they need any help over at the main facility."

Rick peered past her out of the open lock. He saw what he had expected to see, the little maintenance module and beyond it the massive cylinder of CM-31. But there was something else. Off to the left, small but steadily growing, was a feathery plume of brightness.

Should he mention it, or would he seem like an idiot? He glanced at the others, and realized that Vido had seen it, too. They stared at each other, and said in unison, "What's that?"

"It's a ship," added Vido. "Isn't it?"

"Can't be," Jigger said. He was still busy with the two survivors of the accident. "Not for another thirty-six hours."

"But it is." Gina had looked where Rick pointed. "It's not one of ours—it's an Avant Mining vessel."

Rick told himself he ought to have realized that. He had seen such a feathery exhaust before, the result of the pulsed fusion drive used by Avant. But it was so unexpected, out here far from anywhere.

And then he realized that it should not be unexpected at all. This was the very place where you might think to meet an Avant Mining ship—out in the broad region of the valuable metal-bearing asteroids.

The other ship was closing steadily, heading right for the *Vantage*. Rick heard a voice in his headset.

"This is Morse Watanabe, captain of the Avant Mining vessel, *Scarab*. We happened to be in a compatible orbit, and we picked up a Mayday signal on a broad frequency band with these coordinates. Do you need assistance?"

Jigger Tait and Gina Styan said nothing. It was Tom Garcia's voice that sounded in the headsets. "Thanks for the offer, *Scarab*. As you can see, we've had a major accident here, but everything seems to be under control."

"Glad to hear it." There was a pause, then Watanabe

continued, "Unless proprietary elements are involved, would you tell us what happened?"

"We are still in the process of determining that. However, it seems certain that the integrity of the containment cylinder was breached, suddenly and violently. The melted ore spewed out into space in all directions. Unfortunately, the main crew habitat was impacted and destroyed."

Rick heard a grunt in his headset. It came from one of the two women picked up by Jigger Tait and Gina Styan. This must be their first direct evidence that their friends and co-workers were dead.

"I am truly sorry to hear that," Watanabe said. "Any idea what caused the rupture?"

"Not yet. We are working on it. Our preliminary assumption is impact by another body."

"That would have been my guess. Lots of material in this region. Something pretty big, that somehow got past the radar." Watanabe sighed. "Again, our regrets and sympathy. Since we can't help, we'll be on our way."

The feathery plume of the *Scarab*'s exhaust appeared again. The other ship slowly receded. Rick watched it until it was no more than a tiny spark of light, no different from one of the silent stars.

The incident had changed his whole view of Avant Mining. It was a terrible shock to hear Jigger Tait, cycling the lock to fill it with air, mutter to himself, "That slimy bastard. 'Regrets and sympathy'—like hell."

"They were just trying to help," protested Vido. "Weren't they?"

"You can think that if you like." Jigger glared at him, and the two rescued women did the same.

"If you hadn't come along in time," one of them said. "We'd have been dead in another hour or two. With no survivors, CM-31 would have been a derelict. The *Scarab* would have taken possession and filed for full or partial ownership."

"And they'd have got it, too," growled Jigger. "That's space law. Watanabe can say he's glad that things are under control here as often as he likes, but I'll never believe it. He's been robbed of a big gain, and he knows it."

"But the ore's all gone," Rick said. "It was thrown all over the place by the accident."

"Not the ore. That's not what Watanabe wanted. He was after *technology.*" Jigger jerked his thumb at the hovering cylinder. "Avant Mining has nothing like that. They still mine using the old bore-and-scoop method. There's nothing they'd like better than a good look at the inside of CM-31. The general technique may sound simple, but the details aren't. Watanabe's out there now, gnashing his teeth—and wishing that the whole lot of us had died on CM-31."

CHAPTER FOURTEEN

THE two survivors quickly came back to normal health; the bodies of the dead, such as could be found scattered within ten thousand kilometers of CM-31, were given decent space burial; the *Vantage* continued on at a quarter gee to its original destination; and Rick thought that the whole awful episode was over.

He was wrong. The worst was still to come.

It began late on the second night, when someone slipped

into his cabin without knocking. He was lying awake in his bunk, and he sat up pleased. Alice had told him that she had an evening session scheduled for a review of drive mechanisms with Tom Garcia, and would not be able to pay Rick a visit. Something must have changed.

The person who entered was Deedee Mao. "I have to talk to you," she said.

"If it's about—"

"I was told not to talk about this to anyone. But I have to. It's eating me up inside."

She sounded desolate and desperate, in a way that Rick had never heard before. He started to say something, decided that it was a bad idea, and made room for her beside him on the narrow bunk. "I'm listening, Deedee. But if you promised not to talk . . ."

"It's a promise I can't keep." She drew in a deep breath. "Do you know what I did when we got to CM-31?"

"I think so." They had all talked about their roles in the hours that followed. According to Barney French, they had performed better than anyone could have expected. Each of them would receive a note of praise in the record. "You went over near the main cylinder, didn't you? With Marlene Kotite."

"That's right. We were really there to look for bodies. I was picked because I was once in a bad accident myself, and I've seen some pretty gruesome stuff."

"I didn't know that."

"There's a lot we don't know about each other, Rick. That's a pity." She tried to smile at him, and failed. "Anyway, we found one part of the work crew habitat, smashed to pieces by flying jets of molten metal. Seven bodies. They made me feel like throwing up, because they were in pieces. We had to hunt for arms and legs and heads and try to put them together. Two of them were so badly burned I couldn't tell if they were men or women."

"That's terrible, Deedee." Rick put his arm around her shoulders. "I had it easy, but I didn't know it. I didn't have to deal with anything like that."

"I haven't got to the bad part. We came to one bit of the habitat that had been smashed open by flying metal, and then somehow sealed itself back together. It was airtight, but molten iron had splashed all over the place. We found a man there. He was alive."

She paused. Rick, sensing that it was not the time to speak, waited sympathetically.

"He was alive," she went on at last, "but he had no right to be. The iron had burned him, head and body. He must have actually sat for a while in a pool of molten metal. When we found him he was conscious. I didn't know what to do, but Marlene crouched down beside him. 'You're safe now,' she said. 'I'm Marlene Kotite, pilot of the ship *Vantage*. We'll have to move you, so I'm going to give you a shot to knock you out first.'

"He turned his head toward her. I can't say he looked at her, because his eyes had been burned out. They were just black pits in his head. He had no nose.

" 'Thanks, Marlene,' he said. 'I'm Trustrum Keck, chief mining engineer of CM-31.' He sounded absolutely calm and rational. They say that bad burns leave you like that, in shock but not in pain. 'Before you knock me out,' he said, 'how about a little damage assessment?'

"She looked at me, as if she wished I wasn't there, then

she said, 'We met once before, when I was piloting the *Vanity*. It's not good, Rusty. Your eyes have gone, and most of your face.'

" 'I guessed that,' he said. 'And there's more, isn't there.'

" 'Yes. You've lost the flesh of your legs, and your penis and testicles. And most of your right hand.'

" 'I noticed,' he said, 'when it happened. It doesn't feel so bad now.' He was quiet for about half a minute, then he said, 'No chance of real repairs. I don't like the look of the future, Marlene. I want to exercise my option.'

"It was her turn to go quiet, but eventually she said, 'You're in deep shock, Rusty. This is no time to make that decision.'

"But he just gave a sort of coughing laugh and said, 'Tell me a better time. You've seen me,' and after a minute she nodded.

" 'Hold on a little,' she said. 'I'll give you a shot, but I've got a young apprentice with me. She happened to be on the *Vantage* when we picked up your Mayday.' Then she turned to me, and said, 'Step out for a few minutes. Into the corridor.'

"I did. I was totally confused, but it was an order. After about ten minutes she came out again. She had taken off her suit helmet, and her face was dead white. She told me it was all right, I could come back in. I did. He was lying there. He was dead. When I asked what had happened she just shook her head. Rick, she killed him. I know she did. She murdered him."

"No." Rick was suddenly very thankful for the conversation he had had with Jigger Tait, back in the shielded radiation chamber on CM-2. "You can't look at it that way,

Deedee. Would you want to live with no eyes and legs? No genitals, no right hand."

She flinched against his arm. "I couldn't bear to!"

"Nor could I. And nor could he. You heard him say it, he wanted to exercise his option—his right to die."

"But that's murder!"

"Back on Earth it is. Out here, it's a fundamental right. Mine, yours, Barney French's. Nobody can take it away from us. And Marlene Kotite couldn't take it away from Rusty Keck. She just did what he wanted, and helped him along a little. Wouldn't you do as much for me, in the same situation?"

"Oh, Rick, don't say that. Please, don't *ever* say that." Then Deedee was silent for a long time, so long that Rick thought she must be angry. Finally she patted the arm that he had placed around her, and said, "God rest his soul. Thanks, Rick. Thanks an awful lot. I owe you a big one. But I knew I could count on you. I always can."

She left. Rick lay again on his bunk. He was very glad that he had bitten back what he had wanted to say when she first came in: "Chick Teazle is the one you're screwing, not me. If you want to talk to somebody, why don't you go and find him?"

Rick didn't know the answer to his own question. But he offered up a prayer that he had not asked it.

The final arrival at CM-26, their original target, was a big letdown. It took a while to realize why.

The first few hours were the enjoyable confusion of a new home. The apprentices were assigned living quarters—

huge, after the cramped cabins of the *Vantage*—then left free to roam the interior, alone or in groups, and get used to the layout.

Rick was on the same corridor as Gladys de Witt, Lafe Eklund, Polly Quint, and Goggles Landau. He was annoyed that he had not been placed with people he knew well, until he realized that was surely intentional. Turkey Gossage and Barney French had one thing in common: they both insisted that you had to be able to get along with absolutely anyone and learn to work together.

The five apprentices set out as a group to ramble the corridors and tunnels of the mining facility. Rick noted where Alice's cabin was located, though it was probably useless information; she always insisted that she come to him. She was right next door to Deedee Mao, which made Rick feel a bit uncomfortable.

The corridors that led deeper into the interior all ended with flashing lights and warning signs: DO NOT PROCEED BEYOND THIS POINT. MINING OPERATIONS IN PROGRESS.

The five retreated, somewhat irritated. "I thought mining operations were specifically what we were here to learn," Polly Quint grumbled. She was a tall, graceful seventeen-year-old, with an oddly large vocabulary and a flashing smile that at the moment was noticeably absent. "And what type of mining operations are being denied to us, anyway?"

They could hear along the forbidden tunnel the near-continuous rumble of explosions.

"Not what we saw on CM-31, that's for sure," said Gladys de Witt. "There's something odd going on here."

Rick agreed. During their approach to CM-26 he had caught a glimpse of an irregular chunk of rock, with beside it the familiar gleam of a cylinder big enough to enclose it.

But what they had just seen—or rather heard—suggested a traditional mine using ore blasting and excavation equipment.

The mystery remained as they headed in the opposite direction, up toward the outer layers of the mining station. It was compounded when they came to the topmost level and looked out through the transparent bubble of an observation port.

"It's *tiny*," Goggles Landau protested. "Look at the ship next to it!"

They again had a view of the asteroid and cylinder that Rick had seen during final approach. At that time there was no way of judging size, and Rick had assumed that he was looking at something on the same massive scale as the ruined facility of CM-31. Now a maintenance module was floating in space next to the cylinder, and Rick could see that Goggles was right. Instead of the kilometer-plus length and width of CM-31, this cylinder was no more than forty meters in any dimension. The rock next to it was smaller yet, more like a large boulder than a substantial planetoid.

"That's not a mining facility," said Lafe Eklund at last. He was one of the quiet apprentices who rarely said anything, but now he sounded exasperated. "Look at that thing! It's nothing but a *toy*."

No one disagreed. Perplexed, they made their way back to the general living accommodation and ran into two other exploring parties. They had all experienced similar frustrations, of regions denied to them without explanation or mining facilities scaled down to the point where they appeared ludicrous. Without anyone suggesting it, they found themselves moving together to the main dining area.

Chick Teazle, as usual, took the lead. "I think we can all

guess what's happening," he said. "So far as they are concerned, it's business as usual. We're back in the playpen, and
we'll get pushed through the next stage of training as though
we're still babies. But we're not."

There was a mutter of agreement.

"What happened at CM-31 changed everything," Chick
continued. "They still want to treat us as Level Three apprentices, but we showed that we are ready to operate at
Level Five—the highest level. We've grown up faster than
anyone expected. They need to recognize that fact."

"How do we make them?" Alice Klein had been in a
fourth group that had just entered the dining area and added
itself to the discussion. "It's easy to *say* how Vanguard ought
to think of us, but how do you persuade them?"

As usual, Alice had quietly placed her finger on the key
question. There was a long pause, while everyone stared
around at everyone else. Rick tried to catch Alice's eye, but
she looked right through him.

"Only one way," said Chick Teazle at last. "Barney
French is in charge of us. We have to tell her, all of us."

"*All* of us?" Vido repeated. He sounded as skeptical as
Rick felt. "Forget it. You know what she says about committee decisions."

Barney had told them often enough: "Work in ones,
work in twos, even work in threes. But *don't* form a committee, or you'll never get anything done. A committee is a dead-
end street down which ideas are lured and quietly strangled."

"All right, not all of us," Chick said defensively. "Not a
committee, a deputation. Four people, representing everybody. Who'll volunteer?"

"You will," said Goggles Landau, and everyone laughed.

"I guess I have to, if I suggest it." Chick grimaced. "Who else?"

There was another long pause. "I nominate Rick Luban," Gladys de Witt said at last, while Rick stared at her in surprise. "He's one of Barney's pets, you can tell by the way she talks about him."

"Hey!" But Rick's outrage was lost in the buzz of general agreement.

"That's two," said Chick.

"Wait a minute! You said *volunteer!*"

"You've been volunteered." And before Rick could speak again, Chick went on. "Need two more. Who else? Vido Valdez, will you do it?"

"Hold on," Polly Quint said before Vido could reply. "I have nothing at all against Valdez, but you need balance. Better have two of the quartet females."

"Agreed." Vido grinned at her. "Thanks, Polly. Accepted, everyone?"

"Me? I never said *me!*"

But Chick was already looking around the group. "So it's agreed on Polly. Just one more. Gladys?"

"Bad choice. Barney says I complain all the time." Gladys stared around the room. "You need somebody who never bitches. How about Deedee. Will you? You know Barney thinks you walk on water."

"She does not!" But Deedee bit her lip, then slowly nodded. "All right. If you want me to."

"Which makes four. Good." Chick Teazle clapped his hands together briskly. "So there's only one other question: when?"

"Now," chorused a dozen voices.

"I was afraid you'd say that. Rick, Polly, Deedee?" Chick looked to each of them in turn. "All right with you? Then let's get it over with." He started for the door.

"Give 'em hell, guys," Skip Chung shouted after them as they left.

Brave words, but Rick felt the steam going out of him as they approached Barney's office.

She was in. He had rather hoped she would be somewhere else. She greeted them with a raised eyebrow, seated them on uncomfortable chairs made of bare metal struts and mesh, and listened in silence while Chick, with prompting from the other three, explained why they were there.

"I see," she said when he finished. "Level Five." She walked over to the inner door to her office and disappeared through it.

Polly and Deedee looked at each other. "Bad news," Deedee mouthed, and Polly nodded.

"Why?" Rick had seen the exchange.

"Can't you tell?" Deedee was whispering. "She's really angry."

"Or upset."

"Or both."

They were talking only to each other. Before Rick could ask how they knew, Barney was back. She was holding two polished metal cylinders about two feet long. One was thin, the other fat.

"So you're not happy," she said. Rick could see it now, there was a twisted look to the always-asymmetrical face that was new and frightening. "So you don't want to be treated as trainees any more."

Trainees, not apprentices? They had been demoted, but no one was going to correct her.

"Well," Barney went on, "I have a question for all of you. What job do you expect to get when all your training is over?"

The four looked at each other. "Mining engineer?" said Chick Teazle at last.

"Mining engineer." Barney French nodded. "Do you know why you say that? Well, I do. You say it, you overgrown ape, because it's the only goddamn job any of you can imagine. So let me tell you something about Vanguard Mining. Maybe one person in a hundred makes mining engineer. Before you aspire to that, you have to be a real hot-shot—you have to know math, and mechanics, and physics, and metallurgy, and engineering. Most people don't make it. I didn't make it, and I bust my guts trying. Do you think any of you will make it?"

There was a dead silence.

"Well, it's not my job to tell you that you won't. In fact, it's usually my job to tell you that you *can*. But right now you're a million miles away from competence." Barney tossed a sheet of paper across to Chick Teazle. "Read that, and tell me what it says."

He stared at it and shook his head. "I can't. I mean, I can read the words, most of 'em. But it's full of big equations."

"Damn right it is." Barney's face was growing redder. "Those are the equations of motion that describe the stability of a right circular cylinder under forced rotation, with off-axis disturbing forces. In other words, they describe a mining facility like CM-31. Unless you can read that, and maybe write something like it yourself, you'll never make a top-flight mining engineer. And if you do, you won't be getting an easy job. Better men than you'll ever be—and better women—have given their lives for that research." She glared at them, and her voice rose. "You think you're ready for Level Five, do you? You don't know what Level Five means. It means brains and dedication and endless hard work. It means devotion to duty, and sometimes it means sacrifice. The best engineer I ever met, Rusty Keck, was killed in the blow-up of CM-31."

"I was there when he died," Deedee said in a very small voice.

It halted the outburst. Barney stared at her. "So you were," she said at last. "That makes me surprised that you are here."

She put the two cylinders down on her desk, stood up, and left the room again. This time she was gone for more than five minutes, while her visitors sat and asked each other in hushed tones if the meeting was over and they were supposed to leave.

When she returned her face was unreadable. She picked up the two cylinders from her desk as though they weighed a ton each. "The episode at CM-31 gave you a false idea of your own status," she said quietly. "You behaved well, and for an hour or two you did act at Level Five. But in terms of real training, you're still Level Three beginners. Can you tell me why one of these cylinders is stable when it's rotating about its main axis, and the other one isn't? No, you can't. Can you tell me how the stability changes, as the mass distribution changes from being mostly on the central axis to being near the outer curved surface? Again, you can't. But you will know those things, before you leave here, because we'll have done a dozen practical experiments with the centrifuge mining test facility that's waiting outside this station. You'll know what happens in practice. You'll also be able to *calculate* it, so you don't have to do expensive physical tests before you reach the final design stage. You'll know and do all these things, or your future jobs in Vanguard Mining will be cleaning toilets and recycling sewage. If you're lucky."

She sighed, and tossed one cylinder to Rick and the other to Deedee. "Take these and think about them. I should never have told you that you did well. And I ought not to have lost control of myself. I hope you'll forget that. I'm going to forget what you said to me. So far as I'm concerned, you never came here, and you never complained about anything. Now get out—before you make me real mad."

She ushered them out. In the corridor, well away from Barney's office, Chick stopped. "We-e-ll," he said. "Well . . . well . . . I guess . . . shit."

"The *mot juste.*" Polly Quint tried to laugh, and produced only an ugly snort. "My English teacher told me—before he decided that he was more interested in getting into my pants than into my head—that cussing is the sign of an inferior intellect and an inadequate vocabulary. But in certain circumstances, he said, it fulfills a vital function. I guess this is one."

"But what are we going to tell the others? They'll be waiting for us back there, wanting to know how we did."

"We?" Polly shrugged. "It's not *we*, Chick. You are our chosen spokesman and chief representative. What are *you* proposing to tell them?"

To that question, for one of the few times in his life, Chick Teazle had no ready answer.

CHAPTER FIFTEEN

RICK, like the rest, felt crushed and humiliated by Barney French's anguished put-down. It took Alice Klein to offer a different perspective on what was really happening.

"You know what they've been telling us since day one," she said. She nudged him with her elbow to get his attention. *"Things are not what they seem. Expect zingers.* I bet that's what is happening now."

She was snuggled at Rick's side, naked in the darkness of his cabin. It was two days after their arrival at the new training facility, and until now the whole time had been non-stop effort—mostly mental work, which Rick found far more demanding than physical labor. He had spent all day struggling with the unfamiliar notion of moments of inertia. According to the learning machines, moments of inertia were related to advanced methods of ore melting and metal extraction. It was hard to see how, and the problems he had been assigned did not help.

A strong and solid hoop is spinning around a massive central point to which it is connected by thin strings. All those strings are cut at once. What will happen to the hoop, and why? Comment: When you understand the answer to this question, you will know how the great Scottish physicist, James Clerk Maxwell, proved that the rings of Saturn cannot be solid but must be made up of small independent particles.

Rick had about as much interest in dead Scotsmen as Maxwell had in him; but he did have ambition. He wanted to be a success in Vanguard Mining, and visions of a solid hoop spinning around and attracted by a central mass had plagued him all day. After the excitement and horror of the CM-31 disaster, going back to the old routine seemed boring; but he could not get his mind off this particular problem.

Spin the hoop, cut the strings. And then what? What would it do—still spin around the central mass, or something else?

He had been drowsing, his mind filled with rotating rings, when Alice spoke again. "Did you hear me?"

"Uh-huh." He grunted his reply.

She nudged him. "Wake up. I checked the qualities that successful apprentices are supposed to display. Do you know what the most important quality is, according to the manuals?"

"Intelligence?" *A strong, solid hoop.* That meant it was able to stand either compression or tension. As he had learned long ago, the assigned problems did not tell you things that you didn't need to know. And gravity had to be important, too, because the central point was stated to be massive. The hoop and the central mass would attract each other.

"Wrong." Alice wriggled closer. "You only say it's intelligence because you think you're smart. The most important quality isn't knowledge, either. It's *initiative.* But it seems to me that initiative is the exact opposite of doing what you're told and following somebody else's instructions."

"What are you suggesting? That we ignore our assignments? Then we flunk everything and get kicked out."

"No. I think they want us to try things for ourselves. They want us to push the envelope, keep going as far as we can until we're stopped. Unless we're told not to go somewhere, we should make a point of checking it out. Unless something is forbidden, we go ahead and do it."

"Mmm."

"Agreed?"

"Uh-huh."

So far as Rick was concerned that was the end of the conversation. He didn't remember any discussion after that. On the other hand he didn't even remember Alice leaving his cabin. Her words went forgotten until three days later, when the whole group of apprentices were told to put on their suits and assemble inside the Smelting Module.

That was the official name, usually shortened to "the SM," for the cylinder that Lafe Eklund had dismissed as a "toy" the first time that they had seen it. Close up, the SM seemed anything but a toy. Access to the interior was gained through an elaborate triple hatch, more complex than any that Rick had ever seen before. It was located near the edge of the SM's flat circular end, and its three octagonal doors had to be passed through in series, one after another. Each chamber had a little side room with its own door, and every door had a central viewing port of thick transparent glass. From any part of the lock, and even from outside it, you could see all the way along the axis of the cylinder to the other end. That other end was partly open, showing beyond it a disk of star-filled open space.

The size of the Smelting Module was even more apparent once you were inside. Rick, passing through the lock, found himself in a gigantic empty room that towered twenty times his own height. The inner surface of the curved wall was bare, blackened and crusted with hardened ore residue and dross. The flat end of the cylinder through which Rick had entered was covered with instruments, equally dark with dirt and battered as though with long use.

Since they were in free fall it was easy to soar from the "bottom" where they had entered up to the "top," and peer outside. Most of them did that. They saw half a dozen small asteroids, just a couple of kilometers away, co-orbiting with the SM and with the main body of Company Mine 26. They could also see that this end of the SM was made up of flat interlocking sectors, so that the whole end could either close completely or iris wide open. Like CM-31 but on a far smaller scale, the SM could stretch its maw wide enough to engulf any one of the waiting asteroids.

"All right, that's enough boggling at nothing." Barney

French, down at the bottom of the SM, clapped her suited hands together from habit. It produced no sound at all in hard vacuum, but they heard her call through their suit radios: "Let's get down to business."

For the past few days she had been in her toughest and most sarcastic mood, as though she wanted to deny that she had ever displayed any sign of sentiment or human feeling. That had made the returning deputation's job doubly difficult when they went back to the dining-area after their meeting with her. None of the other apprentices believed that Barney was capable of softness, and they had suspected Rick, Deedee, Polly, and especially Chick of being afraid to make their case. Even Alice seemed skeptical when Rick repeated to her what Barney had said during the meeting.

He stared across at her now, floating over at the other side of the group of apprentices. Within her suit visor, Alice's icy grey glance passed over Rick, roamed over Vido Valdez standing next to him, and continued on to stare calmly at nothing.

No one would ever guess what she could be like in private. But Rick didn't have to guess. He had absolute personal proof. He tried again to catch Alice's eye, and was rewarded by what might have been the faintest of frowns. She would probably give him hell for that later, but he didn't care. It was her fault for avoiding him for the past few days.

"Now use your brains if you have any." Barney's voice in Rick's headphone brought his attention away from Alice. "You may wonder," she went on, "why we came in through that odd triple hatch. What is its purpose? Did any of you happen to have your eyes open when you came in, or is that too much to hope for?"

She sounded in savage mood. It was Goggles Landau—always sensitive to any suggestion that he might not see as well as anyone—who risked ridicule.

"It's not just a hatch," he said. "It's an airlock, too."

"Indeed it is. But anybody inside the SM when smelting begins wouldn't last two minutes. Would you like to take the next step, and tell me why a smelting facility *needs* an airlock?"

Rick was just a couple of people along from Goggles and could see his face through the visor. There was a mortified look there that said, *Trapped! Why didn't I keep my big mouth shut?*

Rick didn't feel much sympathy. Hadn't Goggles learned the basic rule back in kindergarten? *Never volunteer. The nail that sticks up gets the hammer.*

And sometimes the nail that doesn't stick up gets it, too. Because Barney was saying, "You do not know, Landau? Then how about you, Luban? That smarmy grin on your face suggests you are feeling highly pleased with yourself. So you tell me why SM needs an airlock."

Another rule, one that Rick had learned more recently: On a test, any answer at all was more likely to be right than no answer at all. He tried the obvious. "It has an airlock so that if the top end of the SM were closed, the inside could be filled with air."

"True, but hardly an earth-shaking conclusion. You are evading the real question. *Why* fill the SM with air? Air would be nothing but a nuisance during smelting."

Rick cast his eye around the interior for inspiration, and saw the grimy and blackened instruments on the flat end of the cylinder. "You fill it with air so that crews can work in here. For—for maintenance."

"Close enough. Of course, maintenance crews could work very well in suits. But I'll accept your answer, because I doubt that any of you could get much closer." Barney looked away from Rick, to his huge relief, and addressed the whole group. "The right answer is, the airlock was put here for *you*. The airtight interior of SM exists for your benefit, and for the benefit of past and future apprentices. I hope you are suitably appreciative.

"This is a real live smelter, although a small one, but it's also intended as a training facility. To this point, you've worked alone or in pairs. Now it's time for a practical effort where you will all work together. That's easiest done when you don't have to wear suits. In the next two weeks we—or rather, you—are going to do three things. First, you are going to clean all the muck out of the SM. Be prepared to eat your meals dirty and go to bed dirty. Second, once this place is clean you are going to learn how each instrument works. You are going to take them apart and put them back together until you can do the whole thing blindfold. And third—the big scary treat—you'll get into your suits, go outside, and work together to bring one of those waiting asteroids in here. You'll melt and centrifuge and tap, and when the molten metal flows I guess you'll feel like genuine miners. And *then*, assuming that goes well, you'll advance to Level Four—and be ready for something difficult. Any questions?"

This time everyone had enough sense to keep quiet. Barney nodded.

"Very well. You are free to make your way back to your quarters and continue with regular assignments. I will post a schedule for SM cleaning and maintenance later today, and work will begin here tomorrow."

She turned and led the way back through the triple-locking hatch. Rick was all set to follow with the others when Alice turned to look directly at him and jerked her head inside her suit. He hung back and waited, until just the two of them were floating in the cavernous interior of the smelter. She gestured to him to turn off his suit radio and moved so that their helmets were touching.

"What?" He knew she would hear him through their direct contact, although no one else would even if they were only a foot away.

"Remember what we agreed? If it's not forbidden, we assume it's permitted. Barney said we were free to go back, but she didn't say we had to. Let's stay and have a look around this place."

Rick had seen as much of the SM as he wanted to. The chance of finding a cozy place where he and Alice could snuggle up and have some fun was as low here as you could get. He wanted her back at the main station, and into his bunk. But he couldn't tell her that, because she had already broken the contact between their helmets and was soaring up toward the other end. He trailed along behind, staring with no relish at all at the SM's crusted sides. In another day or so he would be scraping that crud away—and for what? So that they could melt down an asteroid, and make the whole smelter dirty again.

Alice headed to the very top, out of the open end of the SM and into open space. He followed her, and for the next minute or two they simply hovered, side by side. Rick stared around him, subdued by what he saw. Space felt quite different in a suit than when you looked at it through an observation port. The Sun was far off and small, a brilliant shrunken disk to his lower left. Close to it he picked up Venus and Earth, distinguishable from each other only because Venus was brighter and a little whiter. From this distance you would never know that the two worlds were so different, one bursting with life, the other a dead inferno.

Alice apparently had no interest in surveying the solar system. She was studying the way that the whole top of the smelter could either open wide, or be closed completely to provide an airtight seal. She moved close to Rick and placed her helmet next to his.

"You know, this end could operate as an emergency exit if it had to. There must be control panels, inside and out. I bet that's the external one, under that plate."

Rick had been scanning the starscape for other planets. Mars and Jupiter were easy, but he had not been able to find Saturn. The biggest thing in the sky was the lumpy ovoid of CM-26. From this distance, it and the smelter were the dominant features of the whole solar system.

He brought his attention reluctantly to the feature that Alice was pointing out. It was a white plate, small and almost insignificant, at the extreme outer edge of the flat circular end. Rick could see the big segmented plates that retracted as they opened, into a thick annulus. The white plate sat on the fixed outside edge of that annulus.

"Let's take a look at it." Before Rick could object Alice again had moved away and was zooming down. By the time that he joined her she had the plate cover open and was studying what lay beneath.

Rick put his head next to hers. "Alice! Don't you think—"

"Nothing to it. See." She directed the flashlight in her

suit at one part of the exposed panel and placed a gloved finger on a pair of switches. "Here's the control to open the end of the SM, and here's the safety. This sensor tells you if there's air pressure inside the SM—that light goes on—and if there is, the command to open is automatically cancelled. You'd have to override that manually, if you ever had reason to, and set this timer so you could get away before it opened. But how do you close it?"

Rick had been examining the rest of the panel while she was pondering the controls to open the SM.

"Like this," he said. He pointed out another pair of switches. "This moves the plates that seal the end. No need for a safety to test for air pressure, because when the end of the SM is open there can't be any air inside. But there is an obstruction safety, here. The end won't close if there's anything standing in the way. That's so you can't destroy the plates by asking the end to close when an asteroid or anything else is sitting between them. Agreed?"

"Looks that way to me. Let's give it a try and see if we are right." She reached across Rick and placed her finger on the first switch that he had pointed out.

"Wait a minute!" He put his hand on top of hers and lifted it away from the panel. "You're not proposing to close it."

"Yes, I am."

"Don't be ridiculous. You can't do that."

"I don't see why not." She turned so that their visors met, and Rick was looking straight into those calm grey eyes. "If it's not actually forbidden—and nobody told us we couldn't experiment out here—then we assume that it's permitted. Isn't that the deal we made?"

"Within limits. I mean, you might as well say we could blow up the whole station and kill everybody, because nobody told us that we couldn't."

"Now who's being ridiculous? There's nobody inside the SM, and there's no asteroid anywhere close by. We can't hurt ourselves, and we can't hurt the equipment. I'm sure it's designed to prevent its own damage. Even if we're wrong we'll have done no harm, and if we're right we'll have learned something that I bet none of the others ever think of." Alice placed her finger again on the switch. "And we're showing *initiative*. That's the name of the game for the rest of our training."

She operated the switch.

Rick thought for a moment that he had been wrong about the controls, and nothing was happening; then he saw that the massive silvery segments bounding the periphery of the cylinder were moving, steadily shrinking the size of the circular aperture leading to the interior. The whole operation seemed uncannily smooth and silent, until he realized that any sound of metal moving over metal would not carry to him unless his suit was somewhere in contact with the surface of the SM.

The dark opening shrank and shrank, like a black pupil in a silver iris, until at last it was gone completely. The end of the cylinder formed a flat continuous plate, nearly forty meters across. Rick moved closer, seeking the invisible places where the sectors joined. Alice was still over by the control panel, studying it again. She touched one of the switches and the silver eye began to dilate, metal sectors rolling ponderously back until the aperture was as big as when it started.

Alice came floating across to Rick, grabbed the arm of his suit, and put their helmets together.

"We were exactly right. There's just one thing I can't figure out. Do you see any control that can fill the SM with air from this end?"

They wandered together back to the control panel and Alice waited while Rick made his own examination. At last he shook his head.

"It looks like the air-fill has to be done from the other end. That makes sense. It's where you'd expect the pumps and air supply to be located. This can serve as an emergency exit, but it's not the usual way in."

"I suppose you're right." She touched Rick's helmet. "Radios on. Talking like this is a pain."

Rick agreed—with relief. The end to radio silence meant they must be finished with unauthorized exploration. "Ready to go back now?"

"Might as well. See, I told you that nothing bad would happen if we explored on our own." She grinned at him as they floated together past the outside of the smelter and headed for the main body of CM-26. For someone usually so unemotional she sounded vastly pleased, even excited.

Sometimes Rick was sure that he understood Alice very well; but there were also times, like now, when he wondered if he knew her at all.

CHAPTER SIXTEEN

THANKS to one sort of exploration or another, Rick had lost track of time. When he floated into the dining area for his evening meal he wondered why other people were already eating their final course. Alice was sitting in the middle of one group, relaxed and smiling. She ought to feel as dead and drained as he did, but if so she showed no sign of it. She was talking to Lafe Eklund, and she didn't even glance Rick's way when he entered the room. Rather than going over in her direction he went to another table, where Vido Valdez, Deedee Mao, Polly Quint, and Gladys de Witt were arguing vigorously. They hardly registered his arrival. Rick settled in next to Polly Quint. She was carefully polishing her nails, and he had the random thought that she was going to love scouring out the inside of the smelter for the next week or two.

"The question isn't *when*," Vido was saying. "It's *who*. Is it just another competition? And if so, what are the ground rules?"

"Grow up, Vido." Polly liked Vido, and showed it by putting him down. "You know they won't tell us—they never do. Maybe there are no ground rules."

"Then how will they decide?" Vido frowned at the others around the table. "I mean, none of the things that we've done so far has anything to do with this. So how do they?"

He stared at Rick as though expecting an answer. Rick, in a dreamy daze, paused with a fork halfway to his mouth. He had suddenly realized that he had no idea what they were talking about.

"Do they what?" he said.

"Rick!" said Deedee. But Polly gave him a more useful answer.

"Do they decide which ones of us—if any—will get to go." And then, when Rick sat open-mouthed, "As junior crew members. It's a big swindle. We've had hardly any assignments involving the moons of Jupiter. You'd think that if any of us was going to be involved in mapping and mining them, we'd have been better prepared."

It was dawning on Rick, far too slowly, that there had been some sort of major announcement and he had missed it. "I know quite a bit about the moons of Jupiter," he said slowly. "At least, I know a lot about the big four. I've had three assignments involving Io, Europa, Ganymede and Callisto."

"Which gives you a real leg up," said Gladys scornfully, "given that the exploration team will concentrate specifically on the minor moons: Leda, Himalia, Lysithea, Elara, Ananke, Carme, Pasiphae, and Sinope. What else do you have going for you, Professor?"

Rick decided that it was time for him to shut up, listen, and hope to learn what was going on. By the time that the others were finished and ready to leave, he had managed to piece it together. A new remote survey technique had been developed, capable of detailed analysis of distant objects. The results, still confidential within Vanguard Mining, were startling: the smaller moons of Jupiter, farther out from the planet than the major four, were formed of unique combinations of metals and hydrocarbons. Their value was incalculable. Vanguard was planning a major new initiative to send out a prospecting ship and stake mining claims. It would be a ground-breaking mission, since the Jupiter system was unknown territory. It had been explored to date only slightly and superficially, by pilotless probes.

The whole project was a thriller—but a much bigger thrill was the rumor, sweeping through the group on CM-26, that three apprentices might be included in the team in addition to the seasoned miners and prospectors.

"But it's still *might*, not *will*," Polly said. Everyone from the other tables had already gone, leaving just Vido, Deedee, Gladys and Rick as her audience. "Apprentices *might* be chosen to go. Three of us *may* get lucky."

"That's good enough for me," said Gladys. She stood up from the table. "I don't know about you people, but from now on I'm a reformed character. No binges, no partying, no screwing around, private or otherwise. I'm going to work my tail off—no cracks from you, Vido—and be on my best behavior until further notice. Can you imagine it, being one of the first humans to explore the moons of Jupiter? You know, if you are the first person to land on a body it's usually named after you. How about that? Maybe there will be a Jupiter moon called *de Witt.*"

"More likely *de half-wit.*" Vido fended off her lunge. "Hey! I thought you were on your best behavior."

He ran for the exit pursued by Gladys. Polly soon followed. Rick and Deedee were left sitting alone.

"You look pretty wiped out," she said. "Do you feel too tired to talk?"

The peculiar tone in her voice woke him up at once. "Talk? About what?"

"Not here." Deedee stood up. "If you don't mind, I'd like this to be private. Let's go to my cabin."

Whatever she had in mind, it was surely not what it sounded like. That was just as well. And just as well that she had not suggested his cabin. His bunk still looked as though it had been struck by a tornado. Rick trailed along after Deedee on weary legs, feeling a little uncomfortable as they passed Alice's cabin.

"What's the big mystery?" he said as she closed and locked her door. "Getting paranoid?"

"Maybe I am." She sat down on her bed and gestured to him to use the chair. "I haven't told anyone else about this, because it sounds so crazy. Promise me that what I say to you now won't go any farther."

"I promise. I won't talk."

"Not to anyone. Not even to Alice Klein."

"Alice? What makes you think that I might . . ." Rick saw Deedee's expression, and swallowed the rest of the sentence. "I promise. Not to Alice, not to anyone."

"Thank you. I want to ask you a question about some-body—don't worry, it's not about Alice."

"Go ahead."

"What do you think of Jigger Tait?"

"Jigger?" It was the last name that Rick had expected. He had to stop and analyze his own feelings before he could answer. "You probably know him as well as I do," he said at last. "I think very well of him. He helped me a lot back on CM-2, when I did something really stupid, and he never mentioned it to anyone. He keeps himself to himself, but he's always there when you need him. What are you getting at, Deedee?"

"I'm not sure. Until two days ago I'd have agreed with everything you just said. We've seen a lot of weird things since we shipped up from Earth, and Jigger has been one of our only points of continuity. It's almost uncanny, the way he shows up when anything is happening—like when you had your fight with Vido—but you always felt you could rely on him."

"So what happened two days ago?" It seemed to Rick that she was having trouble getting to the point. Diffidence and uncertainty were not the usual Deedee. "Spit it out, Dee."

"Remember the big group meeting with Barney, the

first one we had after we got here? She started to talk about assignments, and I had left my problem set in my room. I sneaked out while she was going over the list of what came next, and I came back here to pick it up. And I saw Jigger. He didn't see me, but it looked as though he had just come out of my room and was heading away along the corridor."

"Why didn't you say something to him?"

"I was too surprised—and I was in a hurry to get back to the meeting. But it looked like he was going into Goggles Landau's room. After the meeting with Barney was over, I asked Goggles if he had been doing any work with Jigger. He said 'Work? No. I haven't spoken to Jigger since we got here,' and he stared at me as though I was off the wall."

"Why didn't you talk to Barney?"

"And tell her what? I couldn't see any sign in my room that Jigger had been there. I wasn't even sure he had. Barney would have ripped me to pieces."

"She might." Rick tried to sound sympathetic, and failed. "She certainly ought to. You didn't see anything. Nothing happened to your room, or Goggles's. You don't have a thing to go on, except some weird suspicion."

"I haven't finished," Deedee said quietly. "I knew all that, but I was still worried. Today we were all together in the smelter, and it was the first time the whole group had met in two days. I don't know if you noticed, but Gina Styan was there as well as Barney French. Everybody who came out to CM-26 with us was there—except Jigger."

"So? He was busy elsewhere."

"He was. I sneaked out of the SM before the meeting ended, and came back here to my room. I left my door open, but I stayed out of sight on my bunk. If Jigger came along

and saw me I was going to say I wasn't feeling good. And he
did come along."

"Into your room?"

"No. But he went into Alice Klein's, and he went into
Skip Chung's. He was about ten minutes in each one."

"Why didn't you go in after him?" It was the obvious
thing to do, and Rick was losing patience. "Just ask him what
he was doing there."

"This is going to sound stupid, Rick, but I was scared. I
am scared. It's like you feel you know someone really well,
and then they suddenly do something so out of character that
you realize you don't know them at all. Can you understand
that?"

Rick thought he understood exactly. It was his own feeling, right now. This wasn't the Deedee Mao that he knew and
liked.

"What do you want me to do, Dee?"

"I don't know. I guess for the moment, nothing. I'm
going to keep an eye on Jigger, and on anyone else who
comes prowling near my room for the next few days." She
paused. "But if anything bad should happen to me—well, I
want to be sure that at least one person around here will be
asking questions."

Rick didn't forget what Deedee had said, but the activities of
the next few days pushed it away from the center of his attention.

For one thing, he had grappled hard with the problem
of the spinning ring, to the point where he believed that he
knew what must happen. After many hours he could *see* that

hoop, rotating in front of his eyes. It was spinning about the center of attraction. Then you cut all the strings. At that point the ring would wobble, just the tiniest bit, because any real system always did. One side of the hoop would move a fraction closer to the center of attraction. Once that happened that same part would be pulled a little bit harder toward the center by the gravitational force, because gravity was stronger with decreasing distance. At the same time, because that side was closer to the center of rotation but the rotation speed hadn't changed, the outward centrifugal force on it would become a tiny bit less. Both those would act to make that part of the hoop move *toward* the center of attraction.

Meanwhile, because the hoop was strong and solid, the part on the opposite side had to be pushed a little bit farther away from the center of attraction. The gravity force on it would be less, and the centrifugal force bigger. That part of the hoop would feel a force to move it *away* from the center of attraction. In other words, both sides of the hoop would feel forces that amplified the original wobble. The hoop would move more and more off-center, until part of it hit the central attracting point. The strings had been absolutely essential, to prevent any asymmetry in the movement growing and growing.

That was the mental picture. Unfortunately, Rick knew there was no way he could put it into mathematics. The tools were still far beyond him, and his deadline for submission of an answer was close. He wrote out, carefully and laboriously, his train of logic, and added a note: *For the same reason, if the rings of Saturn were solid hoops, their motion would be unstable. They would move until a part of every ring hit the planet and the whole thing would disintegrate.*

He checked the spelling of every doubtful word, worried about what he might have missed, and handed his efforts over to Barney French. She looked at him skeptically when he said he thought he had the answer, but she offered no comment. Even after he had handed in his solution he could not stop thinking about the problem. His obsession ended only when the time came to leave the main body of the station to work on the cleanup of the SM.

The smelter had been filled with air, and after the apprentices had stripped off their suits each one of them was assigned a section of the inner wall to scrape clean.

"Good enough to see your face in every bit," Barney French announced. "Until it's like that, you're not finished. It's possible, because it's been done before. The last group of apprentices managed the whole thing in two days."

She might have meant to encourage, but after four hours of unpleasant work her words had the opposite effect. Every apprentice was filthy, covered by a layer of metallic ash and gritty powder. It was in their eyes, ears, and hair, and when they paused for a meal break they could feel it grinding between their teeth. Rick, looking at the section assigned to him, realized that he had done no more than five percent of the work. At this rate he would be at it for weeks.

When the work first started the apprentices had been cheerful and talkative. During the second four-hour stint they were all looking at their neighbors, wondering if someone else had been given an easier or a smaller section to work on. Not one of them could see any hope of finishing the job in two days.

Finally Barney told them it was time to quit. She was still cheerful—and clean. She had kept her suit on, and ash and grit did not stick to it. Exposed skin was another matter. The grime that went on so easily was the very devil to get off. Rick, after half an hour of effort, still went to bed with matted hair and the taste of metallic oxides in his mouth.

The next morning he returned to the main hall, reluctantly ready to go back to work. He was a little surprised to see Polly Quint already there and standing next to Barney French. Polly was a notorious sluggard, usually the last to arrive at any event beginning before noon. She was grinning all over her face.

That should have been enough to make Rick suspicious. Polly should be anything but pleased with the labor ahead— labor enough to bring a swarm of civil liberties' lawyers if you forced convicted murderers to do it back on Earth.

Barney waited until everyone was there, then took Polly's hand and raised it above her head.

"The winner—and the only one. You ought to give her three cheers."

And, when that was greeted with baffled silence, "The only one to win what and do what, you ask? The only person to use her brains. Did you enjoy yesterday's work? No, I'll bet you didn't, not unless there's something wrong with you. But it wasn't enough to make you *think*. What's the most important quality in this phase of your training?"

"Initiative." The muttered word came from everyone in the group.

"Exactly. Initiative. I'll let you get away with a lot of other things if you show enough of that. Polly, tell them what you did last night."

Polly gave Barney French an imploring "Do I have to?" look, but was offered no way out. She shrugged.

"Like everybody else, I spent two hours trying to remove grit from my hair. After that I went to the data banks, and I made an inquiry. We know that the interior of the SM can be heated, because it is able to smelt ore bodies. We also know that it can be filled with air, because we were there all day yesterday. I asked for the maximum temperature that the inside of the SM can be taken to when it's filled with air—or oxygen—without damaging any part of the structure or the instruments. The answer is, over four thousand degrees. That would be enough to oxidize all the junk on the inside walls, and turn it to gas. Then if you opened up the end of the SM, which we know you can, all the cruddy gas would blow out into space. You'd have a perfectly clean interior. And one person could do the whole job—without even breaking a nail. That's when I went and asked Barney French if what I was thinking of was forbidden, for some reason I did not understand. And it isn't."

It had been dawning on the rest of them, sentence by sentence, that they had been granted a reprieve. Weeks of horrible grimy labor was about to vanish, puffed into space in a cloud of metallic and silicon oxides. What Polly received was not exactly three cheers, but it was lots of whistles, waving arms, and "Yay, Polly."

"Thanks, you beauty," Chick Teazle shouted, loud enough for everyone to hear. "I'll love you forever."

"That's not what I've heard," she called back. "They say you can't last thirty seconds."

His reply was lost in jeers and catcalls.

"All right." Barney clapped her hands. "Anybody have a question for Polly?"

"How did you come up with the idea so quick?" called Goggles Landau.

"You ought to ask, what took me so long?" Polly grimaced in self-disgust. "As soon as I could walk and talk, my stepmother had me helping her in the shelter kitchen. I've known how to use a self-cleaning oven since I was six. It didn't take much brains to apply the same idea to the smelter."

"But you were the only one who did it," Barney said.

"Take credit from me when you can get it—I'm not that way inclined. For the rest of you, since there's no more scraping to be done you are all dismissed for the rest of the morning. Polly will direct the superheated cleanout of the smelter later today, and you will all help. Meet at the main lock at two, in your suits. Until then your time is your own."

The apprentices dispersed in a good humor. Thanks to Polly they were off the hook from days or weeks of pointless labor. In Rick's case the satisfaction lasted only a few minutes. The true situation hit him when he reached his cabin, and found waiting there his solution of the spinning hoop problem along with Barney French's comments.

This is really rather good, she had written on his answer—extravagant praise by Barney's standards. *No one else in the group has managed a solution, and from what I have seen so far I suspect that no one else will. You are still hindered by your lack of mathematics, but that will come with perseverance. You are not a born mathematician, like Henrik Voelker, but I'm rather glad you're not—if you were you'd have been grabbed by the central office—*

Henrik? The Carolina Kid. The central office? It occurred to Rick for the first time that there might be other paths to success in Vanguard Mining. Henrik had flunked the training course, back on CM-2. Rick had felt sorry for him, because he was an OK type but such a goofball. Apparently he was still with the company, performing a different job. The East Coasters who said that Henrik was a mad genius must have been right after all.

—but there are more important things than mathematical talent if you want to be a good mining engineer. Remember, the purpose of mathematical calculation in the physical sciences is not numbers, it is insight. *Your discussion of this question displays both insight and ingenuity.*

If Rick had received that note earlier in the day, he would have been ecstatic. Now, though, he had to compare what he had done with Polly's achievement.

It was no contest. His problem had been explicitly stated and identified. Its solution had to be in a hundred data banks and a thousand textbooks. But Polly had taken a real-world situation, identified it as a problem without being told it *was* a problem, and produced a real-world solution.

No wonder that she had received applause and praise.

And if achievement counted for anything, she was now far ahead of the rest—including Rick—as a candidate for the fabulous expedition to the Jovian moons.

CHAPTER SEVENTEEN

YOU *may feel SICK, you may feel SAD, you may feel STUPID, you may feel SUPERIOR, you may even feel SEXY . . .*

The sign hung prominently displayed at the entrance to the airlock.

. . . but unless you are feeling SUICIDAL you will check every element of your suit before you operate this lock. YOU HAVE BEEN WARNED.

Rick was feeling somber, which was not on the list, but he did not ignore the sign. He carefully made sure of every seal and function of his suit. He had not felt much like eating, and less like talking, and while all the others were still at lunch he had left to come straight here. It would be another hour before the operation at the SM was due to begin, but he wanted to spend time alone. The best place for quiet solo thinking, better even than his cabin, was outside the busy main body of CM-26. Inside the asteroid there was always the subterranean grumble and growl of heavy machinery, a reminder that apart from being a training facility CM-26 was also a producing mine.

It was a surprise and a nuisance to Rick to make his exit from the airlock and see the faint beacon of another suited figure flashing red near the smelter. While he watched it disappeared around the curve of the cylinder, then a couple of minutes later came into view again on the other side.

Who on earth was it? All the apprentices had been in the dining-room. He saw no way that they could have arrived here ahead of him.

There was an easy way to find out: use his suit radio. But then he would be forced into unwanted conversation. Maybe the other would simply go farther away, off toward the cluster of small waiting asteroids beyond the SM, or perhaps around to the other side of CM-26 where the final products of the mine were launched on their trajectories toward distant Earth.

Rick dimmed his own beacon, hovered in space, and watched. The other person's suit was invisible whenever it was in shadow, but the beacon allowed Rick to track every movement. It went round and round the smelter, starting at the bottom and steadily spiraling up to the top. When that was done the flashing red light made a double traverse of each end of the cylinder, and finally the suited figure turned to jet back toward Rick and the main airlock.

He could not avoid contact now. But at least the question of identity would be answered. Rick waited, and knew the exact moment when the other saw him. There was a reflexive jerk in the suit's arms and head, followed by a slight alteration of thrust vector.

"You're pretty early," said a voice in Rick's headset.

It was Jigger Tait, heading straight toward him.

"Yeah. You too." Rick at once thought of Deedee's worried face. There was no reason at all why Jigger should *not* be out here—he was senior enough to go anywhere he pleased—but that did not explain why he would *choose* to be wandering around outside, alone.

"You mean for heat-cleaning the smelter?" Jigger spoke casually, as though meeting Rick was the most natural thing possible. "Oh, I won't be staying for that. I've seen it before, with other apprentice groups, and anyway I have work that needs doing inside. I'll see you later."

He jetted off and entered the open outer door of the airlock, leaving Rick perplexed. Jigger had offered not one word of explanation as to what he was doing. Rick could think of no reason why Jigger needed to be wandering around—*prowling* around, in Deedee's word—the smelting module. On the other hand, if Jigger wanted to prowl the *interior* unobserved, he would soon have the perfect opportunity with the apprentices all busy outside.

Hopes for a quiet half-hour of serious thinking had faded at the first sight of that red spacesuit beacon. It faded farther when the airlock opened again and another suited figure emerged.

Rick's initial thought—Jigger returning—vanished with one look at the newcomer. She was as slim as Jigger was muscular, and considerably shorter. He also knew exactly who it was. An apprentice's style in manipulating the motion controls of a spacesuit was as individual as a walk.

"Hi, Alice." Rick moved toward her. "We're early."

She must have expected to be alone, because he saw the instinctive jerk of surprise.

"Rick? I didn't think there would be anybody else out here yet."

"Me neither." He advanced until they were within a few feet of each other. "But you were exactly right. Initiative is the name of the game, and Polly sure grabbed it."

"For today she did." Alice didn't sound upset, the way that Rick felt. "What was it you told me Vido Valdez said, when the two of you were always fighting? Are you still fighting, by the way?"

"No. We get on just fine."

"But you're not close?"

"No, I wouldn't say we are." The conversation wasn't making a lot of sense to Rick. "What Vido said to me when?"

"When Dr. Bretherton told the two of you to cool it, or get thrown out."

"Oh, yeah. Vido told me, 'It ain't over 'til I say it's over.' "

"That's what I meant. Well, I feel the same about Polly. She's riding high at the moment, but she hasn't won until we say she has. We just have to come up with better ideas."

"Great." Rick knew his skepticism was showing through. "Got any?"

"Not yet. That's why I'm here. But we will have. Come on."

She led the way over to the smelter. It was open and airless and they wandered inside it together, examining the odd airlock, the places where suits could be stored, and the array of monitoring instruments on the lower flat end. They looked at the great inductive heating coils, which would soon raise the whole interior to a temperature of thousands of degrees. At the other end of the smelter Alice made another inspection of the control panel that allowed the segmented metal sectors to iris open or to close for an airtight seal. Finally they moved together along the curved outer surface of the cylinder, studying the little fusion drives that caused the cylinder to spin on its central axis or to slow to a halt.

"Ideas?" Rick asked as they cycled back to their starting point at the base of the cylinder.

"Some. I don't want to talk about them, though—they're still half-baked."

Rick understood that completely. You might get what seemed like the world's greatest idea for the first half hour, and a day later you'd realize that it was a complete crock. In any case, this was no time for discussing secrets. The rest of the apprentices were beginning to appear from the lock, wandering in small groups over to the smelter. Because Rick and Alice were already there, it was natural for the others to treat them as a group center and gather around them.

Polly arrived last, followed by Barney French. "I would like to describe the plan for today," she said in a wobbly voice, while she was still approaching the rest of the group.

She was nervous, and no wonder. Everyone would have a role, but this was Polly's show. Barney wouldn't let her do anything that might destroy or damage the smelter, but it would be almost as bad to be given a public warning, or to have one of the other apprentices point out why what she was suggesting was crazy and dangerous.

Polly moved to stand in front of the triple airlock. "The good news," she said, "is that we won't have to worry about rotating the smelter, because we don't have ore to melt and centrifuge. That means we don't need to inspect the fusion engines on the outside. The other good news is that we won't need to go to four thousand degrees, even though the structure can stand it. Twenty-eight hundred degrees will be enough to oxidize and vaporize all the residues that line the smelter.

"Finally, we won't need anything like full atmospheric pressure for this to work. If we use pure oxygen at one thirtieth of a standard atmosphere, that will do nicely.

"The bad news is something that I didn't realize when I first thought of using heat to clean the inside of the smelter. When you melt a metallic asteroid by electric inductive heating, there is good conduction through all parts of it. In other words, heat travels easily to everything you want to melt. But we are dealing with just a thin layer of residue, too thin in places to conduct much of anything—heat or electricity. That means induction is inefficient, and so is conduction. Instead, we have to make the whole interior of the smelter into a radiating enclosure at a uniform temperature—a black body, that's called in physics. Unfortunately I don't know anything about black bodies—regardless of what some people around here might think."

It produced a laugh, as Polly had intended. Rumors of her affair with Vido Valdez, darkest-skinned of all the apprentices, were widespread.

"I still don't understand black body radiation," she went on. "Chick Teazle did all the work for me, and I want to give him credit."

"Credit for me if it works," Chick said cheerfully. "But Polly's fault if it goes wrong."

"It had better not go wrong." Now Polly was not joking. She had too much riding on this. "I've worked up the inspection schedule that has to be done before we begin, and the assignment for each of you will show on your suit's interior display. If anybody doesn't know what to do, or has trouble when they start doing it, come back to me. I'll be standing right here."

Rick's assignment was straightforward: inspect the power supply for four of the inductive heating units on the periphery of the smelter. As he moved to do it, he realized that Polly had the worst job of all. She would just hover in space with no assignment, waiting and worrying until everyone else was finished.

On the other hand, he wasn't going to skimp his own task for the sake of Polly's peace of mind. He checked the power supply, slowly and systematically, then the transformers, and finally the inductive coils themselves. Beside him, Gladys de Witt did the same thing for four other units. In the well-lit interior he could recognize her by the color coding bars on her suit.

"Sure beats scraping," she said, as they finished the job and moved together back to the exterior of the smelter. "Wish I'd thought of it."

Polly and Barney French were waiting for them with half a dozen of the apprentices. Others came drifting back, in ones and twos, while Polly kept an audible head count. Last of all were Vido Valdez and Alice Klein, appearing together around the outside of the smelter.

"Right," Polly said. She sounded breathless, although she had not moved for the past half hour. "All in working order. Time to pressurize. I'll give the command, but you'll all be receiving the same displays as I will."

Status monitors flashed their reports onto Rick's suit display. There was nothing to see at the smelter itself, where both ends were now closed and airtight. The internal gas pressure crept slowly up to one thirtieth of an atmosphere.

"Now we're going to begin heating," said Polly. "Before we start, we'll all get well out of the way."

She led them away from the smelter and away from the main body of CM-26, to where the cluster of small co-orbiting asteroids waited.

"I don't see how anything can go wrong," she said, "but just in case, we will use one of these as shielding masses. Get close to it, so you can see the SM but if you need to you can duck out of the way."

As the apprentices moved into position, Rick noticed that Barney French was doing her own head count and assessment of position. She moved one person—Rick thought it was Lafe Eklund—back a little, so that he was better shielded by the asteroid's bulk. Finally she nodded to Polly.

"Here goes." Polly's words sounded more like a prayer than a statement. Again there was nothing to see at the SM, but the suit displays showed a massive drain on the central power supply, and almost at once a rapid rise in ambient interior temperature.

Five hundred degrees—eight hundred—eleven hundred.

Rick, like everyone else, stared in fascination at the smelter. He realized that it was another of the million facts he did not know about this sort of mining. How high a temperature did a body have to reach before it turned red-hot? How high before it was orange or white-hot? *Twelve hundred degrees*, read the display. Shouldn't the heated SM be glowing now against its background of stars?

"We don't like to waste power," Barney French said suddenly, as though she was reading Rick's mind, "so there is excellent thermal insulation between the SM's interior and exterior. You won't see a thing from here. But if you were inside—and managed to survive—you would find the walls starting to glow red at five hundred Celsius. If you were inside now, at twelve hundred degrees, they would be white-hot.

"We still have a way to go. To give you an idea of what we're dealing with here, iron and nickel both melt at about fifteen hundred and boil at twenty-seven hundred in a standard atmosphere. Silicon boils at twenty-three fifty, silicon oxide at twenty-two hundred. We don't have any platinum or iridium in the dross, which is just as well, because platinum doesn't boil until thirty-eight hundred and iridium at over forty-one hundred. Mining can be warm work."

The temperature had been climbing fast. It was up to eighteen hundred degrees. Rick tried to imagine the inferno inside the smelter. The oxygen would have gobbled up any pure metal into compounds, and the dross would be beginning to vaporize. The internal pressure had gone up, to more than a fifth of an atmosphere, and it was still rising.

The inside pressure and temperature were now increasing in unison. There must be a simple explanation for that, if only he could think of it.

"Twenty-two hundred," Polly said nervously, although every apprentice could see that on the suit display. "Three more minutes, and we'll hit twenty-seven. I'm going to cut power then and hold it for another two minutes, then give the command to open the big end as wide as it will go."

"And what will happen then?" Barney asked the question in—for her—an oddly gentle voice.

"The gas inside will blow out. The inside will be left clean."

"True. But something else will happen that we have to worry about. I wanted you to have the first chance with this, Polly, but now I'm going to open it up. Anybody. What do we have to do when we let the gas inside blow into space?"

There was a long silence. "Stay out of the way?" Chick Teazle said, in a let's-try-anything voice.

"That, certainly. What else?"

It was a real-time contest, the worst one yet. Rick struggled to visualize the operation. The gas inside was superheated, but there was no way it could damage anything when it came out through the opening aperture at the end of the smelter. It came out hard, because the inside pressure had increased to a third of an atmosphere. *Jetted* out.

"Rocket!" he shouted, afraid that someone else would beat him to it.

"Be more specific, Rick."

"The gas that comes out will be in a jet, it will produce a rocket effect just like the drive on a ship. The smelter will be driven in the other direction."

"So what do we need to do?"

"Balance it." That came as a shriek from Polly, not Rick. "Use the little thrusters on the outside of the smelter to equal the push from the escaping gas. But I don't know how to work out the thrust!"

"Nor does anyone else in the group," Barney said. "But I do! You're feeling crushed, Polly, but you shouldn't. This exercise makes two points. First, you all have a way to go before you look like mining engineers. Second—and more important—what you do when you work for Vanguard will almost never be a solo effort. You are part of a team, and no matter how much you want to succeed you should never forget that. Here's the information for the impulse correction."

Thruster settings flashed onto the suit displays. Obviously, Barney had computed and stored them in advance. The necessary counter-thrust was small. Rick realized that nothing catastrophic would have happened, even if Polly had proceeded as she originally planned. The smelter would have moved away from CM-26 at a modest pace, and a ship would have been forced to go out and bring it back. Barney had interfered to make a point, not to prevent an accident.

"Let's do it," said Barney. "Go ahead, Polly."

At last, there was something to see. The end of the smelter began to open, and a cloud of incandescent gas spewed out into space. At the same moment half a dozen thrust units on the side of the SM flared briefly into action. To Rick's eyes, calibrating the position of the smelter against the starry background, nothing moved so much as a millimeter. From where he was hanging in space he could see into the open maw of the smelter. The inside shone a brilliant white, which as he watched faded to orange, to bright cherry-red, and at last to the dull glow of a dying ember.

"Don't even think of it," Barney said. A few of the suited apprentices were already floating in the direction of the smelter. "You won't be able to go inside and see what it's like without frying for another couple of hours. Let's go and have a meal and come back later. You should be feeling good about things. I told you that the last group of apprentices finished the cleaning job in two days—but I didn't tell you that they needed until nearly midnight.

"You beat them by"—she consulted her suit chronometer—"more than six hours. You've earned a reward. You can tell me later what it will be. Polly gets a veto vote, because you couldn't have done this without her brainwave."

A reward. All through the meal the preferences had been kicked around. A party, a dance, a feast, a day without work assignments.

The knock-'em-dead idea did not emerge until they were back in their suits, examining the results of the fiery purge of the SM.

Those results were spectacular. The smelter wasn't just *clean*, it was immaculate. Not a trace of grime or metal residue or dust of any kind could be seen anywhere. The instruments and walls shone like new.

"So what do you think?" Polly sounded diffident, but Rick could see her eyes, bright behind her visor.

"Super-colossal-amazing." Deedee was standing next to her, and she reached down and ran her glove over one of the plane surfaces. It came away spotless. "Clean enough to eat off."

She paused, and she and Polly stood staring at each other.

"That's it!" Polly exclaimed.

"If we're allowed to," said Deedee.

"Allowed to what?" Obviously, Polly and Deedee had communicated an idea. Just as obviously, Rick had been present but somehow left out.

"Party, of course," said Polly, in tones that suggested any fool would know.

"In *here*," Deedee added. "We said it's clean enough to eat off the floor—so let's do it."

"Eat, and dance, and riot."

"If Barney will let us."

"Why shouldn't she? We'd have to fill it with air, of course, so we won't need suits."

"And we'd have to bring food and drink over—no way we could prepare it here."

"And a little cylinder rotation, to give enough gravity to dance."

"And we'd want partitions, for privacy."

"And couches in them, for you-know-what."

They were off and running, while he was totally ignored. After another couple of exchanges he gave up and moved away. It was obvious that they didn't need him.

Not for the first time, Rick decided that males and females spoke different languages. It was a mystery that they were even considered the same species..

CHAPTER EIGHTEEN

CHICK Teazle had been put in charge of arrangements; not, as Barney French explained to him, because he was especially competent, but because he was so obnoxious that people would do what he asked rather than get into an argument with him.

He was also, though Barney did not mention it, a natural organizer who loved jobs like this. For the past twenty-four hours he had hardly slept, planning out the work needed to make a Cinderella transition from ore smelter to dance hall.

"We spin it *first*, and get some decent internal gravity," he said to the apprentices, assembled in the main training hall of CM-26. "We need gravity for good dancing, and for sitting comfortable. And we fill the SM with air *last*. That way we can bring in partitions and food and drink and everything else through the big open end, and not have to keep using the airlock."

"Suits all the time?" asked Deedee. Even after months of experience, no one really liked working in suits.

"Well, not for the party itself. Just for setting it up. Once that's done and the SM is airtight, we take off our suits." Chick produced a gigantic sheet of hardboard, covered with minute writing. "Here's the schedule for everything, with names attached to individual tasks. We'll eat tonight over in the SM, but that means we have to be finished with everything here before dinner time."

Gladys de Witt was studying the board. "I see my name, and most people's; but I don't see Vido or Alice or Deedee or Rick."

"They go anywhere we have to go, do whatever needs to be done. They're the troubleshooters, along with me."

"What trouble?"

Chick sighed. "If I knew that, it wouldn't be trouble, would it? It would be shown on the board. Trouble is what you don't expect. We've never done anything like this before, I bet we'll run into a hundred things that don't work out quite the way I planned it. Look, do you want a debate, or do you want a party?"

"Party!" Anything that Gladys might have said was drowned out by the shout from everyone else.

"So let's get going." Chick held out the hardboard sheet. "If anybody has questions at this end, Vido and Alice will be here to answer them. Deedee and Rick will handle problems over in the SM. I'll be floating all over."

Any notion that the troubleshooters might have it easier than anyone else was dispelled in the first half-hour. Spinning the smelter on its central axis, to give a comfortable and familiar quarter-gee field at the outer surface, was easy and went exactly as planned. But when the work team went inside they were out again within seconds.

Lafe Eklund came floating over to where Rick and Deedee were waiting. "We're all right for the moment," he said, "because we're getting sunlight in through the open end. But when we close that, the partitions we want will make it too dark for the party. We're going to need more internal lights."

Deedee looked at Rick. She seemed to have something on her mind, and he thought that she had been tentatively working her way around to discussing it. But now she said abruptly, "The lights will have to come from the main base. I'll go get some."

She jetted away, leaving Rick to wonder what was going on. Alice had been with him in his room the previous night. Did Deedee know that? Alice's room was next to hers. Even if she did, why did she care? He thought of the last party, back on CM-2, when he had danced all evening with Deedee. Was she expecting or hoping that he would do the same again? *Would* he do the same again? Did he want to?

Rick was having trouble sorting out his own feelings, but

he had no time to brood on personal matters. Lafe Eklund had been gone less than two minutes, and already he was coming back.

"We could really use another pair of hands," he said. "We can bring partitions in easily through the open end, and we can move them to the curved floor. But because the SM is spinning pretty fast, the floor is moving relative to the partitions when they get there. One person can't handle them."

"How many partitions?"

"Altogether? About forty. And we have eight tables, and forty chairs, and the sound system, and all the food dispensers."

"Then I've got a better answer." Rick felt useful for the first time. "I can slow the spin way down, until all the inside fixtures are on the floor and secured, then spin back up again. Gravity's great for dancing, but it's a pain during installation. Give me five minutes."

As he moved around the outside of the smelter, Rick sent a radio message back to tell Chick Teazle what he was doing. Chick's instinct had been quite right. Plan all you liked, and there would still be a hundred things that had to be done a little differently.

It was easy to see why Lafe had complained. A quarter gee field on the circumference of the SM might be fine for eating or dancing, but to achieve that the whole cylinder was spinning around on its axis once every eighteen seconds. That didn't sound fast—until you realized that partitions you brought in from outside had to be seated on a curved surface moving past them at seven meters a second. That was as fast as most people could run.

Rick used the drives to slow the spin to a more stately

rotation, once every minute. The effective field at the outer curved surface would go down to—what? He struggled to calculate an answer in his head, and failed.

Well, it would go down a lot, from a quarter gee to maybe a fortieth of a gee. Installation work would be much easier.

But it might not be trivial. Rick headed around to the open end of the smelter and moved inside, to see how things were going. Lafe Eklund gave him a thumbs-up sign. The partitions were floating down easily into position and being secured by a super-glue that held at anything from absolute zero to a thousand degrees.

It was tempting to join Lafe and his group at their work. Rick told himself that was not his job. He was supposed to save himself for things that weren't going well. But when Deedee returned with a dozen light fixtures, he helped her to pick good positions and install them. This was a task that had not been anticipated, so it was a natural for the troubleshooters.

He was half expecting Deedee to pick up their earlier conversation, but apparently in her absence she had changed her mind. Her comments were all technical. It was Rick, to his surprise, who found himself gesturing to her to turn off her radio. He placed his helmet next to hers. "Got any plans for the party?"

She stared at him, but even with the bright new lights he could not see her eyes inside her suit's visor. "What do you mean, plans? Maybe I do. Why?"

"I thought you might be willing to give me dance lessons again. I mean, if you still like to dance with fire hydrants.

I'm the nearest thing to it within three hundred million kilometers."

"Is that your idea of a graceful invitation?" But she didn't sound angry, only amused and thoughtful. "I sort of told Chick Teazle that he and I might make a couple."

"Oh." Rick bit back a question about Chick and Deedee. "Pity."

"It wasn't definite, though. I can tell him I changed my mind." Deedee turned, so that at last he could see her face. She was frowning. "But what about you—and Alice? I mean, I thought that you two . . ."

"It's nothing definite." Rick knew that was a whopping lie, and he could be getting into big trouble. It was true that he and Alice had never gone public, but in private they had done things that Rick never dreamed of before. Maybe Alice would want him to dance with her tonight. Maybe she would finally forget her worries about what the instructors might think of affairs between apprentices—certainly, no one else seemed to care.

"I'd like you to go to the party with me." Rick spoke to end his own uncertainties. "And I'd like you to dance with me."

"Just you?"

Rick swallowed, and took the plunge. "Just me. Nobody else."

"Then I will." Deedee gave Rick a glowing smile, and squeezed his arm in a gloved hand. "Damn these suits. I can't even touch you."

"We won't have to wear suits at the dance. Assuming there is a dance, which there won't be unless we get everything ready." Rick moved his helmet away from Deedee's and gestured to her to turn her radio on. "We'd better get back to work. There could be a million problems going on right now, and we'd never know it."

"No. If there were, Chick would be buzzing all over the place. But I'd better go talk to him and tell him about tonight."

"Do you think he'll be upset?"

"Suppose he is. Do you want to call it off?"

"No way!"

"Then don't ask stupid questions. I'll be back as soon as I can."

Deedee jetted up to the open top of the smelter and vanished around the outside. Rick realized that he ought to have his own conversation with Alice—and soon. He was probably a jerk, but if Deedee wanted to do more than dance tonight he knew he would not hesitate.

Alice was over at the main station, handling problems there with Vido. And Rick, with Deedee gone off to talk to Chick Teazle, was the only assigned troubleshooter at the smelter. He had to stay until she got back.

Before he could fret over that, other matters took over. Lafe Eklund called to say that the interior work was all done, and Rick could spin the SM back up to a quarter gee field. While he was doing it, what seemed like an army of suited apprentices appeared from the main body of CM-26 and came streaming over toward the smelter.

"What's wrong?" he called on his suit radio.

"Wrong?" That was Vido. "Nothing's wrong. That's why we're here."

"We're all done back there." That was Chick, jetting along beside Deedee—if he was heartbroken he certainly didn't sound it. "We have all the food and everything else with us. As soon as you are finished we can fill the inside with air, get out of these suits, and start the party."

"We're done, too," said Lafe. He was standing on the inner surface up near the top of the smelter, checking the apparent gravity as the cylinder gradually leveled off its rate of spin. "Come in through this end. Once you're all inside I'll close it so we can pressurize."

Deedee was moving past Rick, giving him a jaunty wave and a nod that said that she had talked to Chick, and everything was all right.

But it wasn't. Rick hadn't spoken to Alice. He hovered outside as person after person passed him, moving down into the bright and transformed interior of the smelter. Tables and chairs now ran top to bottom along one quadrant of the curved interior, with the food service area taking up another quarter. Half of the other side of the cylinder was a generous dance area. The remainder was cubicles with their own couches, walls, doors—and ceilings. No one would be able to look up from the dining area across the middle of the cylinder, and see what was going on in one of the private rooms on the other side.

Where was Alice? He felt sure that he hadn't missed her.

"Are you coming in?" That was Lafe, waiting at the big open end of the smelter. "We're set to close and fill."

"I'll be another few minutes. Go ahead and don't worry about me. I can use the airlock at the other end."

It occurred to Rick as he spoke that Alice might be doing exactly that. Maybe instead of moving with the main group into this end of the SM, she was entering instead through the triple airlock at the other end.

The metal sectors close to him began their ponderous pincer movement, narrowing to seal the circular aperture of the smelter. While they were still closing Rick headed along the outer edge of the cylinder, reflecting that it would be just his luck if Alice happened to be going the other way, out of sight on the far side.

Well, if that were the case she was too late. She would have to return and use the lock, just like him.

He came to the triple airlock and moved into the first of its three compartments. This one could be held at vacuum, or pressurized to the same level as the interior, or partially pressurized at any level in between. The chamber beyond had the same feature, plus enough rack space for dozens of suits. At the moment both locks were hard vacuum, but the pressure gauges showed that the inside of the SM was already filling with air.

Rick remained in the second of the locks and peered through the thick glass port. He saw Barney, he saw Gina, he saw Vido and Lafe and Gladys. He surveyed the whole group, climbing out of their suits. Everyone except Alice was there.

So where was she?

He turned, and was just in time to see a suited figure glide across the edge of his field of view and disappear from sight around the side of the smelter. Whoever it was had come from the direction of the main body of CM-26—and it was surely not Alice. The suit was far too big and bulky.

It was Jigger Tait. Rick was almost sure, even from that brief glimpse. There was no reason why Jigger should not come to the party; but if that was his intention, why hadn't he headed straight for this airlock?

Rick thought again of Deedee's suspicions that Jigger, with his secret prowling around the mining asteroid, was up to something sinister. The party was a perfect time for anyone to snoop through the apprentices' rooms. But it made little sense to explore out here. And why stay *outside* the SM if you did?

Rick went back through the locks and floated cautiously in the direction that Jigger Tait had taken. He paused as he rounded the end of the smelter. There was no sign of a suit anywhere along the smooth curved side of the cylinder. Open space in all directions seemed just as empty.

Where could Jigger have gone? The only hiding place left was the end of the cylinder, its flat circle still invisible to Rick. He used his suit jets at their lowest setting and crept forward to where he could peer over the curved cylinder edge.

What he saw was totally bewildering. There was not one suited figure, but two—and they were fighting. They were grappling with each other, turning and rolling and kicking in a jumble of arms and legs.

Jigger Tait—and Alice. From this distance there was no doubt at all.

As Rick watched, Jigger used his superior strength and mass to spin Alice around and lock a forearm viciously across her suit's flexible neck piece. He levered hard, cutting off her breathing and resisting her desperate efforts to break free. She kicked and beat at him, but it did no more than turn them end over end in space.

Rick watched, open-mouthed. He was oblivious to his own movement, and he was slowly drifting higher over the cylinder's end plate when the interlocked bodies turned far enough for Alice to catch sight of him.

"Rick!" Her cry was faint and agonized, from lungs starved for air. "Rick. Help me!"

Jigger was killing her. Rick responded instinctively. He jetted right at Tait, hoping to separate the two of them by the sheer force of his collision. It didn't work as planned, because Jigger turned somehow and dipped his shoulder. Rick drove feet-first into that shoulder and the side of Jigger's helmet, partly breaking his hold on Alice and sending them toward the rigid side of the smelter.

Jigger seemed stunned. As his grip loosened, Alice gave a cry of triumph. She turned, wrapped her long legs around Jigger's middle, and fired her suit's jets at maximum impulse. Jigger was driven backwards, headfirst toward the solid wall. It seemed inevitable that the helmet and face plate of his suit would shatter as he hit, but at the last moment his own jets fired laterally. He and Alice spun giddily about their common center of mass. It was her helmet that smashed at high speed into the unyielding cylinder.

Not even hardened plastics could withstand such an impact. Her face plate burst open at eye level. Rick heard a whistling scream on his suit radio as air exploded from Alice's lungs. Her body bounced one way, while Jigger Tait's suit with jets still flaring went spinning off crazily in another direction.

"Rick!" The cry came this time from Tait, flying farther off and struggling to get his suit's movements under control. "Rick—the panel. Hit the Abort key."

Rick, ready to plunge after Alice, paused. If he reached her he did not know what he could for her. But what was Jigger Tait shouting about, with such desperation in his voice?

Rick turned.

The panel. There it was, the control panel, its white cover open. It was right next to him. What did Jigger mean, hit the Abort?

Rick stooped over to look more closely. The control that would open the end of the smelter had been switched to the ON position. The safety override was in operation. The timer was set and counting down even as he watched—eight seconds to go—seven.

His thoughts ran faster than his gloved hand as it slammed for the Abort key.

Seven seconds—the plates at the end of the smelter would be preparing to open.

Six—the apprentices inside were out of their suits and would take minutes to get back into them.

Five—the countdown had not stopped, they would be blown out with the rush of escaping air.

Four—his friends would all die in the naked vacuum of space.

Rick stared, close to hysteria, as the changing digits kept counting down. At last they froze. Three seconds. The override light went out. And then Jigger Tait was standing next to him, his breathing—or was it Rick's own?—harsh and rattling over the suit radio.

"Close," he said. "Too damn close. You almost killed all of us, coming when you did."

"Alice . . ."

"She's gone. Come on. We have to collect her body."

He jetted off toward a stiff-limbed suit that turned in the

Sun's harsh light. Its red beacon light was still forlornly blinking. Rick trailed after him.

"What do we do now?" he said, as they reached Alice.

"Now?" Jigger gathered the body in his arms, staring down into the silent but agonized rictus of death by sudden vacuum. "That's one hell of a question. Now, I guess that you and I go and ruin a party before it's had a chance to get started."

The apprentices were chatting to each other as they wandered through the inside of the smelter, examining and admiring all the new fixtures. The noise level had been growing steadily.

Then Jigger appeared from the inner airlock. Alice's dead body, still in its suit, was cradled to his chest. Many people had been looking the other way, but somehow the whole giant enclosure at once became uncannily silent.

"Alice?" said an uncertain voice. It was Vido Valdez, standing like a statue near the lock. "Is that Alice?"

"Not really." Jigger, with Rick right behind him, moved to the area equipped for serving food and laid the body gently onto one of the tables.

"But it is," said Rick, wondering if Jigger had lost his mind. It was understandable if he had. Rick himself did not feel like a human being, he was numb and dead inside. "It's Alice—Alice Klein."

"No. You thought she was Alice Klein, but this woman is Moira Lindstrom." Jigger lifted his head and stared around at the closing circle of apprentices. He inhaled and exhaled deeply, like a man who has been holding his breath for a long time. "I received a confirming call less than an hour ago from headquarters. She is twenty-six years old. And she works—worked—for Avant Mining, not Vanguard Mining."

Gina Styan and Barney French stepped forward to stand by Alice's body.

"She's the one?" said Gina.

"No doubt about it. We caught her in the act. She had overridden the safety and she was all set to open the smelter. If Luban and I hadn't come along when we did, she'd have killed the lot of you. The whole group of apprentices, plus Gina and Barney."

The expression on Jigger's face ordered Rick, about to blurt out that he had been no help, to keep quiet.

Gina was nodding slowly. "So that was it. I wondered." She turned to face the shocked group. "It's time to explain a few things that we couldn't tell you about before. For over a year we've known of efforts to ruin Vanguard Mining operations. We were pretty sure that it was Avant Mining's work, but we had no proof. The 'accident' that you saw on CM-31 was a good example. It was deliberate sabotage, a planted explosive on the outer surface of the smelting cylinder. Jigger and I suspected as much when Morse Watanabe and the Avant Mining ship, the *Scarab*, just 'happened' to come along at precisely the right time to claim a derelict. He had no way of knowing that two survivors had avoided the blow-up by being outside the habitat, or that we would arrive on the scene so quickly.

"We had suspicions, but that was all. And we had no proof that a saboteur had been planted in the latest group of trainees. So far as we were concerned, every one of you was suspect. But we were able to narrow it down, bit by bit. When

Alice Klein told Barney that she didn't feel well, earlier today, we didn't like the sound of that. It meant that she, and she alone, might not be here at the smelter tonight. Jigger agreed to hang behind and keep an eye on her."

"I nearly failed." Jigger again stared straight at Rick. "She was a smart operator, smart enough to fool any of us most of the time. She sneaked out of a cargo lock instead of the usual exit, and she was on the way here before I knew it. Good thing I was already in my suit, just in case. But you're all lucky to be alive."

"We *are* alive. That's what matters." Barney French had been watching the apprentices closely, monitoring their expressions. "Look, it's quite obvious that this is no time for any sort of party. We are going back to the main station. On the way you can think about this whole thing, and when we get there we'll meet in the main hall. If you have questions, I'll try to answer them."

"But what—" Chick Teazle started.

"I said *there*, not here." Barney clapped her hands. "Come on, do it." She turned to Rick and added in a lower voice. "You join us later if you want to. For the moment, you go with Jigger. No questions—just go."

No questions.

Rick drearily followed Jigger Tait, away from the smelter and into Jigger's private room in the main body of CM-26.

No questions—when he had a thousand, starting to percolate up from the depths of his numbed brain. But more disturbing than any question was a growing conviction. If Alice were a saboteur, planted in the group way back at the time of the first tests on Earth, then her whole relationship with Rick had been a lie.

"I'm afraid you're right." Jigger Tait agreed when Rick suggested it. He sat draped over a chair, his forearms along its back and his chin on his fists. "She picked you out, but I doubt that she had any special fondness for you. She was working on Vido Valdez, too, just in case."

"She thought I was an idiot," Rick said bitterly.

"Not an idiot, or you would have been no use to her. She probably thought you were bright. But intelligence and experience of the world are two different things." When Rick grunted at his own stupidity, Jigger went on, "Don't feel too bad about that. Men and women have manipulated each other right through history, everyone from emperors to peasants."

"What did she have in store for me?"

"I don't know. My bet is that it would have been something deadly to you. You're very lucky to be alive. She saw an opportunity tonight to wipe out the entire group of apprentices in one go, so she grabbed the chance without calling on you. If she had succeeded, I think she'd have tried to make the whole thing look like an accident, the way that the destruction of CM-31 was supposed to be an accident. If the *Scarab* had arrived before us you can bet that all evidence of sabotage would have disappeared before anyone else could see it."

Rick recalled Jigger's face, glaring at the vanishing plume of the *Scarab*'s exhaust. "You knew all that, didn't you, when the *Scarab* first appeared? That's why you were so angry and rude. But *how* did you know? I mean, what made you suspicious when the rest of us didn't have a clue?"

"I was afraid you'd ask me that." Jigger's big moon face was gloomy, and he shook his head. "I could make up a story, but one of you would see through it. Didn't it strike you as strange that Gina and I have been with you all the time, right from your flight from Earth up to CM-2?"

"I never thought it was anything out of the ordinary. Deedee did, though. She said you'd been snooping. She pointed it out to me, and said we ought to keep an eye on you."

"Deedee is one with-it girl. But I guess it's time to tell the truth. Gina and I work for Vanguard Mining, just as we said. We don't work for Operations, though. We work in Security. We were assigned to tag along with your group because there was word of a possible saboteur. The problem was, we had no idea who it might be—you, or Deedee, or Alice, or Vido, it could have been anyone. Actually, our first clue that it might be Alice came from Turkey Gossage."

"Did he see her doing something?" Rick was beginning to suspect that he was the only blind person in the solar system.

"Not in the usual sense. He had been reviewing her test results, and he noticed that she always scraped through with a score just a few points above the pass mark. That can happen a few times by accident. But if it happens *consistently*, that's unnatural. It suggests that the person taking the test really knows the right answers, and is deliberately giving enough wrong ones to keep her down in the pack. Scraping through was intended to make Moira Lindstrom inconspicuous. Thanks to Turkey's experience and shrewdness, it had the opposite effect.

"That gave a starting point. But of course it wasn't anything like proof. It could have been just a statistical fluke."

Jigger had been studying Rick as they talked. He had noticed the yawns and the drooping eyelids.

"Rick Luban!" And, when Rick jerked to attention, "You don't realize it, but you've had more shocks than a person can stand in one day. Stress exhausts more than anything. We still have a lot to talk about, but we won't do it tonight."

"The other group, with Barney . . ."

"Will still be there in the morning."

"I can't possibly go to sleep. Everything inside my head is a big jumbled-up mess."

"I'm sure it is. But you need rest." Jigger pointed across to his own bunk. "I'll tell you what. Stretch out on that for a little while. If you're still awake in ten minutes, you can get up again and we'll talk some more. But it's my bet that you'll fall asleep."

"I bet I don't. I can't possibly sleep." Rick went over to the bunk, lay down on it, and reluctantly closed his eyes.

He lost his bet with Jigger by eight and a half minutes.

CHAPTER NINETEEN

RICK emerged from a vivid nightmare, a chaos of screams and freefall darkness and bursting bodies. He came suddenly awake, opened his eyes, and sat up.

He stared around him. He was not in his own familiar cabin. When he realized where he was, he knew that part of the nightmare was no dream. Alice had died, in an agony of ruptured lungs and exploding air that turned to a fog of ice

crystals. Every other apprentice had come within seconds of
that same fate.

He rolled off the bunk and lurched to his feet. His stomach hurt, and he felt drunk or drugged. How long had he
been asleep? Where was everyone else?

There was no sign of Jigger Tait, although it was his
room. Rick went outside and staggered along the darkened
corridor to the dining area. Everywhere seemed oddly quiet,
with the hushed silence of a hospital or a church. All Rick
could think of was a drink. His throat was parched and his
tongue felt like a withered lump of flesh in his mouth.

He walked into the bright room, squinting his eyes
against the sudden light. Only after he had bent over the
spigot and allowed cold water to run into his mouth and over
his whole face did he take any notice of the people at the tables.

There were three of them. Deedee Mao, Vido Valdez,
and Polly Quint were sitting with drinks in front of them, but
they were not talking to each other. All of their faces had a
pale, waxen look.

Rick moved unsteadily over to them and slumped onto
a hard chair. "What time is it? I mean, is it night or morning?"

"Half and half," said Polly. "It's the middle of the night.
We've tried but we haven't been able to sleep. Even after Barney's explanation, we can't decide what really happened."

"I wasn't there with Barney." Rick paused. Was he ready
to talk about this? "But I was there when Alice died."

"Moira," said Deedee. "That's what Jigger Tait called
her. But I'm like you, I can't think of her any other way than
Alice."

"And twenty-six years old." Vido shook his head. "First time I saw her, I guessed she was thirteen. She could have passed for it, easy."

"How *did* she die?" Polly asked. "Barney didn't actually say."

"Jigger killed her." Rick felt obliged to add, "In self-defense. And I almost screwed that up, and killed all of you."

While the others stared, everything came blurting out. Rick made no attempt to excuse his own naivety and incompetence. The others did not offer a word of criticism, though he knew it was well-deserved. They didn't seem in the least surprised that Rick had been seduced by Alice, and it turned out that Gina Styan had already told them that she and Jigger worked for Vanguard Mining's security office.

The surprise was on Rick's side, when after describing Alice's terrible death he said gloomily, "The rest you know. Jigger didn't come right out and blame me for getting in the way, but I'm sure he thought it. I guess you can cross my name off the short list for exploring the moons of Jupiter."

The other three exchanged looks. "Jigger didn't tell you?" Deedee said.

"Tell me what?"

"That the whole thing was a set-up. Security knew there were information leaks somewhere in Vanguard. The people from Avant Mining had been finding out about valuable asteroid discoveries made by our surveys, and flying out there to stake claims before we did. So Security planted stories, different ones in different places. Then they watched to see what Avant did. And Avant took the bait on this one."

"You mean the Jupiter moon exploration—"

"Isn't real," said Polly. "Not a word. And I had my heart set on it."

"Yeah," Vido snorted. "You and everybody else. Move over, lady."

"Outer System exploration will happen, maybe in another ten years," said Deedee. "It won't be those moons, though. So far as Vanguard's remote surveys can tell, the lesser moons of Jupiter are just big useless lumps of rock. But Gina has been monitoring the shipping records, and a few days ago three of Avant's main prospecting vessels went whomping out through the Belt at maximum acceleration—heading for Jupiter."

"Pulsed fusion, two and a half gees on and off every few seconds," Vido smiled with vicious glee. "Serves the bastards right. Let's hope it takes 'em a long time to get there and longer to come back."

"No Jupiter project." Rick leaned forward and rested his head on the table. "What else have we been lied to about? I've had it. I say screw Avant Mining, and screw Vanguard Mining, and screw everything. We'd be better off in the Pool, back on Earth."

"Amen," said Vido.

The other two seemed to have nothing to add, and after a long pause Vido stood up. "Well," he said, "I've been to bed twice, and I've got up twice because I couldn't sleep. I'm going to take another shot at it. Third time lucky. Good night, all."

"Wait for me." Polly dragged herself to her feet. "Anything you can do, Vido Valdez, I can do better."

Rick and Deedee were left alone at the table. He did not speak or lift his head, and after a while she sighed and stood up. "Maybe they have the right idea. I'm going to give it a try."

She began to leave the table, then reached across and gently ruffled Rick's hair. "You too, hero. That's what Barney and Gina told us you are, even though you don't think so. Jigger says you saved everybody. Better get used to fame."

She was at the door before she turned and spoke again. "One other thing you may have missed. Barney says that a day to get over shock is the maximum allowance when you work for Vanguard. She told us the party is scheduled for tomorrow night, come meteor shower or solar flare. And it's going to take place the same as before, in the smelter. Still want me to give you dance lessons?"

She waited. Rick did not speak or move. Finally Deedee shook her head and said, "Why don't you sleep on it? But do it in your bunk and not here. Even a bonehead deserves a softer pillow than a table."

And she was gone.

Morning was not pleasant. But it was tolerable, as the middle of the night had not been tolerable.

Work helped. For reasons either therapeutic or punitive, Barney French drove the apprentices as never before. She piled on cleaning chores and exercise fatigues and maintenance details with a vicious disregard for human limitations. Rick reeled through the day from one assignment to the next, without time to rest or think or even eat a proper meal, until a general siren sounded. He realized with astonishment that it was the signal to down tools and head for the smelter.

All for a stupid party.

Rick felt that he wanted nothing in the world less—until he reached the racks at the exit port and saw his suit. He stared at it with a distaste that bordered on horror. More than avoiding a party, more than anything, he did not want to put himself inside that suit and drift through open space to the SM. His mind flung at him a vivid image of Alice, face plate smashed, limbs contorted, dying in the airless void.

He was still standing and staring when Jigger Tait and Gina Styan arrived. They did not notice—or chose to ignore—his frozen immobility.

"This is a bit of luck," said Jigger. "I've been wanting a quiet word with you all day, but Barney told me she had you fully scheduled and I was to stay out of your way. Let's take five minutes when we get over to the smelter, all right?"

It was easier to go along than to admit the truth. Rick found himself climbing lethargically into his suit while he read the sign on the wall.

You may feel SICK, you may feel SAD, you may feel STUPID . . .

He felt all of those, as well as scared. But he followed protocol, and together with Jigger and Gina performed the thirty-six point check of the suits. That ritual somehow helped.

They went into the airlock together, and he floated across to the smelter with one of them like a guard on each side of him. In the pressurized second hatch of the SM's airlock, Jigger halted.

"You go through, Gina," he said. "Rick and I will get rid of our suits and stay here for a few minutes. See you later."

He motioned Rick to the chamber off the side of the room and followed him in.

"You may wonder what the hell this is all about," he began, even before the door was closed. "I'll get to the point right away. I want to talk about your future. I know how it is at this stage of your training, because I went through it myself. You feel as though the assignments and tests will go on forever. But they won't. They'll be over before you know it. So I want to ask, what do you see yourself doing afterwards?"

"Yesterday, I thought I might have a chance at the Jupiter expedition. Early this morning I was ready to call everything quits and go back to Earth. Now?" Rick shrugged. "Now I don't know what I want."

"I understand about the Jupiter moons. That story paid off for Vanguard, but no one thought through what the effect would be on your group. I can't change that, but I can tell you that even if the Jupiter expedition were real, it still wouldn't be the toughest job in the solar system. Do you know what is?"

"I guess I don't. All through training we've been told that the most challenging job is out here in the Belt, mining and refining and carrying finished products back to the Earth-Moon system. Are you saying that's wrong?"

"That's a tough job, and a rewarding one. Almost all the apprentices will be doing some piece of it. For you, though, I want to suggest an alternative. I want to ask you to consider a career with Security."

The idea caught Rick totally unprepared. "Security?" He stared at Jigger. "Why me?"

"I think—and Gina and Barney agree—you probably have a talent for it."

"But I don't know a thing about security operations."

"Of course you don't. You'd have to learn new things.

But that will be true wherever you work. Education isn't like a video, with a beginning and a middle and an end. It has a beginning, then it keeps going until you're dead. If it stops you *are* dead, even if you don't know it. And Gina and I will be learning, too. Vanguard is about to start a completely new project, tougher than anything we've ever tackled before. We'll need all the help we can get."

"You mean—Avant Mining?" Rick thought he knew where Jigger was heading.

"There's certainly opportunities there, if that interests you. Beating Avant won't be easy. They draw their people from the school system's absolute cesspools, the hardest, most cynical kids they can find. You only met one of them—Alice Klein—and she was nowhere near as bad as some of the others. Compared with them, the toughest of your group is Mr. Nice Guy. But I'm going to surprise you: the hardest job isn't fighting Avant. It's a job where Avant and Vanguard are in total agreement about what needs to be done, and will probably have to join forces to do it. Know what it is?"

Rick shook his head. Vanguard and Avant, working together? He couldn't imagine any area where the two companies had a common interest.

"In fact, if we don't cooperate," Jigger went on, "I don't think we can possibly win. We have to fight a monster that's effectively immortal, a monster with a billion arms, one with a million times more power than Vanguard and Avant combined. A monster not in space, but back on Earth. Do you remember what it was like in school?"

"Very well." Rick's confusion had become total.

"Do you think you're smarter now than you were then?"

Rick had to consider that. He wasn't sure what Jigger

was asking. "Smarter, no. My brain's the same. But I know a lot more, and I understand more of what I know."

"Very true. And do you know *why* that's true? I'll tell you. Back on Earth you were being strangled by the biggest, most inefficient, best entrenched bureaucratic system in the history of the world. You were in school, adrift within an education system that had lost any interest in the value of knowledge, or truth, or discipline, or self-evaluation. Like all monopolies, it was more interested in perpetuating and protecting its own territory than in anything else. The men and women who emerge from the school system know less and less—and then wonder why they find themselves unemployable." Jigger paused. "My God, I'm starting to spout the official company line. Let me get to the point. For every bright bored kid like you who gets kicked out of the system, another thousand stay inside it and are stifled for life. We have to change that. The toughest job in the solar system isn't on the moons of Jupiter. It's not beating Avant Mining. It's back down on Earth."

"No!" Rick finally thought he knew where Jigger was heading, and for the first time since Alice's death he was flooded with powerful emotion. He saw in his mind Mr. Hamel, the patient turtle, bowed down by thirty years of frustration and indignity. "If you think I could ever go back there and put up with all the bullshit—"

"You told me that early this morning you were ready to go back. But this would be different. Forget the way we operate today. We're talking something a lot more direct. We have to infiltrate the education system, and either transform it or destroy the whole mess. That needs older people, like Turkey Gossage and Coral Wogan—they've both volunteered—but we also need younger people, too, like me and Gina and—"

"No. Absolutely no. I'm not interested." Rick backed toward the door. "I don't want to talk about it any more."

"All right." Jigger nodded and sighed. "I thought you would say that. I've had my five minutes, and more. The party and the dance will be starting now, and you've earned the right to be there. I didn't expect you to say yes, you know. I just wanted to plant the seed of an idea that might grow into something five years from now. Any questions before you go?"

"No." But Rick paused. "Did you ask anyone else in our group?"

"Two other people. I spoke with Vido Valdez, and Gina spoke with Deedee Mao."

"I see. Can you tell me what they said?"

"Yes. Vido told me no way—no goddamn way, to be precise. Deedee told Gina, no, never, not if she lived to be a thousand. Then she asked if we had asked you. Gina told her we had not, but I was going to."

"I see. Thank you. May I go now?"

"Sure. Have fun. I'll be there myself in a few minutes."

Rick closed the door and entered the second chamber of the airlock. He went through, but at the inner hatch he paused and stood motionless for a long time. He had not thought about Mr. Hamel for months, until today; but suddenly his mind was full of their final meeting, the small stooped figure sitting on the bench in the fading light of late afternoon. He heard again that dry, dusty voice: *Not an easy job, but a worthwhile one. The most rewarding jobs are always the most difficult ones.*

Could that be true? On Earth, in space, everywhere?

Maybe; but not for Rick Luban. Not tomorrow, not ever. And certainly not today, with Deedee waiting for him. He moved to operate the hatch.

Beyond it, the party was getting into its stride. From where Rick was standing the sound through the closed door was no more than a confused hubbub, like the first distant swell of a revolution.